The Black Wolf's Breed

"Come, fellow, thou art trapped ; give me up my purse."   p. 76.

The
Black Wolf's Breed,

A Story of France
*In the Old World and the New, happening
in the Reign of Louis XIV*

By

Harris Dickson

Illustrations by

C. M. Relyea

NEW YORK
B. W. DODGE & COMPANY
PUBLISHERS

TO THE MEMORY OF

BIENVILLE

THE SOLDIER-GOVERNOR OF LOUISIANA
OUT OF WHOSE
MIGHTY PROVINCE HAS GROWN NEARLY ONE-HALF
OF THE
WORLD'S GREATEST
REPUBLIC

CONTENTS

CONTENTS

CONTENTS

*F*RANCE—*In the old world and in the new!*
    *The France of romance and glory under Henry
of Navarre; of pride and glitter under Louis XIV, in
whose reign was builded, under the silver lilies, that empire—Louisiana—in the vague, dim valley of the Mis-
sissippi across the sea: these are the scenes wherein this
drama shall be played.   Through these times shall run
the tale which follows. Times when a man's good sword
was ever his truest friend, when he who fought best commanded most respect.   It was the era of lusty men——
the weak went to the wall.*

    *King and courtier; soldier and diplomat; lass and
lady; these are the people with whom this story deals.
If, therefore, you find brave fighting and swords hanging too loosely in their sheaths; if honor clings round an
empty shadow.and the women seem more fair than honest, I pray you remember when these things did happen,
who were the actors, and the stage whereon they played.*

                                        THE *A*UTHOR.

THE BLACK WOLF'S BREED

—

FOREWORD

*I*T is fitting that old men, even those whose trade is
war, should end their days in peace, yet it galls me
grievously to sit idly here by the fire, in this year of
grace 1746, while great things go on in the world about
me.

The feeble hound at my feet, stretching his crippled
limbs to the blaze, dreams of the chase, and bays delighted in his sleep. Nor can I do more than dream
and meditate and brood.

News of Fontenoy and the glory of Prince Maurice
thrills my sluggish blood; again I taste the wild joys of
conflict; the clashing steel, the battle shouts, the cries
of dying men—yea, even the death scream of those
sorely stricken comes as a balm to soothe my droning
age. But the youthful vigor is gone. This arm could
scarcely wield a bodkin; the old friend of many cam-
paigns rusts in its scabbard, and God knows France had
never more urgent need of keen and honest swords.

(1)

Thus run my thoughts while I sit here like some de-crepit priest, bending over my task, for though but an in-different clerk I desire to leave this narrative for my children's children.

My early life was spent, as my children already know, for the most part in the American Colonies. Of my father I knew little, he being stationed at such re-mote frontier posts in the savage country that he would not allow my mother and myself to accompany him. So we led a secluded life in the garrison at Quebec. After the news came of his death somewhere out in the wilder-ness, my brave mother and I were left entirely alone. I was far too young then to realize my loss, and the mem-ory of those eaceful years in America with my patient, accomplished mother remains to me now the very happiest of my life.

From her I learned to note and love the beauties of mountain and of stream. The broad blue St. Lawrence and the mighty forests on its banks were a constant source of delight to my childish fancy, and those mem-ories cling to me, ineffaceable even by all these years of war and tumult.

When she died I drifted to our newer stations in the south, down the great river, and it is of that last year in Louisiana, while I was yet Captain de Mouret of Bienville's Guards, that I would have my children know.

Along the shore of Back Bay, on the southern coast of our Province of Louisiana, the dense marsh grass grows far out into the water, trembling and throbbing with the ebb and flow of every tide.

Thicker than men at arms, it stands awhile erect where the shallow sea waves foam and fret; then climbing higher ground, it straggles away, thinner and thinner, in oaken-shaded solitudes long innocent of sun.

Beginning on the slopes, a vast mysterious forest, without village, path, or white inhabitant, stretches inland far and away beyond the utmost ken of man. There the towering pines range themselves in ever-receding colonnades upon a carpet smooth and soft as ever hushed the tread of Sultan's foot. Dripping from their topmost boughs the sunlight's splendor flickers on the floor, as if it stole through chancel window of some cool cathedral where Nature in proud humility worshiped at the foot of Nature's God.

It was in those wilds, somewhere, the fabled El Dorado lay; there bubbled the fountain of eternal youth; through that endless wilderness of forest, plain and hill flowed on in turbid majesty the waters of De Soto's mighty grave.

CHAPTER I

THE MASTER

IT was late one clear moonlight night in the spring of
17—, when three silent figures emerged from the
woodland darkness and struck across the wide extent of
rank grass which yet separated us from the bay. Tuskahoma led the way, a tall grim Choctaw chieftain, my
companion on many a hunt, his streaming plumes fluttering behind him as he strode. I followed, and after me,
Le Corbeau Rouge, a runner of the Choctaws. We
were returning to Biloxi from a reconnaissance in the
Chickasaw country.

Each straight behind the other, dumb and soundless
shadows, we passed along the way, hardly bruising a
leaf or brushing the rustling reeds aside.

"See, there is the light," grunted Tuskahoma, pointing to a glimmer through the trees. "Yes, the White
Prophet never sleeps," assented Le Corbeau Rouge.

The light which marked our almost ended journey
came from a window in one of those low, square log
houses, fortress-dwellings, so common in the provinces.

Here, however, the strong pine palisades were broken
down in many places; the iron-studded gate hung un-

(5)

hinged and open, the accumulated sand at its base showed it had not been closed in many years.

But the decay and neglect everywhere manifest in its defenses extended no further, for inside the enclosure was a garden carefully tended; a trailing vine clung lovingly to a corner of the wide gallery, and even a few of the bright roses of France lent their sweetness to a place it seemed impossible to associate with a thought of barbaric warfare.

I loved this humble home, for in such a one my mother and I had spent those last years of sweet good-comradeship before her death—the roses, the rude house, all reminded me of her, of peace, of gentler things.

The character of its lone occupant protected this lowly abode far better than the armies of France, the chivalry of Spain, or the Choctaw's ceaseless vigilance could possibly have done. He came there it was said, some fifteen years before, a Huguenot exile, seemingly a man of education and birth. He built his castle of refuge on a knoll overlooking the sheltered bay, hoping there to find the toleration denied him in his native land. The edict of Nantes had been revoked by King Louis, and thousands of exiled Frenchmen of high and low degree sought new fortunes in newer lands.

Many had reached America, and strove with energetic swords and rapacious wallets to wrest blood and gold and fame from whatsoever source they might.

This man alone of all those first explorers had shown no disposition to search out the hidden treasures of the wilderness, to prey upon the natives. He became their friend and not their plunderer.

His quiet life, his kindness, his charity, his knowledge of the simple arts of healing, so endeared him to every warring faction that at his house the Choctaw and the Chickasaw, the Frenchman, Spaniard and the Englishman met alike in peace. So the needless fortifications fell into unrepaired decay.

Many an afternoon I had paddled across the bay and spent a quiet hour with him, as far from the jars and discord at Biloxi as if we were in some other world.

As, this night, we drew nearer the house we saw no signs of life save the chinks of light creeping beneath the door. I rapped, and his voice bade me enter.

The master sat at his table in the center of a great room, about which were a number of surgical and scientific instruments, all objects of mistrust to my Indian friends.

These curious weapons of destruction or of witchcraft, for so the Indians regarded them, contributed to make him an object of fear, which doubtless did much to strengthen his influence among the tribes.

He was at this time somewhat more than sixty, slender and rather above the medium height. With his usual grave courtesy he welcomed us and readily loaned the small pirogue necessary to carry our party across the bay.

The Indians were restless and the governor waited, so I only thanked our host and turned to go.

He rose, and laying his hand upon my arm detained me. "Wait, Placide; I am glad you returned this way, for I have long wished to speak with you; especially do I wish it on this night—on this night. Sit down."

Mechanically I obeyed, for I could see there was something of more than usual import on his mind. The Indians had withdrawn, and the master, pacing uncertainly about the room, paused and regarded me intently, as if he almost regretted his invitation to stay. After several efforts he abruptly began:

"I fear I have not very long to live, and dread to meet death, leaving a solemn duty unperformed. It is of this I would speak."

I listened in silence. He spoke hurriedly as though he doubted his resolution to tell it all.

"You, and every one in these colonies, know me only as Colonel d'Ortez, the Huguenot refugee. So I have been known by the whites ever since I came here to escape persecution at home, and to get forever beyond the sound of a name which has become hateful to me—my own.

"The Counts d'Artin have been a proud race in France for centuries, yet I, the last d'Artin, find the name too great a burden to bear with me in shameful silence to my grave. See this," and he took from his throat a pearl-studded locket, swung by a substantial golden chain, which he opened and handed to me. Inside were the arms of a noble family exquisitely blazoned upon a silver shield.

"What is it; what device is there?"

I knew something of heraldry and read aloud without

hesitation the bearings upon the shield, prominent among which were three wolves' heads, chevroned, supported by two black wolves, rampant, the coronet and motto "Præclare factum."

"Aye," he mused half coherently, "the wolf; 'tis the crest of the d'Artins, quartered with those of many of the most ancient houses of France. So do those arms appear to men. But see."

He took the locket quickly from me and with a swift forceful movement turned the plate in its place, exposing the reverse side.

"What is this? Look!"

I glanced at it and started, looking inquiringly into my old friend's face. He avoided my eye.

I saw now upon the plate the same arms, the same quarterings, but over all there ran diagonally across the scutcheon a flaming bar of red which blazed evilly upon the silver ground. I understood.

"What is it?" he demanded impatiently. I still could find no word to answer.

"Speak out boy, what is it?"

"The same, but here, over all, is the bendlet sinister." I scarcely dared to look up into his face.

"Aye," he replied, his countenance livid with shame. "It is the bar sinister, the badge of dishonor. So do those proud arms appear in the sight of God, and so shall they be seen of men. And for generations each Lord of Cartillon has added to that crimson stripe the indelible stain of cowardice."

The master, his features working convulsively with

humbled pride, his eyes never leaving the floor, continued resolutely.

"The story is short. Over a hundred years ago the Count d'Artin was murdered in his castle by the son of a peasant woman, his half brother, who assumed the title and seized the estates. This was easy in those times, for the murdered man was a Huguenot, his slayer a Catholic in the service of Guise, and it was the day after St. Bartholomew's. The count had sent his infant son for safety to an old friend, the abbott of a neighboring monastery. This child was brought up in the Catholic faith, and in him and his descendants resided the true right of the Counts d'Artin. Of this they have always been ignorant. The usurper on his death bed repented, and calling his own son to him, told him the whole story, exacting a solemn oath that he would find the disinherited one and restore to him his own. This oath was kept in part. His son, Raoul d'Ortez, found the child, then an officer in the army, but lacked the courage to declare his own shame, and relinquish the price of his father's crime. By that Raoul d'Ortez this locket was made, and the same vow and the same tradition were handed down to me. I have no child. God knows I would give up the accursed heritage if I could.

"During all these years a careful record has been kept of the true lineage, which was only broken in my father's time. Here in this packet are the papers which prove it; I confide them to you upon my death. After I am gone I want you to find the last d'Artin."

He was silent now a long time, then continued in a lower tone: "My mother was of the reformed religion and I embraced her faith. It seems like a judgment of God that I, a Huguenot, should lose under King Louis what my Catholic ancestor gained under King Charles. Now go, lad."

I could say nothing, but touching his hand in mute sympathy turned away without a word.

I had almost reached the door when he sprang after and again detained me. His glance searched apprehensively into the shadowy corners of the room, his voice wavered, the look of a hunted animal crept into his eyes.

"'Tis said," he whispered, "the restless spirits of my fathers yet haunt our castle in Normandy—oh, merciful God, do you believe it? Oh no, no, after all these troubled years I fain would find a dreamless slumber in my grave."

I soothed him as I would a frightened child, and left him standing at the door.

CHAPTER II

BIENVILLE

MUSING on this strange story, and the old man's unwonted fear, I walked on down to the water's edge where my Indian friends, already in the pirogue, awaited me. Another half hour and we were in Biloxi.

When we reached the barracks I found orders to attend the governor at once.

Bienville stood before his fire alone, quiet, but in a very different mood from any in which I had theretofore seen him.

"Captain de Mouret," the rough old warrior began, without any prelude or indirection, "I desire to send you at once to Paris on an errand of the utmost importance to myself and to this colony. I select you for this task, though I can ill spare you here, because it is a delicate matter. I believe you to be honest, I know you are courageous."

I bowed, and he went on. Something had evidently occurred to vex and irritate him.

"You know the people who surround me here, the weak, the vicious, the licentious of all the earth. A band of unprincipled adventurers, vile Canadians and half-breeds, all too lazy to work, or even to feed them-

selves out of the bountiful earth which would give everything we need almost for the asking. The air is full now
of rumors of a Spanish war, and a Natchez-Chickasaw
alliance. If these things are true we would find ourselves entirely cut off from French supplies, and this
colony would literally starve to death. Yes, starve to
death with untold millions of fruitful acres all about us.
Had we strength to fight I would not care so much.
With but two companies of undisciplined troops, a mere
straggling handful, officered by drunkards, we could not
defend this post a day against any organized attack.''

All this I knew to be true, so I made no comment.
He pursued the conversation and evidently relieved his
mind of much that had troubled him for months.

"Then this beggarly commissary of mine, and the
trafficking priest, de la Vente, they are constantly stirring up strife against me here, and putting lies in the
hands of my enemies at court. The king, too, is wearied
out with this endless drain upon his treasury for money
and supplies, and is now, so I am informed, almost
ready to accede to Crozat's proposition, and turn over
to him the revenues and government of the colonies.''

The old man grew earnest and eloquent.

"What! turn over an empire such as this to a miserable trading huckster, the son of a peasant—permit him
to name the governors and officers! Why, under his
rule, such cattle as la Salle and de la Vente would feed
fat upon the miseries of the people! Great God,
Placide, do you appreciate what that means? To
create this peddler of silks and laces lord of a bound-

less domain, more magnificent than Louis in his wildest schemes of conquest ever dreamed? Why, boy, the day will come when for a thousand leagues the silver lilies will signal each other from every hill top; marts of commerce will thrive and flourish; the land will smile with farms and cities, with proud palaces and with granite castles. The white sails of our boats will fleck every lake and sea and river with their rich burdens of trade, pouring a fabulous and a willing wealth into the coffers of the king. Gold and silver mines will yield their precious stores, while from these niggard natives we will wrest with mighty arm the tribute they so contemptuously deny the weakling curs who snap and snarl at my heels. Grey tower and fortress will guard every inlet, and watch this sheltered coast. In every vale the low chant of holy nuns will breathe their benediction upon a happy people. And hordes of nations yet unknown and races yet unborn, in future legends, in song, in story and in rhyme, will laud the name of Bourbon and the glory of the French. Oh lad! lad! 'tis an ambition worthy a god.''

The governor had risen, and waving his long arms this way and that, pointed out the confines of his mighty dreamland empire with as much assurance as if cities and towns would spring up at his bidding

His whole frame spoke the most intense emotion. The face, glorified and transfigured by the allurement of his brilliant mirage, seemed that of another man.

''Ah, Placide! Placide! it stings me that this chivalrous king of ours, this degenerate grandson of Henry the Great, should think of selling for a few paltry livres such an heritage as this. Shame to you Louis, shame!"

His tone had grown so loud, so peremptory, I interrupted.

"Caution, sire; who knows what tattler's ears are listening, or where your thoughtless words may be repeated."

He stood moodily with hands behind him gazing into the fire. For years I had known Bienville the soldier, the stern and unyielding governor, with the hand of iron and the tongue of suasion.

Now I saw for the first time Bienville the man, Bienville the visionary, Bienville the enthusiast, the dreamer of dreams and the builder of castles. I watched him in amazement.

"Then these miserable women whom our good father, the Bishop of Quebec, was so kind as to send us, bringing from their House of Correction all the airs and graces of a court. Bringing hither their silly romances of a land of plenty; they vow they came not here to work, and by the grace of God, work they will not. They declare they are not horses to eat of the corn of the fields, and clamor for their dear Parisian dainties. Against such a petticoat insurrection the governor is helpless. Bah! it sickens me. I wonder not that our men prefer the Indian maidens, for they at least have common sense. But by my soul, Captain, here I stand and rant like some schoolboy mouthing his speech. Tush, it is forgotten.

"Tell me, Captain de Mouret, what have you learned of the Chickasaws, for our time grows short.'

Glad to change the current of his thought I went on in detail to give the results of my reconnaissance. Everywhere we found preparations among the allied tribes, and felt sure we saw signs of a secret understanding between them and the Spaniard.

The governor made many notes, and carefully examined the charts I had drawn of the Chickasaw towns, systematically marking down the strength and fortifications of each. When I had finished my report we sat for quite a while, he silent and thoughtful, watching the thin blue smoke eddy round and round then dart up the capacious chimney.

"And they charge me at the court of France," he soliloquized, giving half unconscious expression to the matter uppermost in his mind, "they charge me at the court of France, what no man save my king dare say to me—that I divert the public funds to my own use. I, a Le Moyne, who spend my own private fortune in protecting and feeding these ungrateful people. But we waste time in words, like two chattering old women. We need ships and money and men—men who fight like gentlemen for glory, not deserters and convicts who fight unwillingly under the lash for gold.

"What can I do with troops who would as gladly spoil Biloxi as Havana?

"Captain de Mouret, you will sail on le Dauphin tomorrow at daylight. Place these dispatches in my brother Serigny's hands immediately upon your arrival.

From that time forward act under his instructions. Remember, sir, your mission is a secret one."

I knew well the name he gave me, for next to Iberville, Serigny was reputed the most accomplished of all the Le Moyne's. To his fame as a soldier, his attainments as a scholar, he added the easy grace of the courtier. His position at the court of Louis gave him great prestige throughout the colonies; he being a sort of adviser to the King on colonial affairs, or so we all then thought him. Little did I then know how scant was the heed paid by power and ambition to real merit and soldierly virtues.

This while we sat without passing a word. Truth to tell I was loath to leave the Governor, for I knew even better than he how much of treachery there was in those about him. Besides that I had no confidence in my lieutenant, and yet hated to acquaint Bienville with the fact for fear he might mistrust my motives. I was heavy at heart and dreaded the future.

When, somewhat after midnight, I arose to go, he came around the table and taking me by both shoulders gazed steadily into my face. I met his glance frankly and quailed not.

"Forgive me, Placide, these are such days of distrust I doubt every one about me. Forgive me, lad, but your old commander's reputation, aye, his honor even, depends now so much upon your fidelity."

I could say nothing. I felt a stealthy tear tremble in my eye, yet was not ashamed, for its mate glistened in his own, and he was a man not given to over-weeping.

2—BLACK WOLF

CHAPTER III

ABOARD LE DAUPHIN.

THE morning dawned moist and cold, with a stiff westerly wind. Just before daylight a small boat pushed off the low beach, scraped along the shallows, skirted the western edge of the island which there lies endwise across the harbor, and put me aboard le Dauphin.

I alone had no part in all the noisy preparation for departure, but sat absorbed in thought near an open port listening to the straining of the masts, the flapping sails, the low complaining beat of the wind-tormented waters.

Above the creak of the windlass raising anchor, I could catch snatches of whispered conversation just outside the port. The two men were beyond my range of vision. One seemed to be tossing in a boat, the other hung down the vessel's side by a ladder. I made out, disjointedly:

"Along in September—as soon as you return—all will be in readiness—two thousand Creeks, Chickasaws, Natchez—we ought to have no difficulty—Yvard—Spanish ships. The fall of Biloxi will be a great thing for us." And much more that I could not hear clearly.

(18)

But I had heard enough to know there was some truth in the rumor of a Spanish-Indian alliance, and an attack on Biloxi. And the name Yvard, being unusual, clung somewhat to my memory.

I immediately ran on deck and sauntered over towards that side, seeking to discover the traitor. No one was there, only a little group of officers walking about; towards the shore were the retreating outlines of a light boat. I knew none of these officers, any one of whom might have been the man I overheard, and so I durst ask no questions. I could therefore confide in no one on board for fear of making a mistake, but must rely upon giving Bienville prompt warning upon my return, and I must needs hide my reluctance and mingle with officers and men, for perchance by this means I might uncover the scoundrel.

Although I made free with the men, pitched quoits, and joined in their rough play, I trusted none, suspected all. No, not all. There were two young fellows whom I was many times on the point of calling to my confidence, but, thinking it wiser, kept my own counsel. Treason could ever wear a smiling front and air of frankness.

Levert was a man much older than myself, of gloomy and taciturn manners, yet something there was so masterful about him men obeyed him whether they would or no. A more silent man I never knew, yet courteous and stately withal, and well liked by the men. But it was to Achille Broussard my heart went out in those days of loneliness. His almost childish lightness of disposition and his friendly ways won me completely, and we became fast comrades. A noble looking lad, with the strength of a young Titan, and the blonde curls of a woman. During the long idle hours of the afternoon it was his custom to banter me for a bout at swords, and Levert generally acted as our master of the lists. At first he was much my superior with the foils, for during his days with the Embassy at Madrid, and in the schools at Paris, he had learned those hundreds of showy and fancy little tricks of which we in the forests knew nothing. However, I doubted not that on the field our rougher ways and sterner methods would count for quite as much.

With all the five long weeks of daily practice, I gathered many things from him, until one day we had an experience which made us lay the foils aside for good.

We had been sitting after the dinner hour, discussing his early life in Paris. He wound up with his usual declaration, "As for myself, give me the gorgeous plays, the fetes and smiles of the Montespan, rather than the prayers, the masses and the sober gowns of de Maintenon. And now it is your turn, comrade; let us know something of your escapades, your days of folly in dear old Paris."

"I have never seen Paris," I answered simply.

"What! Never been to Paris? Then, man, you have never lived. But where have you spent all your days?"

"In the colonies—Quebec, Montreal, Biloxi. But now I will have an opportunity, for I am going—"

I had almost told something of my mission, ere I checked a too fluent confidence.

Levert, who had been pacing up and down the deck in his absorbed and inattentive way, dropped his blade across my shoulder and challenged me to the foils.

"No, it is too early yet," Achille replied, "besides, we were talking of other things. As you were saying, comrade, you go—?"

"Oh, you two talk too much," Levert broke in again, "let us have a bout; I'm half a mind I can handle a foil myself. A still tongue, a clear head and a sharp blade are the tools of Fortune."

It seemed almost that he had twice interrupted purposely to keep me from talking. I thought I read that deeper meaning in his eyes. Somehow I grew to distrust him from that moment. What consequence was it to him of what I spoke?

It was not Levert's business to govern my tongue for me, so I only said:

"Nay, we'll try our skill somewhat later; not now," and resumed my conversation with Achille.

While his manner showed a concern I deemed the matter little to warrant, yet it did make me consider, so I determined not to speak truly of myself.

"Well, now, comrade, of your own intrigues. You were saying—?"

"Nay, nothing of that kind. I journey to Paris simply for my own pleasure." Levert, who half listened at a distance knew I was going to heed his advice, though

I misdoubted his motive, and again took up his pacing to and fro.

"Aye, my dear Captain, but 'tis a long trip for such an errand·?"

"Yes, quite a long trip, but I weary of the life at Biloxi, and would amuse myself for a while in France."

"But the garrison at Biloxi; is that strong enough to spare so good a soldier? then the Indians, do you not fear them?"

I glanced at him quickly, only half betraying my thought, but replied nonchalantly:

"No, the Indians are quiet, at least so our scouts tell us, and as for the state of the garrison, you were long enough ashore to know we are strong."

"Ah, then, there is another motive; a woman. Come, is it not true? Confess?"

I blushed in spite of myself; it was an idle way I had, for I had seen little of women. My confusion threw him completely off the track; had I only guessed it, would have taken refuge in that device sooner.

"No, no, comrade; you are wrong"—but still somehow my color came and went like a novice out of the convent. His good-humored raillery continued until I became annoyed in earnest, yet was glad he took the matter so seriously. When Levert passed us again on his walk I spoke to him.

"Now, my dear Levert, we will try our fortune with the foils if it pleases you."

"No, my humor is past. Do you try with Broussard;

methinks he had rather the better of you yesterday.
You agree, Broussard?"

"Yes, yes," he replied, eagerly, "let us at it."

He fenced rather worse than usual, so I had no trouble
in touching him as I pleased. This begat an irritation
of manner, and noticing it I suggested we leave off.

He would not hear to it; I saw the color slowly leave
his face; his thin lips curled back and showed his teeth,
until, fearing a serious outbreak, I stepped back as if I
would lay aside the foil. He pressed me close, so close
indeed I could not if I would drop my guard. He
touched me once or twice.

"I call the bout a draw," declared Levert, who had
himself observed Broussard's unusual energy.

"Nay, not so, not so; he gives back. I've much the
better," and he lunged at me so vigorously I was forced
to act with more aggression. The button snapped from
the point of his foil; I cared not, and he affected not to
see it, though something made me sure he realized his
advantage. I determined now to show him a trick of
my own.

From my youth I had the peculiar faculty of using
one hand quite as well as the other, and had often practiced changing my sword swiftly from right to left. It
was a simple feat, much more showy than difficult, yet
exceedingly bewildering to an adversary. In this in-
stance it afforded me an easy means of reaching his
undefended side. So I feigned to be driven back, and
watching for a more headlong and careless rush, my
weapon was apparently twisted from my hand and for an

instant seemed to hang suspended in the air. I caught
it in my left and before he recovered his footing had
thrown his foil from him, sending it whizzing overboard.
It took but an instant to press my point firmly against
his chest, as he stood panting and disarmed. Never
was man more surprised.

"Bravely done," cried Levert.

"A most foul and dishonorable trick," Achille
snarled.

"Not so," Levert corrected him gravely, looking at
me to observe the effect of the insult. I stood still at
guard, but made no move.

"Broussard, you are angry now, and I'll take no
heed of your heated words. But to-morrow you must
make a gentleman's amends."

"Tush, tush," Levert interposed, "'tis the quarrel of
a child. He means nothing."

Broussard said no more, but looked surly and ill
pleased. I was secretly elated at the success of my coup
against such a skilled swordsman, and only remarked
quietly:

"Broussard, when your anger has passed I trust you
will do me the honor of an apology."

Behind it all I cared little, for I felt myself his master with his chosen weapon and could afford to be generous. He came up in very manly fashion, after a time,
and craved my forgiveness, but we played at foils no
more.

The lookouts were beginning to watch for land, I
growing more and more impatient as the end of our

voyage drew near. And now I had much leisure to contemplate, and wonder at the strange turn of fortune which had called upon me to play a part in the affairs of state, though what the drama was, and what my lines might be, I could only guess. The story of Colonel D'Ortez, too, furnished me much food for reflection these long starlit nights, when I sat in my favorite seat in the very prow of the vessel. There would I sit night after night, watching the phosphorescent waves rippling against the vessel, gleaming fitful in the gloom; there observe the steadfast stars, and seem alone with darkness and with God.

One wet morning, pacing the slippery deck, the sailing master called to me:

"See, sir, yonder dim outline to the nor'east? 'Tis the Norman coast; this night, God willing, we sleep in Dieppe."

My errand now consumed my entire attention, so I thought no more of my companions of the voyage, bidding them both good-night before we had yet landed.

CHAPTER IV

THE ROAD TO VERSAILLES

A T the break of day, rumbling out of the little fish-
ing village, I was surprised to see both Broussard
and Levert astir as early as myself, each in a separate
coach, traveling the same direction. I thought it strange
that they chose to go separately, and that neither had
told me of his expected journey. However that might
be, as it suited my purpose well to be alone, I disturbed
not myself with pondering over it. Yet I wondered
somewhat.

The King and Court were at Versailles; so judging to
find Serigny there I turned aside from my first intention
and proceeded thither. I was shocked by the universal
desolation of the country through which I passed. Was
this the reverse side to all the *Grand Monarque's* glory?
I had pictured *la belle* France as a country of wine, of
roses and of happy people. These ravaged fields, these
squalid dens of misery, the sullen, despairing faces of
the peasantry, all bore silent protest to the extrava-
gances of Versailles. For the wars, the ambition and
the mistresses of Louis had made of this fair land a
desert. Through the devastated country roamed thousands of starving people, gaunt and hungry as the wild

(26)

beasts of the forest; they subsisted upon such berries as they found, but durst not touch a stick of their lord's wood to thaw out their frozen bodies.

Young as I was, and a soldier, the sight of this wide-spread suffering appalled me, though being no philosopher I reasoned not to the cause. Yet this was the real France, the foundation upon which the King had reared the splendid structure of his pride.

It was some time during the second day, I think, when we passed a few scattering hovels which marked the approach to a village where we were to stop for dinner. At the foot of a little incline the horses shied violently, and passed beyond the man's control. My driver endeavored in vain to quiet them, and then jumped from his box and ran to their heads. I looked out to see what the matter was, and observing a squad of soldiers, followed by quite a concourse of villagers, I sprang to the ground.

Down the hill they marched, some ten or fifteen fellows in a dirty half uniform, I knew not what it was, while straggling out behind them seemed to follow the entire population of the hamlet. The old and gray-haired fathers, the mothers, the stalwart children and toddling babies, all came to stand and gape. In the lead there strode a burly ruffian, proud of his low authority, who shouted at intervals:

"So-with-the-H-u-g-u-e-n-o-t-s!"

Behind him skulked four stout varlets, bearing between them a rude plank, on which was stretched a naked body, the limbs being not yet stiffened in death.

I hardly credited my sight. Before they came abreast of us I inquired of the driver what it all meant. He only shrugged his shoulders, "A dead Huguenot, I suppose," and gave his care to the horses. Verily this was past belief.

I placed myself in the road and bade the leader of the procession pause. He stopped, staring stupidly at my dress.

"What is here my good fellow? what crime hath he committed?"

He, like the driver, answered carelessly:

"None; she is a Huguenot."

"*She*," I echoed, and stopped the bearers who laid their ghastly burden down, having little relish in the task. Yes, it was in very truth a woman.

"For the sake of decency, comrade, why do you not cover her and give her Christian burial?"

"It is the law," he replied stolidly.

"Yes, yes, it is the law," eagerly assented the people who gathered about the corpse, not as friends, not as mourners, but as spectators of the horrid scene. Among them, unrebuked, were many white-faced children, half afraid and wholly curious. I looked at them all in disgust. They went their way and came to the outskirts of the village, where they contemptuously tossed the woman from the plank across a ditch into the open field. In spite of my loathing I had followed.

I perceived now a feeble old woman hobble up toward the body and try with loud wailings to make her way through the guard which surrounded it. They

shoved her back with their pikes, and finally one of
them struck her for her persistence.

"Pierre, look at her old mother; ah, Holy Virgin,
what a stubborn lot are these heretics."

Her mother! Great powers of heaven, could it be possible? My indignation blazed out against the inhuman
guard.

"Why do ye this most un-Christian thing?" and
to the crowd:

"Do you call yourselves men to stand by and witness
this?"

At my words one sturdy young fellow, of the better,
peasant-farmer class, broke from those who held him
and would have thrown himself unarmed against the
mail-clad guard. Many strong arms kept him back.
He struggled furiously for a while, then sank in the
sheer desperation of exhaustion upon the road. As soon
as he was quiet the mob, gathering about the more
attractive spectacle, left him quite alone. I went up to
him, laid my hand upon his shoulder, and spoke to him
kindly. He looked up, surprised that one wearing a
uniform should show him human sympathy. He had
a good, honest face, blue-eyed and frank, yet such an
expression of utter hopelessness as never marred a mortal
countenance. It haunts me to this day.

I was touched by the man's sullen apathy, succeed-
ing so quickly to the desperate energy I had seen him
display, and asked concerning his trouble.

"Oh, God, Monsieur, my wife, Celeste, my young
wife! Only a year married, Monsieur." He raised upon

his elbow, taking my hand in both of his, ''We tried to go; tried to reach England, America, anywhere but France; they brought us back, put us in prison; she died—died, Monsieur, of cruelty and exposure, then they cast her out like some unclean thing; she, so pure, so good. Only look, lying there. Holy Mother of Christ, look down upon her.''

He turned his gaze to where his wife lay and sprang up.

''She shall not—shall not,'' and cast himself again towards the guard. A dozen men seized him.

Deeply pained by his misery and the horror of the thing, I made my way to the front, near where the body lay.

''What is this foul law of which you spoke? Tell me?''

My tone had somewhat of authority and anger in it, so the fellow gave me civil answer.

''The law buries a Huguenot as you see—such unholy flesh could never sleep in holy earth. The beasts and birds will provide her proper sepulcher.''

''Nay, but compose her fittingly; here is my cloak.''

''It is not the order of the King,'' he sullenly replied. The brutal throng again gave assent.

'' 'Tis not the law, 'tis not the law, and bowed their heads at very name of law.

I remembered the Governor's errand, and could waste no time in quarrel which was not mine, yet willingly would I have cast my cloak about her. I inquired of the man:

"And what is the penalty should the hand of charity take this woman from the highway?"

"On pain of death."

"Then death let it be," screamed her husband, and breaking through the line of guard, he threw himself upon his wife, protecting her with his pitying garments.

Whilst I had been talking to the officer, no one observed the man come stealthily to the front, coat in hand, until, seeing his chance, he broke through their line. But these staunch upholders of the law would not have it so. They tore him viciously away, and I, sickened, turned from a revolting struggle I could do nothing to prevent. All these long years have not dimmed the memory of that barbarous scene.

CHAPTER V

THE DECADENCE OF VERSAILLES

IT was nearly noon on the fourth day when I alighted at the Place d'Armes, the grand court-yard of Versailles, and I fear I cut but a sorry figure for a governor's messenger. It appeared that my dress at best was unlike that worn at the court; my fringed leather leggings, hunting knife and long sword differed much from the wigs and frizzes worn by the officers of the guard. However, I made bold to seem at ease and accustomed to court as I addressed the officer of the watch.

"Can you direct me, sir, to M. de Serigny? I have business with him."

The man smiled, I knew not at what, and regarded me curiously. I felt my face flush, but repeated the question.

"M. de Serigny," he replied, "is with the court. Seek him at his apartments. Pass through yonder great gate, turn to the left and inquire of the guard at the door."

I walked on hastily, glad to be quit of his inspection. Such a throng of fine gentlemen in silks, satins and ribbons I never dreamed of; even the soldiers seemed dressed more for bridals than for battles. I held my peace though, walking steadily onward as directed, yet itching to stick my sword into some of their dainty trappings. At the door I came upon a great throng of loungers playing at dice, some throwing and others laying their wagers upon those who threw.

Standing somewhat aloof was a slender young fellow who wore the slashed silver and blue of the King's own guard—I knew the colors well from some of our older officers in the Provincial army. They had told me of men, soldiers and hard fighters, too, wearing great frizzled wigs outside their natural hair, with ruffles on their sleeves and perfumed laces at their throats—but I had generally discredited such tales. Here was a man dressed more gaily than I had ever seen a woman in my childhood—and he seemed a fine, likely young fellow, too. I fear I examined him rather critically and without proper deference to his uniform, for he turned upon me angrily, catching my glance.

"Well, my good fellow, didst never see the King's colors before? Where hast thou lived then all these years?"

He seemed quite as much amused at my plain forest garb, leggings and service cap, as I had been at his silken trumpery. I replied to him as quietly as might be:

"In our parts beyond the seas we hear often of the King's Guard, but never have my eyes rested upon their uniform before."

Observing my shoulder straps he unbent somewhat and inquired:

3—BLACK WOLF

"Thou bearest the rank of captain?"

"Aye, comrade, in the service of the King in his province of Louisiana. I pray you direct me to the apartments of M. de Serigny, I would have speech with him."

He was a manly young lad, of soldierly bearing, too, despite his effeminate dress; he turned and himself guided me through the many intricate halls and passages until we reached a door which he pointed out as Serigny's, where, with polite speeches, he left me alone.

Monsieur was out, at what business the servant did not know, but would return at two of the clock. In the meantime I sought to amuse myself strolling about the place. I knew I could find my way along the bayou paths of Louisiana the darkest night God ever sent, for there at least I would have through the trees the glimmer of a friendly star to guide me. But here in the King's palace of Versailles, with the winding passages running hither and yonder, each as like the other as twin gauntlets, I lost myself hopelessly.

Clanking about alone over the tiles in great deserted corridors I grew almost frightened at my own noise until I passed out into an immense gallery, gaily decorated, and thronged with the ladies and gentlemen of the court. I could not make much sense of it all except it seemed greatly painted up, especially overhead, and nearly every figure bore the face of the King.

From the windows I could see a strange forest where every tree grew in the shape of some odd beast or bird, being set in long rows, and among them were white images of some substance like unto the Holy Mother at the shrine in Montreal. Some of these graven stones were in semblance of men with horns and goats' legs, and some of warrior women with plumed helms upon their heads. Verily I marveled much at these strange sights.

The pert little lads who idled about the hall began to make sport of me concerning my dress, and laughed greatly at their own wit. I paid no heed to their foolish gibes, there being no man among them. It irked me more than good sense would admit, and I left the hall, and after many vain endeavors made my way out into the open air—being right glad to breathe again without a roof above my head.

I was ill at ease among all these gay gallants who minced and paced along like so many string-halted nags. It was said the King walked much in that way, and so, forsooth, must all his lords and ladies go. Perhaps it was the fashion of the court, but I stuck to the only gait I knew, a good, honest, swinging stride which could cover fifteen leagues a day at a pinch.

Off to one side the water kept leaping up into the air as I am told the spouting springs do in the Dacotah country. I walked that way and was soon lost in wonderment at the contemplation of a vast bronze basin filled with curious brazen beasts, half men half fishes, the like of which I had never seen. Some had horns from which they blew sparkling streams; others astride of strange sea monsters plunged about and cast up jets of water. It all made so much noise I scarcely heard a voice behind me say:

"I'll lay a golden Louis his coat is of as queer a cut as his nether garment—whatever its outlandish name may be."

"Done," said another voice.

I gave no heed, thinking they meant not me, until a dapper little chap, all plumed and belaced, stepped in front of me with a most lordly air.

"Hey, friend, who is thy tailor?" and behind me rang out the merry laugh at such a famous jest.

I turned and there being a party of fine ladies at my back full gladly would I have retired, had not the young braggart swaggered to my front again and persisted:

"Friend, let us see the cut of thy coat."

We men of the forest accustomed to the rough ways of a camp, and looking not for insult, are slow to anger, so I only asked as politely as might be, because of the ladies:

"And wherefore?"

"Because I say so, sir," he replied, most arrogantly and stamping his foot, "cast off thy cloak that we may see."

I still stood undecided, scarce knowing what to think, and being ignorant of fashions at court. De Brienne—for that was his name—mistaking my hesitation, advanced and laying his hand upon my cloak would have torn it off, had I not brushed him aside so vigorously he stumbled and fell to the ground.

I had no thought of using strength sufficient to throw

him down. He sprang up instantly, and, furious, drew
his sword. I felt my own wrath rise at sight of cold
steel—it was ever a way of mine beyond control—and
asked him hotly:

"How is it affair of thine what manner of coat I
wear?"

He made no reply, but, raising his arm, said, men-
acingly:

"Now, clown, show thy coat, or I'll spit thee like a
dog."

I glanced around the circle at the blanched faces of
the ladies, seeing such a serious turn to their jest, and
would not even then have drawn, but the men made no
effort to interfere, so I only answered him, "Nay, I'll
wear my cloak," when he made a quick lunge at me. I
know not that he meant me serious injury, but taking
no risk my blade came readily, and catching his slen-
derer weapon broke it short off, leaving him raging and
defenceless—a simple trick, yet not learned in a day.
It was a dainty little jewel-hilted toy, and I hated to
spoil it.

"Now, sir, thank the King's uniform for thy life,"
my blood was up, and I ached to teach him a lesson,
"I can not turn the King's sword against one of his
servants."

The ladies laughed now, and the hot flush mounted
to my cheeks, for I feared a woman, but their merriment quickly died away at sound of an imperious voice
saying:

"For shame de Brienne, brawler!" "And thou, my

young coxcomb of Orleans," he continued, addressing
that dissolute Prince: "How dare you, sir, lead such
a throng of revellers into the King's own gardens? Is
not your own house of debauchery sufficient for Your
Grace? Have a care, young sir, I am yet the King,
and thou mayest never be the Regent."

The Duke simulated his profound regret, but when
Louis' back was turned made a most unprincely and
most uncourtly grimace at his royal uncle, which set
them all a-laughing. Whereat all these noble lords and
ladies made great pretense of gravity, and ostenta-
tiously held their handkerchiefs before their mouths to
hide their mirth.

Already these satellites began to desert the sinking
to attach their fortunes to those of the rising sun. I
marvelled at this, for the name of Louis had been held in
almost Godlike reverence by us in the colonies. Meanwhile he had turned to me.

"Well said, young man; thou hast a loyal tongue."

"And a loyal master, sire," for it needed not the
mention of his name to tell me I faced the King. That
face, stamped on his every golden namesake, had been
familiar to me since the earliest days of my childhood.

"Thy name, sir?"

Kingly still, though a little bent, for he was now well
past sixty, Louis stood in his high-heeled shoes tapping
the ground impatiently with a long cane, his flowing
coat fluttering in the wind. For a period I completely
lost my tongue, could see nothing but the blazing cross
of the Holy Ghost, the red order of St. Louis, upon the

Monarch's breast, could hear nothing but the grating of
his cane against the gravel.   Yet I was not ashamed,
for a brave soldier can proudly fear his God, his conscience and his King.

"Thy name," he sharply demanded, "dost hear?"
"Placide de Mouret, Captain of Bienville's Guards,
Province of Louisiana, may it please you, sire," I stam-
mered out.

"Attend me at the morning hour to-morrow," and
he strutted away from the giggling crowd.

I too would have turned off, had not my late antagonist proven himself a man at heart.   He quickly moved
toward me holding out his hand in reconciliation.

"I ask thy pardon, comrade; I too am a soldier,
though but an indifferent one in these peaceful times.
We mistook thee, and I humbly ask thy pardon."

Of course I could bear no malice against the fellow,
and he seeming sincere, I suffered him to present me to
his friends.   First among these, de Brienne presented
me to His Royal Highness, the Duke of Orleans, "First
Prince of the Blood, and the coming Regent of France."

This latter speech was given with decided emphasis,
and a malicious glance toward a pale, studious looking
man, a cripple, who, the center of a more sedate group,
was well within hearing. The deformed Duke of Maine,
I thought, rival of Orleans for the Regency.   The
ladies I would have willingly escaped, but they would
not hear of it, and soon I was surrounded by a chattering group, asking a thousand questions about the
fabled land of gold and glory beyond the seas.   Right

glad was I when one of the gallants pointed out a thoughtful looking gentleman who walked slowly through the eastern gate.

"There is M. de Serigny, a brother of Bienville, your Governor."

"That de Serigny?" I repeated, "then I must leave you, for I would speak with him," and I bowed myself off with what grace I could muster, knowing naught of such matters. A brisk walk fetched me to Serigny's side. In a few words I communicated my mission. His quick, incisive glance took in every detail of my dress and appearance, but his features never changed.

"Wait, my dear Captain," he drawled out, with a polite wave of his perfumed handkerchief, "time for business after a while. Let us enjoy the beauties of the garden."

My spirits fell. Could this be a brother of the stern Bienville, this the man upon whom my governor's fortunes now so largely depended? His foppish manner impressed me very disagreeably, and, in no pleasant frame of mind, I stalked along by his side listening to the senseless gossip of the court. We soon passed out of the gardens into the great hall, and reached his own apartments.

No sooner was the valet dismissed and the key turned in the lock than his face showed the keenest interest. After satisfying himself of my identity and glancing through the packet which I now handed him, he gave vent to an exclamation of intense relief.

"Not a day too soon, my dear Captain, not a day,

not a day, not a day,'' he kept repeating over and over,
looking at the different documents. ''The King promises to act on this matter in a few days, to-morrow,
probably. Chamillard is against us; he seems all powerful now; the King loves him for his truculence. But
these will help, yes, these will help.'' And again he
ran through the various papers with business-like swift-
ness. His fashionable air and the perfumed handkerchief were alike laid aside. Now I could see the re-
semblance between him and his sturdy brother.

''To-morrow, yes, to-morrow, my lad—pardon me
the familiarity, Captain de Mouret,'' he apologized,
waiving aside my hand raised in protest. ''To-morrow
we must act. We must gain the King's own ear. These
must not go through the department of war. Chamillard will poison the King's mind against us. Most
likely they would never reach the King at all. Louis
will hardly listen to me even now.''

''Then let me speak to the King,'' I blurted out before I thought.

''You?'' he repeated in unconcealed astonishment.

''Yes, I,'' I replied, for I was now well into it, and
determined to wade through; besides I loved my old
commander, and would venture much in his service.

Then I told Serigny of the occurrence in the garden,
or enough to let him understand why I was summoned
to the morning audience.

''Thou art lucky, lad; here half a day and already
have an appointment with the King.'' ''Yes,'' he
mused half aloud, ''Louis likes such things. He grows

suspicious with age, and doubts even his ministers. It
is quite possible he may question you of affairs in the
colonies. If so, speak out, and freely, too, my lad;
Louis loves the plain truth when it touches not his
princely person or his vanities. God grant that we may
win.''

Serigny then told me much of the petty trickery of
the court in order that I might understand how the land
lay.

"It may be of service to you to know something of
the many webs which ambition, cupidity and malice
have woven about us here in this great government of
France,'' he went on, speaking bitterly. "We never
dare speak our thoughts, for blindness, silence, flattery
and fawning seem surer passports to favor than are gallant deeds and honest service. The King grows old,
and it is feared his end is near. Of this, men scarcely
whisper. His death, as you know, would leave all
France to the frail little Duke of Anjou. Looking to
this, the court here is already divided in interest between the rivals for the regency, Philip of Orleans, and
the Duke of Maine. The Orleans party is the stronger,
though the Duke stands accused in the vulgar mind of poi-
soning all who may come between himself and the throne,
save this Anjou child, who will probably die of sheer
weakness. The King has recently had his de Montespan
children legitimated and rendered capable of inheriting
the crown, though the legality of this action is bitterly
contested by the Orleanists. He has also, it is said,
left a will in favor of the Duke of Maine, giving him all

real power, while nominally making Orleans the Regent.
And strange as it may seem, it is said this will was made
at the persistent request of de Maintenon, so viciously
hated by the proud de Montespan. But you know she
was the teacher of this little Duke, and they are very
much attached to each other. Were the Duke of Maine
a more vigorous man, there would be no doubt of his
suceess. If 'that little wasp of Sceaux,' as Madame
Orleans calls the wife of the Duke of Maine, were
the man of the family, she would surely be the Regent.
She's a wonderful woman. Madame du Maine hates
Bienville because she can not use him in her dealings
with Spain. She has duped the Bretons by the promise of an independent provincial government, but Bienville stands true to his King. So they seek by every
means to discredit him. You may surmise from this
how unfortunately our affairs here are complicated in
the affairs of great personages, where lesser men lose
their lives at the first breath of suspicion.''

After a little I had ample opportunity to observe
the man more closely, for he kept his seat to examine
at leisure the dispatches I had brought. He was evidently not entirely pleased with this inspection, giving
vent at times to low expressions of annoyance.

''Always the same trouble, la Salle and de la Vente,
spies in Biloxi—Ah, here is the fine hand of Madame
du Maine, currying favor with the Spaniard in aid of
her cripple husband. If we could only make this plain
to Louis; this stirring up of strife. Fancy a son of de
Montespan on the throne of France. Yes, yes, yes,

here is the awkward work of our old friend Crozat, the tradesman, who would purchase an empire of the King. See how clumsily he throws out his golden bait.''

I could but listen and observe. Now, more than ever, in the sternness and decision of his countenance he resembled his famous brothers, Iberville, Sauvolle and Bienville—and yet beyond them all he possessed the faculties of a courtier.

"Captain, are you acquainted with the nature of these dispatches?'' he asked directly.

"No, sire, only in general, and from my knowledge of affairs at Biloxi.''

"My brother tells me I may trust you.'' My face flushed hotly with the blood of anger.

"Oh, my dear Captain, I meant no offense; I speak plainly, and there are few men about this court whom you can trust. There is an adventure of grave importance upon which I wish to employ you. Your being unknown in Paris may assist us greatly.''

I signified my attention.

"It is supposed we are on the eve of war with Spain, and it is my belief the colonies will be the first objects of attack. Some person, and one who is in our confidence, is now carrying on a secret correspondence with the Spanish agent at Paris. Cellamare, the Spanish Ambassador, is concerned in the intrigue. This much we know from letters which have fallen into my hands, and I have permitted them to be delivered rather than interrupt a correspondence which will eventually lead to a discovery of the traitor. We have now good rea-

son to believe that dispatches of a very serious nature are expected daily by Yvard—Yvard is the Spanish
spy—''

"Yvard, Yvard," I mentally repeated, where had I
heard that name?

"These papers are to give our exact strength at
Biloxi, the plans of our fortifications, and a chart of all
the navigable waters of Louisiana. We can not afford
to let the Spaniards have this information, even if thereby we should capture their agent."

I maintained a strict silence.

"You understand le Dauphin is the last vessel over,
and no other is expected for months, so we think all
this information came over with you."

When he began I instinctively thought of Levert, who
set out alone for Paris just behind me. As he proceeded, the name "Yvard" again fixed my attention.
The very name I had heard mentioned by one of the
men the morning I left Biloxi. Serigny was right in
his surmise, but I let him go on without interruption.

"If I am correct, these plans will be perfected in Paris
before le Dauphin sails again. The spy, whoever he
may be, will perhaps want to return in her. Now you
can see what I want. You can understand what a help
you may possibly be in this matter. You doubtless
know every person who came over in le Dauphin, yet
you must avoid notice yourself, for they would suspect
you instantly."

I still said nothing to him of the conversation I had
overheard, or of my own suspicions, childishly thinking

I would gain the greater credit by unearthing the whole affair and divulging it at one time.

"We have some reliable fellows in Paris, and I will send such letters as will put you in possession of all the information they have. You and they, I trust, can do the work satisfactorily, but in no event shall my name, or that of Bienville, be connected with the enterprise. If the matter should come to the King, we would lose what little hold we now have upon him. It is not an easy or an agreeable task. The Spanish spy bears the name of Carne Yvard, a man of good birth, but a gambler and a profligate. He is known throughout Paris as a reckless gamester, but no man dare question him, because of his marvellous skill with the sword. He spends much of his time at Bertrand's wine and card rooms, though he has the *entree* at some of the most fashionable houses in the city, even at Madame du Maine's exclusive Villa of Sceaux. But thereby hangs his employment; we do not know how far Madame is involved in this intrigue with Spain and the Bretons."

Verily I felt encouraged as Serigny unfolded his charming plans for my entertainment. In a strange city to hunt up and dispossess a man like this of papers which would hang him. A delightful undertaking forsooth!

"But we plan in advance, my dear Captain. We must wait the pleasure of the King concerning you. We will renew this subject to-morrow."

That night I lodged with Serigny.

CHAPTER VI

LOUIS XIV

EVEN at this time I remember how nervous I was when I dressed for my interview with the King. What it was for, or how it might result, I could form no idea, so I did not trouble myself with vain thinking.

Promptly at ten I presented myself at that famous door which led to the room where Louis held his morning levee. Already the approaches were crowded, and the officer on watch was busy examining passes and requests for admission. Some there were who passed haughtily in without even so much as a glance at the guard or the crowd which parted obsequiously to let them through. Most probably favorites of the King, or perchance his ministers. When he reached me the officer of the guard, noting my uniform, inquired:

"Captain de Mouret of Louisiana?"

"Yes."

"You are to be admitted, sir," and I found myself ushered immediately through the opening ranks of Swiss mercenaries into the audience chamber of the King.

Louis no longer held his levees in the great vaulted chamber into which I was first shown, but in a smaller

(47)

and more sombre room, that of de Maintenon. The
character and dress of those present reflected with a
chameleon's fidelity the change in His Majesty's habits.
Madame sat near the King, working upon a piece of
tapestry which, when she was interested in what went
on, lay idle in her lap. Behind her chair stood the
sour-visaged Jesuit confessor, Letellier.

Death, which spared not even the Bourbon, had
taken away the Dauphin and his son; leaving as the
King's successor an infant yet in his cradle. This em-
bittered every thought of the King's declining years,
made him gloomy, petulant and querulous. And yet
there were many men still about him capable of upholding the dignity of the throne. I heard announced, one
after the other, Grand Marshal Villars, lately placed in
command of all the armies of France; the Duke of
Savoy, a famous soldier, but a deserter from the En-
glish; the brothers de Noailles, one bearing a Marshal's
baton, the other, cold, cynical, austere, robed in
churchly garments, Archbishop of Paris. There were
Villeroi, de Tourville, the admiral; and Marshal Tal-
lard—he who lost the bloody field of Blenheim to the
Englishman Churchill.

I confess I was abashed at the sound of so many
great names, and advanced in hesitating fashion across
the floor, to kneel before the King.

"Tut, tut, Captain de Mouret," he said, kindly,
"Rise, we would hear somewhat from you touching
matters in our Province of Louisiana, and particularly
of their safety in case of war—say, with Spain."

He then asked a few questions about things familiar to me, which put me quite at ease. What I said I can scarce at this time recollect, but I know I spoke with all a soldier's enthusiasm of my beloved commander, of his diplomacy in peace, of his war-won successes.

It did not pass unnoticed that many a venomous glance was shot towards me from that little group behind the King, but in the King's presence I feared nothing, and spoke on, unrestrained.

Once a tall man whom I took to be Chamillard interrupted; the King motioned me to proceed, and I told him all the strength and resources of the colonies, their weakness and their needs. When I thought I had finished, the King's face hardened, and looking me straight in the eye, he inquired:

"What is this I hear of Bienville's presuming to criticise me—me, Louis, his King—for contemplating such a disposition of the colonies as suits my royal pleasure? Can you tell me that as glibly, sir?"

For the moment I was astounded and had no word to say. I could see a faint smile run round the circle as they exchanged glances of intelligence. Serigny was right. The spy had already arrived. His eavesdropping news had reached the King. In my indignation I forgot the man I addressed was the Imperial Louis. Defending my master I spoke vigorously the truth, and that right earnestly.

"Your Majesty is a soldier, and will forgive a soldier's blunt speech. I beg you, Sire, to consider the services and the sorrows of Bienville's people, the loyal le

4—BLACK WOLF

Moynes. Where rests his father? Where his valiant brothers, Ste. Helene and Mericourt? Dead, and for the silver lilies! Where's Iberville, the courteous, the brave; he who ravaged the frozen ocean and the tropic seas in his royal master's name? Dead, Sire, of the pestilence in San Domingo. Does the King not remember his good ship Pelican? Has the King forgotten Iberville? Hast forgotten thine own white flag cruising on thine enemy's coast, borne down by four vessels of superior weight? Did the Eagle stretch her wings to escape the Lion?

Did the Silver Lilies flee before St. George's Cross? No, by the deathless glory of the Bourbon, no! And who was he that dared—following the example of his King, the Conqueror of the Rhine—who was he that dared meet such enemies and engage such odds? Whose was that boyish face of thirty, waving his curls upon the quarter deck, with the noble front of a very God of War? Iberville! Who is he that brushes away a tear to gaze upon his stripling brother beside the guns, soon to be exposed by his command to such a fearful danger? Iberville, again! Who is that fiery soldier, recking nothing save his duty, who seeth without a tremor that beloved brother lying mangled at his post, where the storms of hell do rage, and flames consume the dead? Who, when the enemy lay dismantled, their hulks afire, their colors struck, their best ships sunk, when the glorious standard of France triumphant dallied with the breeze—who is that dauntless gentleman who kneels

upon his battle-riven but victorious deck and sobs aloud
in agony above his writhing brother? Who is this
stricken gentleman, who, having won that most heroic
fight for his King, now prints a kiss, as a tender maiden
might, upon the pale lips of a dying lad? Ah, Sire,
it was Iberville, it was Iberville, my King, Iberville the
gentle, Iberville the true! Hast thou forgotten that
wounded lad who lived to serve his King so well on
other fields? Dost remember his name? Let me remind you, Sire, that lad was Bienville de la Chaise, your
loyal governor of Louisiana. Did the King but know
the trials and sufferings of my master in upholding the
royal authority, he would forgive him much. Nor do
I fear to say it even here, that those men who seek his
downfall would as lief line their wallets with Spanish
doubloons as with honest Louis d'or. De la Vente, the
renegade priest, the center of strife and discontent in
the colonies, traffics with the Indians and brings oppro-
brium upon your Majesty's name. It is he or la Salle
who sends this idle tale—la Salle, who, from your
Majesty's commissary, supplies this de la Vente with his
merchandise. Who their friends are here to tell your
Majesty these tales, I care not. Saving the royal presence, I would be pleased to discuss the matter with them
elsewhere.''

"Thou art a bold lad,'' observed the King.

I had noted his eyes flash, and the thin nostrils dilate
at mention of the passage of the Rhine; so, emboldened
by the surety of success, I kept my own courage up.

"Aye, Sire, truth need have no fear from the greatest of all the Bourbons. Bienville is a soldier, not a courtier, and stung beyond endurance by the threat of his enemies that they would yet beguile your Majesty to sell your fair Province of Louisiana, and turn the royal barracks into a peddler's shop—mayhap he did use some such hot and thoughtless expressions to me. These, some spy may have overheard and forwarded here to his hurt. If it please you to hear the words, I will repeat them upon the oath of an officer."

"Go on," he commanded drily.

"Bienville did say it was a matter of shame to forego such a broad domain wherein lay so much wealth, because of present troubles. It is his ambition to found there a new empire in the west, to add a brighter glory to the name of Bourbon, to plant the silver lilies upon the remotest boundaries of the earth, calling it all Louisiana, a mighty continent, without a rival and without a frontier. Ah! Your Majesty has in Bienville a strong heart and a firm hand, a man who prefers to devote his life to your service, rather than live at ease in France; a man who carries more scars for his King than your Majesty has fingers—poorer to-day than when he entered your service, though others about him have grown rich."

I told him, too, without reserve, of the contemplated Indian attack in the spring, of my own haste to return. His face lighted up with the fire of his thought:

"Then, by my faith," he broke in, "you need a bold, ambitious soldier for your Governor. What think you, Villars, Chamillard—gentlemen?"

None dared oppose the King.

"I overheard you, Captain, in the gardens yesterday, and think the master who has taught you such sentiments is a man the King of France can trust. Convey to the trusty and well beloved Governor of our Province of Louisiana our renewed confidence, with our assurance he is not to be disturbed. We make you our royal messenger for the purpose.'

Then he gravely inclined his head to signify the interview was done.

As soon as I decently could I left the royal presence and repaired at once to Serigny. I found him still in his apartments waiting me with every appearance of intense impatience. Almost as I rapped he had opened the door himself. The valet had been dismissed. My face—for I was yet flushed with excitement—told of our victory. He grasped my hand in both his own and asked:

"We have won? Tell me, how was it?"

"Aye, sir, and nobly. I have the King's own warrant that our Governor is not to be disturbed."

Every shade of anxiety vanished, and he laughed as unaffectedly as a girl.

"Thou art a clever lad; but tell me of it, tell me of it!"

I told him then of the audience, neglecting not the minutest detail, not even the black looks of those who thronged about the King.

"Chamillard's doing, and Crozat. Crozat the par-

venu—Marquis du Chatel, forsooth, with his scissors
and yardstick for device.''

He questioned me closely concerning the personages
present, and what they said. After having heard on to
the end he was quite composed and broached again the
subject of the previous night.

"Well, Captain " he commenced, half banteringly,
"if thou hast done thy conferences with the King, we
will talk of your next adventure. Time presses, and
you see from what Louis said, our enemies are already
at work.''

I hearkened with many misgivings, for I felt of a
truth uncertain of myself in this new character—and
shall I confess it—a trifle ill at ease concerning this
bravo, Carne Yvard, the duelist of the iron hand, and
the gamester with the luck of the devil. However, I
put upon myself a steadfast front and listened.

"We have a fine lad at Paris in our service," said
Serigny, "and with him four as staunch fellows as ever
dodged a halter. De Greville—Jerome de Greville—
has his lodgings in Rue St. Denis, at the sign of the
Austrian Arms. The host is a surly, close-mouthed
churl who will give you little information until he knows
you well. Then you may rely upon him. Jerome has
been watching our quarry these many weeks; we hold
him in easy reach, as a bait to catch his accomplice.
Then we will put them both where they can spy upon
us no longer. I desire them to be taken alive if possible, and by all the gods, they shall hang.''

Verily, this was a pleasant adventure for me to contemplate, taking alive such a desperado, who handled his sword like a hell-born imp.

"I would not expose you to this," continued Serigny, "but for the stern necessity that those papers should reach me unopened. They are to be delivered to you, and I hold you responsible. You understand?"

I bowed my acquiescence.

Then he went on, talking more at ease, though I was far from placid at the prospect. He told me of the different streets, the lay of the town, and the various men with whom I would be thrown.

"Beyond all," and in this I afterward acknowledged his foresight, "do not neglect the women, for their hands now wield the real power in France.'

I must own I thought more on the nature of my new errand than on what he was saying. I felt no small degree of distrust, yet, for my honor's sake, kept it to myself.

"And when shall I set out for Paris?" I asked.

"To-day; at once. Le Dauphin has already lain four days at anchorage, and we know for a surety that the expected spy has come. We can not act too promptly."

And so it came about that I left within the hour.

A carriage had been made ready, and I bade Serigny good-bye in his own rooms. He feared our being seen together too frequently about the palace.

"But one other thing, my lad," he stopped me as I would go, "you must need have other garb than that. Your harness of the wilderness but ill befits a gay gallant in Paris—for such you must now appear. You visit the capital to see the sights, understand; a country gentleman—Greville will instruct you, the rascal has naturally a turn for intrigue and masquerading. A dress like yours would mark you apart from the throng and perchance draw upon you the scathe of idle tongue. Here is gold to array yourself as becomes a well-to-do gentleman, and gold to spend at wine and on the games withal—for, thank Providence, the ancient House of Lemoyne is not yet bankrupt.''

I fain would not take his proffered coins, but he urged them upon me with such insistency that I, seeing the good sense of doing as I was bid, placed them in my meager purse, and with a light heart I set out upon my doubtful journey.

The fear of which I spoke died away, for since our success with the King, my spirits rose, and I deemed all things possible. Besides, was I not in the personal service of my beloved commander who never knew a fear?

* * * *

The postilion whipped up his horses, and we turned towards the old city of Paris, that treasure-house of varied fortunes whence every man might draw his lot— of poverty or riches, of fame or obscurity, of happiness or misery—as chance and strength directs.

CHAPTER VII

AT THE AUSTRIAN ARMS

IT was well into the night when the first dim lights of Paris came into view, and perhaps some two good hours afterwards before we drew up in front of the "Austrian Arms."

It was not a new or prepossessing place, yet much better than those I had seen along the road from Dieppe.

The host well deserved Serigny's appellation of a churl, for he looked suspiciously at me, and when I asked for de Greville replied he knew nothing of him. I could get no satisfaction from him, so I determined to take up my abode and wait. In I went and heeded not the surly host who regarded me askance.

The small public room was vacant, and I possessed myself of it with the settled air of a man who has come to stay. Verily the fire felt most grateful, and it did me much comfort to stretch as I listed, after the tedious confinement of the coach. Mine host busied himself about mending the fire, but whenever I raised my eyes I caught his gaze fixed doubtingly upon me. Evidently the man knew more than he told, and I planned to test his loyalty.

(57)

"Here, my good man," I called to him, "dost know anything of this Jerome de Greville? Where is he?"

"By our Lady, noble sir, I know him not. Paris is a great city, and many noble gentlemen come and go at their will."

"But M. de Greville lodges with you, I am told. My business is urgent."

"I do not recall such a name? Jerome de Greville?" and the rascal turned his eyes to the ceiling in the attitude of deep contemplation. I smiled inwardly.

"If it please you, sir, to write your name in my guest book, should Monsieur de Greville call I will show it him. You may tell me where you can be found."

He fetched out a worn and greasy book from a chest in the rear, and handed me a pen, watching, as I thought, with some interest, what name I would write, though I much questioned if he could read it. I pushed the book aside.

"Oh, it matters not, my name; it is an obscure one, and M. de Greville would not recall it. See here my good fellow, here is a gold piece to aid thy memory. At what hour will M. de Greville return?"

He took the coin, and turning it over and over in his palm, said, as if to it:

"If Monsieur will write a note and leave it, I will send to other inns and see if such a man be in Paris. Monsieur is of Gascony?" he ventured.

The Gascons were at this time regarded with distrust, it was such an easy matter for them to carry news into Spain, being on the border.

I soon found there was nothing to be gained from the fellow, and becoming convinced of his steadfastness was willing he should keep the coin as earnest money for future services. De Greville not coming in, I grew restive, and concluded I would stroll about the city. Claude, for so the landlord styled himself, directed me to the principal thoroughfare, and I thought by walking straight along one street I could easily return. There was nothing unusual in the neighboring buildings to make a landmark of, so I chose a great round tower not far away, and carefully laid my bearings from that.

The landlord watched me taking my observations and felt sure I would shortly return; the more so that my few articles of apparel and necessity were left stowed in the corner by his hearth. These I had purposely so arranged that I could detect any meddling. Throwing my cloak about me I took the way he indicated, and soon passed into a wider and more handsome street, which I came afterward to know. Walking idly on, without thought of distance or direction, I tired after a while, and began to think of getting back to the inn fireside. I retraced my steps perfectly, I thought, and if my calculations were right should have stood where the broad, well-lighted street I had traversed corners on Rue St. Denis. But the locality was entirely strange, and I had lost sight of the great tower which I thought would guide me home, when a squad of the watch halted me and questioned my errand.

"I am a gentleman, and officer of the King," I replied with such an air they passed on.

"I pray you, gentlemen, direct me to the Rue St. Denis, thence I can find my way."

The man gave me directions which simply confused me, and, ashamed to confess my ignorance, I blundered on to where five or six narrow, crooked streets ran together, branching out like the fingers from my palm. I paused now uncertain which way to go amid so many devious courses, and deciding almost at hazard, turned down the best paved of all those dingy streets. I had hardly gone past more than two cross streets, when there stood at a corner, looking timidly this way and that, a slight girl, with blonde hair and eyes of Breton blue. She seemed so brave, yet so out of place and helpless at that hour of the night, on such an unfrequented road, I almost made so bold as to address her, thinking I might be of service to a lady in distress. But my tongue was not formed for such well chosen words and polite phrases, so I merely held to one side, she standing to the outer edge to admit of my passage.

At the moment I got opposite her, it seems she had misjudged the width of the pavement, for I heard her give a slight ejaculation, and one foot slipped off the paved way as if she would fall into the muddy street. I passed my arm quickly about her, and raised her to a place of safety, but even then could bring no word of courtly elegance to my assistance.

She thanked me prettily and daintily, and as I pursued my course, I could but turn and give yet another glance in her direction. She caught my eye, and again looking each way, bent her steps down a by-way leading off to the left, which we were that instant nearest. There was that in her manner, I could not say exactly what, which led me to follow her at a respectful distance, seeing which she turned her head, and I fancied I could observe a thankful little smile playing about her lips. At any rate she quickened her pace and walked with more assurance, no longer in doubt about her movements.

For many rods at times she would be lost to view in the dark, and her tread was so light it scarcely made a sound—or the great, clumsy clattering I created drowned it entirely. Just at the time I thought I had lost her, I could catch a glimpse of a flitting skirt beneath one of the flambeaux, which, stuck in niches of the wall here and there, lighted old Paris.

In a very pleasant frame of mind, I strode along behind her. It was wonderful, I thought, how readily a woman's intuition recognizes a protector. And I— for I must admit I was young then; in the ways of women, far younger than my years—I amused myself with many conjectures concerning what manner of errand had taken this young woman abroad alone on such a night. A lady she plainly seemed. Disguised a little, that might be, for her quiet dignity did not fully comport with the style of her dress.

A thousand airy castles I built for my fair heroine to live in, and I, like the knightly heroes of the Crusades, was ever her defender, ever her champion in the lists.

Busied with these fancies and romantic thoughts, I lost count of streets and passages, turning this way,

that and the other, through many narrow and tortu-
ous byways and alleys, until I realized I was hopelessly
lost. With my fair guide in front and my good sword
by my side, lightly I recked of streets or houses. Yet
I dared not forget I was on an errand for the Governor
and must not expose myself to bootless peril.

At last, and somewhat to my relief, she stopped before a great oaken iron-studded gate, possibly of five
good paces width, in one corner of which was cut a
smaller door so low a man must stoop to pass. Upon
this smaller door she rapped and stood in the attitude
of waiting.

I had a moment now to look about me. It was in a
quarter of the town that was forbidding. Here were
two huge, dismal, gray-stone mansions, separated by a
court-yard of probably forty paces across; a high wall
fronted the street, flanked by a tower on either side
the gate. On top, this wall was defended by bits of
broken glass and spikes of steel, stuck into the masonry while it was yet soft. More than this the flickering brazier would not permit me to see. All of this I
took in at a glance; across the street the murkiness of
the night shut out my view. She rapped again, impatiently, but in the same manner as before. A trifling
space thereafter the smaller door was opened, whoever
was inside having first peeped out through a round hole,
which closed itself with a shutter no bigger than his eye.

The lady looked first to me, then stepped inside and
stood back as if she bade me enter.

This was an adventure I had not bargained for.

Thinking only to see that the lady reached her destination in safety, here was a complication of which I had
never dreamed. What her singular errand was, or
wherein she desired my assistance, I could not even
hazard a guess. Yet there she stood and beckoned me
to enter, and I moved forward a pace or two so I could
see within the door.

The *concierge* held the door ajar, and a more repul-
sive, deformed wretch I never laid eyes upon. His left
arm hung withered by his side; at his girdle he swung
a bunch of keys, with any one of which a strong man
might have brained an ox. Every evil passion which
curses the race of men had left its imprint upon his lowering countenance. Yet for a moment, when his gaze
rested upon the girl, it was as though some spark of her
loveliness ·drove the villainy from his face. He was
hardly so tall as she who stood beside him watching me,
the semblance of a mocking sneer about her lips. Looking past them both I could see what manner of place it
was. A smoky oil-lamp sputtered in the rear, sufficiently distinct to disclose the paved court-yard, covered with the green slime which marks the place where
no sun ever shines. Further than this I could see nothing except the tall gray buildings which shut in every
side and this wall in front. That door once locked
upon the intruder there would be no easy egress. Instinctively I held back

"Monsieur is afraid?" she inquired, then tossed back
her head, and laughed such a low, disdainful, mean
laugh, as fired my every nerve to hear. I hesitated no

longer. Let come what will, let the Governor's errand
look to itself, for no man or no woman could ever laugh
at me like that.

Holding my blade at easy command, I stepped inside. Immediately the door closed, and the rasping of
the key told me it was securely locked as before.
Then came regret, but came too late. What I had
so foolishly commenced, I must now see finished. The
cup had been taken in hand and the dice must be
thrown.

As we came, I followed her again, though at much
closer range. We crossed the yard diagonally, across
the broken panes, bits of casks, wine bottles and other
refuse scattered about. I liked not the aspect of the
place. As the girl was about to enter a door leading
inside the building, a man came down the inner stairs
and passed out, coming in our direction. For the moment he was under the light I had good sight of him.

A rather low, dark fellow, dressed in the height of
the fashion, yet somewhat flashily withal; not too foppish, he was evidently a young gallant of the better
class. He staggered somewhat from wine, and carried
a magnificent breadth of shoulder, denoting considerable
strength. This was my mental catalogue from the
glimpse I caught.

By this time, the lady had got rather within the
range of the light; the man came straight at her, and,
to my amazement, despite her struggles, seized and
kissed her. This was before I could reach them.

I was upon him in an instant. Another, and he had

reeled back against the wall, drawing his weapon as he
fell. He recovered his feet, my blade met his, yet each
paused, well knowing the deadly lottery of such a duel
in the dark.

The lady ran up as nearly between us as she dared,
and besought:

"Oh, Messires, Messires," she plucked me by the
sleeve, "do not fight; there is no need of it."

"Get out of the way you impudent hussy," he commanded, "I'll kill your meddling lover, like the varlet'
hound he is."

I went at him in earnest. His further insult to her
made every muscle a cord of steel. I soon found this no
mere sport, for the fellow was a thorough master of his
weapon. I was a trifle the taller and had a longer reach;
this, with my heavier blade, gave me well the vantage.
Besides I had touched no wine, and my nerves were
steady.

However, I had the light full in my face, and he was
not slow to see the annoyance it caused me. I knew I
could not maintain such a fight for long, so I pressed
him sternly and the bright sparks flew. Backwards,
step by step he retreated, until he had almost reached
the door out of which he came. I durst not withdraw
my eyes from his, yet I had seen the lady run swiftly up
the inner stairs, whether for help or for other assassins
I could not guess.

Still back, ever pressing him desperately back, the
fight went, and he stood again inside the door, at the
very foot of the stair. Now every advantage was mine,

5—BLACK WOLF

for he was well within the glow of the lamp, every movement distinctly visible, while I yet stood in darkness.

"For the sake of mercy, my lord, come quick." It
was the girl's voice at the head of the stairs; "there
they are. They will desist if you command it." And
I heard the heavy tread of two men coming down the
stairs, a lighter step behind them. My foot touched
something which lay in the dense shadow of the door-
step. It felt soft, a package of some kind. Then I remember seeing something fall from the cloak of my adversary forgotten in the heat of the fray. I placed my
foot upon it.

"What quarrel is this, gentlemen? Put by your
swords?"

The voice was that of a man accustomed to obedience. My antagonist stood entirely upon the defensive;
I stepped back a pace and we rested at ease. He
leaned heavily against the balustrade; his breath came
hard; I could see he was nearly spent, so furious had
been our short contest. His face showed, besides, the
flush of too much wine, or perchance I had not been so
fortunate.

"What mean you, gentlemen? Your quarrel?"

"I did but kiss the wench, and this fellow set upon
me in the dark."

"Aye, my lord," I replied stoutly, according to the
stranger the respect he seemed to command. "A wan-
ton insult to this lady whom I met unprotected in the

streets, and saw her safely to her gate. Who she is, or
what, I know not."

The two men looked at each other, from the girl to
me, then burst into such peals of incredulous laughter
as roused my anger again. Even my late foe joined in,
but faintly.

"Would either of you, my lords, be pleased to take
the matter up?" for I was hot now indeed.

But they only laughed the more. The lady looked
much confused.

"Thou art not of Paris?" the taller man asked.

"No, this is my first night in Paris."

"I thought as much. This *lady*," the tall man continued in a sarcastic tone, "permit me to present you to
Mademoiselle Florine, waitress and decoy pigeon for
Betrand's wine rooms, where gentlemen sometimes play
at dice."

He laughed again, and even the girl could muster
up a smile now that the danger had blown over.

"That is true, Mademoiselle?" I asked. She nodded.

"Then, good sirs, I'll fight no more in such a matter."

"And by my soul, comrade, right glad I am to hear
you say it; for you fight like a very devil of hell, and
Carne Yvard knows a swordsman."

Carne Yvard! The very fellow I had been sent out to
find, now by a queer chance thrown full in my way.
Verily, I was relieved to know I could hold my own
against this famous—or infamous—bravo. Another
thing gained; I knew my man while yet a stranger to

him. And further, I stumbled on the very place which of all others I desired to find. Truly the chance was odd.

The two gentlemen upon the stair had not yet staunched their merriment, while these thoughts coming so unexpectedly had swept from me every recollection of the fight.

"Thou art not of Paris?" the spokesman asked again.

I heard him as a man hears something afar off, for my foot resting upon the package which had been dropped, sent my mind a wandering again. Could it be that this was a paper of importance, or possibly the very one I desired? Why not? I resolved to possess it at every hazard. Yet were I to stoop and pick it up now, and they saw me, I knew of no means by which I might leave the place in safety. So I carelessly shoved it with my foot farther into the shadow of the step. I answered the question asked me so long before.

"No, my lord, the city is a strange one to me."

"Of what place, did you say?"

Now I had purposely refrained from saying, and did not know what reply to give. I hated to appear boorish, besides it would not serve my purpose. My father being of Normandy, I deemed I would have nearly the accent of those people, so I made a venture to say:

"Of Normandy, sir," in such a way he did not pursue the subject further.

"We thought you no Parisian, or this lady would not have made so easy a conquest," and they laughed again.

"Do you play?" he queried.

"But rarely, my lord," the fact was I knew little of the dice.

They put about and ascended the stair, the two together, then Yvard, I coming on behind, but not until the packet, from which I hoped so much, was safely in my bosom. This was easily accomplished when Yvard had turned his back.

We climbed the stair, and after some forty or fifty paces stood inside the room of which Serigny had spoken to me. I could recognize the place from his description.

The gaming tables were ranged about in the center of the room, and about them sat many men—and women, too—at play. On three sides of the place a row of columns ran some four or five yards from the wall. These pillars formed convenient alcoves for those who would sit and sip their wine. Some were curtained, the better to screen their occupants. Others stood broadly open.

The four of us walked over to a table well out of view and sat down to wine. It was then I regretted not having already heeded Serigny's admonition to provide myself with garments more suited to my character, for I felt I attracted some attention as we passed through the room, and this was most to be avoided.

We seated ourselves about the table and ordered wine; mine remained untasted while the others drank. I determined to touch no wine that night.

"Comrade, you do not drink," Yvard remarked, "is your blood still hot with the clash of steel?"

"No, by my honor, that is long forgotten; it is my oath, an oath, too, that can not be broken."

"Ah, to a lady?"

I nodded, and he smiled.

We talked indifferent gossip, and after awhile the Spanish troubles were mentioned; I think the tall man first spoke of it. Somehow I felt Yvard's carelessness to be assumed, and that he very much desired to hear what these two gentlemen would say on a matter so important. His manner made it plain to me he knew the two gentlemen, and also that they were men of rank. However, they were quite discreet; while they talked much, yet they said nothing which was not common talk on the streets. After a bit they arose to leave, and I was sorely perplexed whether it were better that I depart with them, now that papers which might be valuable rested safely against my breast, or had I better stay and endeavor to learn more from Yvard, who was beginning to drink heavily. Perhaps a little more liquor might loosen his tongue, and I might even capture him or his confederate. Discretion would have taken me away, for that these two gentlemen were powerful enough to protect me in case of trouble in the house I did not doubt. The bearing of the elder man especially was such as to inspire confidence.

The adventure, though, was too enticing, and the hotter counsels of youth prevailed. I bade the gentlemen good night, and remained sitting at table with Yvard. It was but a few moments before I regretted my unwise decision.

Yvard leaned forward, the edge of the table pressing against his breast, and in so doing noticed the absence of the paper which he had forgotten in the fight. His face changed instantly, the drunken leer vanished. At first there was merely a puzzled expression, as of an intense effort to remember. He looked swiftly at me. I gave no sign. The two men were gone. His anxiety convinced me of the importance of the papers. He thought for a moment, then excused himself and went out the way we came. As he passed through the room, I saw him stoop and whisper a word to one of the men at the dice table. In a minute the fellow shifted his seat, and though he continued to play, he had taken a position where, as I imagined, he could watch me that I did not leave. I became uneasy now, for I could not tell how many there were, and my principal thought was how to get out of the house. Assuredly not by the way I entered.

Looking about more carefully to note the different means of egress, my attention was attracted by a carven shield above the main door. The arms were the same as those graven on the locket shown me by Colonel d'Ortez the night I left Biloxi. There, standing out boldly above the door, was the same sable wolf, the crest of the d'Artins. For a moment his story filled my mind again; but I had no time then for such reflections, and dismissed them to a future period of leisure. The question how to leave the house on that particular night gave me infinitely more concern than the idle speculation as to who had probably owned it long years before.

CHAPTER VIII

A NEW FRIEND

I RAPPED on the table, called a waitress, and ordered a bottle of light wine, which I knew would not hurt me.

"Send for Mademosielle Florine," and before many seconds were gone that lady presented herself, and perched upon the edge of the table where I sat. Her humor was gay, her laugh was keen; she smiled and asked, "Has Monsieur forgiven?" with such a penitent little look I bade her be at ease.

"Mademosielle, sit down, I pray you," and she saw by my serious face I was in no mood for chaffing, so she seated herself with a pretty air of attention. I could see the fellow at the dice watching, but now he appeared quite satisfied I intended to stay and drink with the girl. She was evidently a great favorite with the habitues of the place. He looked at me less frequently than at the door, and I guessed he expected Yvard's return.

Now I grew certain. Yvard had merely gone down the stair to see if he had dropped the papers in the fight. As soon as he found they were not there I felt morally certain he would come and demand them of me. I had begun the game, and must play out the hand. So

I reached across the table, filled the glasses for myself and Florine, raising mine high as if I would propose a toast. I tapped her banteringly on the cheek, for the benefit of him who watched, and said in a low tone, trying to maintain my nonchalant manner.

"Listen to me a minute, and I beseech you smile, do not look so serious. You brought me here, and now I trust you to get me out alive. Is there any other way than that I came?"

She looked about her apprehensively, so I cautioned her again.

"For heaven's sake smile; I am closely watched, and you must laugh and be merry as if I drank with you and made love."

She comprehended, and well did she play her part. The tones of her voice were light and playful; she lifted the glass to her lips, tasting as a connoisseur, and said between her sips:

"Yes, Monsieur, there is—another way leading out— on an alley—in the rear."

"How do you reach it?"

"The door behind the table—where they play for highest stakes—leads to the passage. Do but cast— your eyes that way—and you will see."

"Then let us—"

"Wait, Monsieur, not yet. If Monsieur would go and seat himself at that table, as if he desired to play, I will slip around and make ready the door for him. Monsieur was kind to me, and Florine is grateful. Even we women here respect a gentleman."

I pitied the woman from the bottom of my heart. I took out my purse, paid the reckoning, and together we wandered aimlessly toward that table, laughing and looking on at the various games. The fellow watched us as we went, but was pleased, and seemed satisfied the woman but carried out the purposes of her employment.

I took a seat at the table, laid a wager or two and made myself intent upon the game. Florine stood behind my chair for awhile, watched my play, then disappeared. After a little she returned and again took her place behind me. Directly she laughed out merrily, and in a tone loud enough to be heard by the man who listened as well as watched, cried:

"Monsieur plays the stakes too low. Fortune favors the brave," and reaching over she took several gold pieces from my store, laid them out and leaned close beside me to watch the throw. In this position she whispered:

"I have the key to the outer door. The inner door will be unlocked. Monsieur will play twice more, and by that time I will be in the passage. Arise, and when you lay your hand upon the door I will open it from the other side." I lost the throw.

"Double the wager, and better luck next time," she laughed as she moved off, and joking lightly to different men she knew, made her way beyond my range of vision. During the play I saw Yvard come in hurriedly and question the man at the door. He shrugged his

shoulders and shook his head. Yvard evidently asked
who had passed out or in.

The doorkeeper then recollected, and I imagined he
was telling of the two gentlemen who had just gone
down the stair. Yvard stood an instant as if uncertain
what to do. He was much agitated and perfectly sober.
He glanced toward the table where he had left me. I
was gone. He strode over to his confederate, yet engaged in play, and made no pretense of concealing the
abruptness of his question. The man, in reply, indicated
my position at the other table. Yvard appeared somewhat relieved. Again he spoke, and this time the man
at the table gathered up the money in front of him and
replaced it in his purse. Then he cried loud enough
for me to hear:

"What?"

And sprang up instantly. They both looked at me
and held a hurried consultation, then separated, and one
going one way, one the other, came over toward where
I sat. By this time my second throw was made, and I
felt if Florine played me false the game was lost. Yet
hoping for everything I rose quietly, and thrusting my
winnings in a wallet—for I had been fortunate—stepped
back and laid my hand upon the knob. It was locked.
I had no time to think, but saw the whole trick; lured
to my destruction, hemmed in beyond hope of escape.
Bitterly I repented my folly.

I have heard men say they faced death without a
tremor, and so for that matter have I, yea, many times,
but it was upon an honest field in lawful fight for honor's

sake or duty's. My cheek paled in spite of me, at sight of the men who now came on. Three others with blades half drawn pressed close behind Yvard. How many more there were I had no knowledge.

It was a sore test to my courage thus to meet the ugly chill of death in a Parisian gambling hell—in a place of such ill-repute. But there was no escape, and even if I fell in fight, they would brand me as a thief. Should the papers be found on my body, then honorable men would execrate my memory as a traitor to country and to King, for had not Serigny told me he could not avow my connection with him? The lust of life still surging strong within me, I drew my sword. Its point effectually guarded the narrow space in front from post to post. They parleyed a time, and I rested firm against the door.

"Come, fellow, thou art trapped; give me up my purse."

"Spit the thief, run him through," came from one of those behind—for the rear guard, beyond the reach of steel, was ever loud and brave. But Yvard, being in front, was more cautious. He well knew the first man who came against me would be badly hurt. And, I rather fancied, he respected my blade.

As they took counsel together, dozens of voices from the hall swelled the din, yet above it all I caught a light step without. My heart bounded to my throat; I felt the door give way at my back, and before they understood what had happened, I was safe on the other side, with the stout oaken boards well locked between.

I heard Yvard yell: "To the great gate, my bullies, and I will follow here," and at once a great pressure was cast against the door, but it bravely bore the strain.

"Come," Florine said; and taking me by the hand together we sped through many dark and devious windings, until I stood once more in the open street.

"Hurry, Monsieur, take that street; it leads to Rue St. Antoine, whence Monsieur can find his way."

I would have paused a moment to thank the girl, but she bade me haste. I pressed a piece of gold into her hand; she would not have it.

"No, Monsieur, not for your gold," and the woman of the wine shop shamed my thought. "Good-night, Monsieur." She kissed my hand, and drew back into the darkness.

I turned hastily down the street, but had not made more than the distance of three rods when I heard a scream, and looking back saw two men dragging Florine back into the street.

"Which way did he go?" Yvard demanded fiercely. She made no reply.

"Speak quick or I'll kill you as I would a hare." Still she kept her tongue.

"She makes time for her lover, Carne," the other man suggested, and as I feared he would strike, I called out loudly to them:

"Here he is," to draw them off from the girl.

They dropped her at once and started in my direction. I ran on ahead, yet at a disadvantage, for I knew not where to go, knowing, too, that I could not fight them both. Yet more than all I dreaded falling into the hands of the city guard with the papers I had upon me. I ran under a street lamp, and taking up a position some twenty feet beyond in the dark, waited. The knife for one, the sword for the other, was my thought. Holding my long sword in my left hand, I swung my right free, and catching my knife by its point, stood my ground. The younger man was swifter, yet seemed afraid to lead Yvard. So they passed under the lamp side by side.

Selecting Yvard as my mark, I made a quick cast, and had the satisfaction of seeing my knife glitter as it struck him full in the shoulder, and bury itself well to the hilt. It was a trick I had learned from the Indians, and it had not been lost.

"A million devils, who was that?" screamed the stricken man, tugging to free the knife. Out it came, followed by a widening dark stain upon his doublet.

"He had others with him—hidden in the dark," and at his companion's suggestion, they stood back to back, in readiness for their imaginary foes.

This gave me an opportunity to slip away, they pursuing no further. I dodged round the next corner and took my way up a street running parallel to the one I left.

When they no longer came I slackened my pace to a walk, trying in vain to recall how I came and how to reach Rue St. Denis. There was nothing for it but to keep straight on. The streets grew broader and travelers were not so few. I questioned several, and for a coin secured an honest-looking idler to guide me. It

was not so very far after all to my inn, yet right joyful I
was to see the place again and to find a cheerful fire
blazing on the hearth. I stood before the homelike
warmth and chuckled to myself at the success of my
adventure.

The host and some crony of his sat at table with their
cards and ale. I overlooked the game They exchanged glances and prepared to leave off, whereat I
apologized and begged them not to let me disturb them.
Claude declared he had only waited for me, and being
tired he would shut the house. He went on up to bed
and his friend took a seat beside me at the fire.

He was a simple-looking young fellow, dressed after
the fashion of a peasant farmer, with mild blue eyes,
and straggling yellow whiskers on his chin. I thought
to question him about the city.

"Well, friend, how goes the world in Paris?"

"Much the same as ever, yet your Paris is new to
me."

"Indeed? You are not of the city; of what place,
then?"

"Of Languedoc, in the south, where the skies are
bluer and the wind does not cut you through as it does
in this damp Paris of yours."

"Yes, I thought you of Languedoc, from your
speech. So the climate is with us in our parts bey :d
the seas. Beneath our southern sun ice is a thing almost unknown, and the snow never comes."

"And where do you live, my lord?" his eyes wide
open and shallow.

I felt somewhat flattered at his artless recognition of the difference in our stations.

"In Biloxi; the Southern Provinces, Louisiana," I explained, "whereof Bienville is governor."

Afterward I thought I could remember a knowing twinkle in the fellow's eye, which passed unnoticed at the moment.

"Ah, I hear much of the colonies; it must be a goodly land to dwell in, but for the savages and the cannibals."

I laughed outright.

"Verily, friend, we have no cannibals worse than the barbarous Spaniards who wait but the chance to slaughter our garrison," and before I was aware, I had told him of my voyage from Biloxi, and of going to Versailles, stopping short only of giving the purpose of my visit to Paris. I was sore ashamed of the indiscretion. When I looked I found him laughing silently to himself, laughing at me.

"Then you are Captain de Mouret?" he asked with purest Parisian intonation, and the courtesy of a gentleman.

"How do you know?" I attempted to be stern, but somehow my effort fell flat. "How do you know?"

"Well, I've been expecting you," and he brushed his hand across his chin, wiping the yellow whiskers away before my astonished eyes.

"I am Jerome de Greville. Claude told me of your coming, but I wished to make sure. We have examined your baggage," he went on frankly, unmindful of my ill-concealed disapproval, "but found nothing in the way of identification. You see," he apologized, "these things are necessary here, in affairs of this nature, if a fellow would preserve the proper connection between his head and his body."

He rolled up his whiskers, laid aside a yellow wig, and I could see he was as Serigny had described. He was not as tall as I, but strongly built, and some two good years my senior.

"Captain, if you will allow me I will take these traps of yours to our apartments. You lodge with me."

I was nettled that I should have spoken so freely to a stranger, and felt ill-disposed to be pleasant, but he soon drove away any lingering animosity.

When we had settled in our rooms, which adjoined, de Greville threw himself across his couch and said:

"Look here, de Mouret, we have a hard task before us, and you may as well know it. M. de Serigny tells me he has instructed you himself, but details he would leave to me. What's your name?"

"Placide," I replied as simply as a lad of ten.

"Well, I'm Jerome. We are to stand together now, and men engaged in business like ours have no time for extra manners."

His *bon camaraderie* was contagious, and I gladly caught it. "Agreed, Jerome; so be it. Go on."

"First we must locate our friend Carne Yvard, the very fiend of a fellow, who stops at nothing. Then to catch him with the papers, take them, cost what it will.

6—BLACK WOLF

For that work we have strong lads enough and true. Above all we must make no mistake when we strike, for if he scents our suspicions of him he'll whisk them off to Spain before you could bat your eye."

I listened to him intently, yet enjoying to the utmost my prospective triumph. He went on:

"Then there is that other fellow; we don't know who he is, the one that came over with you. He will probably exchange dispatches with Yvard, then off to the colonies again. There is not so much trouble about him, for he can be captured aboard ship. It is Yvard we want, and his dispatches."

I said very quietly, still looking into the fire:

"That much is already done."

Jerome raised up on his elbow and stared at me as if he thought me mad.

"I have taken those dispatches from your friend. Here they are."

"The devil you have," he cried out, reaching the middle of the floor at a single bound. "How and when?"

He would not leave off until I had related the whole of my adventure beginning with meeting the girl, and ending when I found him, at the inn. He was as happy as a school-boy, and laughed heartily at my being so readily made a victim of by the girl Florine.

"Such tender doves to pluck she does not often find, and I warrant you she lets not many go so easily."

I thought it unnecessary to tell him of my encounter

with Yvard, only that I had found the packet where he
dropped it.

"You lucky dog; it's well he did not see you, or
you might not now be talking to me with a whole skin."

It was better though to let him know of Yvard's
wound, for that would perhaps assist us in a measure to
determine upon our future course. So that part of the
affair I detailed in full.

"Verily, lad, your savage accomplishment stood you
in good stead."

He recognized the description I gave of the fellow
with Yvard, but said he was a bully, hired merely to
fight, and perhaps knew nothing of consequence. Then
we examined very closely the envelope containing the
papers. It had, from all appearance, come over from
the colonies, and bore traces of having long been carried about a man's person. This settled one matter.
The go-betweens had met, and the traitor on le Dauphin
was most likely in possession of the instructions from
Spain. This made his capture the more important.

De Greville well merited all Serigny had said of his
shrewdness, and more. Now see what a simple scheme
he laid.

We were first to find where Yvard was hidden. He
would certainly go into hiding until his wound was
healed; the finding of the papers upon him making it
necessary he should not be seen in Paris.

Where would he be likely to secrete himself? Ah,
trust a woman for that; so reasoned Jerome. What
woman? L'Astrea, of course. Of her intrigue with

Yvard, de Greville, who was a handsome gallant with a
smooth tongue, had learned from a waitress at Bertrand's.
This was the more probable because, Bertrand's being a
public place, the confederate could seek him there without suspicion. This confederate being unknown and
unsuspected could come and go unchallenged. Jerome's
deductions were plain enough when he told me these
things and the wherefore.

It was agreed our plan would be to watch L'Astrea;
she at least would enable us to find Yvard, or his accomplice whom we most wished to discover.

Who would do this? Why I, of course, for no one
knew me, or would know me when I had wrought the
miracle of shining boots, blue coat, curly wig, laces at
throat, in all which small matters Jerome was a connoisseur, and so it was laid out with much care; run
the quarry to earth, then continue the chase as needs
demanded.

Yet folly of follies; how lightly are such well arranged plans broken into. Through a woman came all
this scheming, by a woman's hand it was all swept into
naught. Both innocent of intention, both ignorant of
effect. Yet it was true. Jerome and I, as we then
thought, disposed our pieces with great care and cir-
cumspection, advanced the pawns, guarded the king,
and made ready for the final checkmate. Yet a woman's
caprice overturned the board, scattered our puppets far
and wide, and by the tyranny of an accident recast our
game on other lines, without rule or rhyme or reason.

CHAPTER IX

MADEMOISELLE

IN the morning of the following day we were engaged about a business which troubled me no little. Had it not been for Jerome I fear I had never come through it at all with credit.

First, we repaired to another house which Jerome possessed in a more fashionable quarter, and thither by his directions came a fawning swarm of tailors, boot-makers, barbers, wig-makers; vendors of silken hose and men with laces, jaunty caps, perfumes—it was a huge task, this making a gentlemen of me—as Jerome phrased it.

I worried over it grievously in the beginning, but at length sullenly delivered myself into his hands, murmuring an abject prayer for the salvation of my soul. That, at least, was not to be remodeled by all their fashionable garniture. These heated discussions concerning what I was to wear were not for me to put a voice in. Verily, I knew nothing and cared naught for the cut of a shoe my Lord of Orleans had made the style, nor did it matter whether my coat was slashed with crimson or braided with golden furbelows. Like some wretch a-quivering of the palsy I heard the learned doctors wrangling over my medicine, which they must needs hold my nose to make me swallow. For all their biases and twistings I knew full well they could carve no sprig of fashion from so rough a block as I. Certes, I must now have a squire to fasten this new harness well upon me, for by my word, I knew not one garment from the other by sight of it. Jerome went off into fits of laughter seeing me trying to struggle into things I could not even guess the use of.

When the worst was over, late in the afternoon, I felt like a play-actor, dressed for his part, but who, for the life of him, could not recall one syllable of his speech, nor breathe because of his wig. Jerome surveyed me with a half-critical, half-approving scrutiny, until I essayed to buckle on my sword.

"By my lady, fine sir, that dingy old cutlass will never do for a drawing-room. As well a miller's dusty cap to cover those glorious borrowed curls of thine; we must get thee one shaped in the mode." This quip exterminated my patience.

"To the foul fiend with all this everlasting style of thine. I know this blade, have tested it on many fields, and by all the gods at once I'll not replace it with a silly toy."

"A most virtuous resolution, a most godly oath, but my mettlesome friend, I'll point out thy error."

To his insinuating argument, even in this matter, at length I yielded; surrendered with the better grace perhaps, that he provided a most excellent piece of steel, which he said had seen good service. I tried its temper, and the edge being keen, I laid my own aside with sore misdoubtings, casting off an old friend to strap on a new. He now added a touch of rouge here and there, a black line to my brows and in the corners of my eyes, stepping back ever and anon to observe the effect. It galled me raw, yet I must perforce submit. When the whole job was finished, and I was allowed to sit, I gained no comfort. My clothes were too tight in some places, while in others I rocked about as loose as a washerwoman's arm in her scrubbing tub.

Jerome must now give me some lessons in deportment, he called it. It was but another name for a smirking and a-bowing and a-grimacing, what was denominated the "etiquette of the court." Jerome sat himself contented down, and put me through my paces like some farrier showing off a foundered nag. I more than half believed he was all the while making game of me, yet I knew no better. At any rate it was the veriest nonsense.

After a series of rehearsals Jerome withdrew to make himself ready, leaving me to practice my new acquirements of gait, of gesture, and of speech. What had taken me the better part of a laborious day he accomplished in a short half hour. Coming back unannounced he caught me bowing and scraping before a mirror, like a man stricken with idiocy. I felt as shamed as though I had been detected hiding in face of the enemy.

Jerome mocked and taunted me into a fine rage, which he deftly pacified in wonderment at himself. I should never have known him again for the plain Jerome.

Arrayed in much the same character of finery which be-
decked me, I could give no accurate description of his
dress, except that with glossy wig and a bit of color in
his cheeks he strutted valiantly as a crowing cock in his
own barnyard.

"Come, Placide, we are going to a ball; we can do
nothing in our quest to-night."

"To a what?"

"A ball. I thought it might be well to have you
look in upon Madame M——'s and recite your lessons.
It is to be a famous gathering and well worth your seeing."

I was in a whirl, a stupor, by this time, and obeyed
implicitly; beside, it required such an infinite skill to
keep my sword from swinging between my legs and
throwing me down, I had no time to consider of minor
matters. He led the way and I followed meekly as a
lap-dog.

At the great entrance gate we became entangled in a
medley of soldiers, coachmen, torch-bearers and servants coming and going—such a babel of strange oaths—
I wished I were safe again in the quiet of Biloxi. I
pleaded with Jerome to turn again, but he was inexor-
able.

"I expect to find out something to-night," he explained.

Of this ball I remember nothing but that the slippery
floor, in which a man could see his own face, kept me
in deadly fear lest my sword trip me. Jerome was gay
and talkative, pointing out many people of whom I had
heard, but they did not look so great after all.

"For sake of heaven man, wear not so long a face;
it is not the funeral of thy mistress I have brought thee
to."

I marveled that so many old ladies should carry
such young faces or perchance their hair had turned
gray earlier than was its wont in the colonies. And, too,
they seemed sadly disfigured with boils, for on the chin
or cheek of nearly every one there showed a patch of
black sticking-plaster. Poor things! I sorrowed for
them, it was so humiliating. Verily, I pitied them all,
and speculated on the wonderful compensations of Providence.   With all their wealth and rank, their lordly
castles and their jewels, these noble dames could not
purchase that which the humblest serving-maid in Quebec had, and to spare—a clear skin and sunny locks.

I touched upon these matters to Jerome, but he only
laughed immoderately.   He was ever a light-headed
young spark who gave no contemplation to deeper
questions than present enjoyment.

Of a sudden my wits almost left me at a terrible out-
cry from one end of the great hall, a cry not of human
beings but of wild beasts, muffled and menacing.   The
dancing, the music, the hum of voices ceased, and a
thick silence as of direst fear fell upon them all.   Then
there came a loud crackling and shattering of glass, a
woman's scream, the first of very many.   This for
aught I know might have been a usual happening at a
ball, I had never been to one before.

I looked for Jerome.   He was gone, speeding toward
a young lady surpassing fair, with whom he had been

speaking but a few moments since. I fain would have assisted him, for the damsel appeared wofully beset, but the whole throng of mincing lords and screaming ladies, in the rankest riot, over-ran me. They swept me from my feet and bore me back to the farthest wall, where I found myself pinned tight and fast against a window.

What the danger was I could not see, but it must have been dolorous from the headlong terror of their flight. Soon by the thinning of the crowd through the doors I saw the cause. It was a motley and a moving spectacle. For by some mischance a flock of sheep had broken into the ball-room, and frightened out of their shallow senses by the lights and music, they rushed pell-mell here and there, upsetting without discrimination whatever stood in their path.

Verily such an onset would do brave work against an enemies' ranks, for could our knights but make a gap like that, an army of children might march through un-hindered. All went down alike before their charge, my lord and my lady, the Prince of the Blood, and the humblest page who bore his pouncet box. Such a slip-ping and a sliding across a floor slickened with much wax and polishing, was never in a ball room before, nor ever was again. One old ram regarded each mirror as a certain avenue of escape, and the radiating fracture of each taught him no greater wisdom concerning the others.

Standing spellbound as a statue in the midst of the ruins, I caught sight of a florid, rotund lady, speechless in her horror and her misery.

"The Duchess does not enjoy her quaint surprise," laughed a light voice behind me, and a slim finger directed my gaze toward the lady whom I had just noted.

I observed then at my back, standing upon a chair where she could see the better, a young woman of distinguished appearance, rather more plainly attired than the balance. She appeared greatly to enjoy the confusion.

"That is the reward for her romantic and pastoral 'tastes," and she laughed till the tears dripped down her cheeks. Her hair was still black, and neither paint nor sticking plaster marred the whiteness of her skin. I asked no questions, but regarded more closely this young woman with whom I now drifted naturally into conversation. Her manners were strikingly free and unconstrained. There was, however, an air of reserve, of dignity—of majesty even—about her, despite her frankness, which forbade anything but the utmost deference.

"Does my lord understand—that?" and she pointed her finger to the servants who were chasing and capturing the refractory sheep one by one.

I shook my head, for, in all seriousness, it was a queer proceeding.

"Well it's too merry a jest to keep long a secret. Beside I'm weary of these eternal shackles of court which forbid me to speak to those whom I please." A certain defiance gave an undercurrent of sadness to her voice, a mounting rebellion to her tone.

"And I *will* talk if I want to; there's no harm, is there?"

I gravely assured her not, and wondered what was coming.

"Well, you see," she dried her eyes on a hand-kerchief of costliest lace, "you see my—that is, the Duchess, is of such a romantic temperament, so enamoured of rural scenes, idyllic meadows, pretty shepherd-esses, and the like—all the court makes merry at her foible. She thought to astonish Paris to-night by a lavish display of sweet simplicity—did Monsieur see it? That big dark place back there, behind the glass partition, was arranged as a meadow, with a stream winding through it, and rocks and trees, and what not. She had a flock of sheep washed clean and white, penned up and in waiting. At a signal from her during the ball, lights were to have been turned on, and Mademoiselle, the pretty opera singer, was to come gracefully down a curving pathway, dressed as a shepherdess, singing and leading her sheep. Oh, it was to be too pure for this earth. The Duchess fretted for the opportune time. But the sheep escaped from their keepers, and, oh, isn't it too ludicrous?"

Thus she chattered on with the naive freedom of any other young demoiselle. I agreed with her, and was inwardly glad the affair turned out an accident, for were this the custom of balls I'd go to no others.

We continued to chat gayly together; she was of a lively wit, and surprised me by her knowledge of dogs and horses, of the chase, of sword play and of fire-

arms.   Odd tastes for a gentlewoman, most of all for
one of her exalted rank. Of this latter I had no doubt.
I knew none of the people she mentioned, nothing of
the drawing-room gossip, and she very naturally remarked.

"My lord is a stranger?"

"Only yesterday in Paris," I assented.

"From what place comes my lord?" and for the
second time in a day I was driven to a direct lie.

"From Normandy," I replied.

"To live in Paris?"

"No, unfortunately; my affairs will be finished in a
few days at most. Then I return to the country." The
lady was pensive for a space, hesitated in a pretty perplexity and then spoke doubtfully.

"You can be of a service to me if you will."

I immediately signified my willingness to render her
aid, in the courtliest speech I could muster. She looked
at me long and seriously again, then again pursued the
subject of her thought.

"It is a mere woman's whim, but *I* gratify *my* whims.
Perchance it is not a proper wish for a lady of birth,
yet I have it, and if you will but aid me, I will carry it
through."

Moved as much by curiosity as by any other motive,
I inquired of her what so weighty a matter could be.

"Come, let us go into this ante-room that we may
converse undisturbed," she said, and led me into a
quiet corner where there were seats.   I would have

thoughtlessly taken a place by her side, forgetful of Jerome's teachings, but she commanded coldly:

"Monsieur will stand."

And I stood.

"You are a stranger in Paris, you seem a man of honor; for those reasons I choose you. I would not care to have one of my own gentlemen know what I wish to do. All Paris would talk of it to-morrow. We in the palace see naught of the common people, and I have long dreamed it would be a brave adventure to go unknown among them, to their inns and gathering places. I have always desired to know more of our Paris, especially one place which I hear mentioned frequently of late. My position will not permit me to visit it openly—you understand."

I protested that knowing naught of the streets I should be but a blind guide.

"I know where I would go," she said, determinedly, brushing aside the difficulties I would suggest, "and I will go; you will go too."

I was vastly troubled at this, for might it not lead to such another escapade as came so near costing me dear? Her eyes fixed full upon me, her voice blended a command which no man dared disobey, with an entreaty which none would willingly run counter to, and I gave reluctant assent.

"Will you await me here?" she demanded rather than asked. "My apartments are in this building. I will return very briefly."

When the lady came back she would never have been

taken for a woman; her long cloak, such as men wore, reached to her boots, identical in all respects with my own. Her hat, plume and sword were correct and bravely worn. Her maid, a trifle nervous over the adventure, but who said nothing, bore a similar cloak for me, and held two masks in her hands.

"Will my lord throw this about him?" and without any question I assumed the cloak.

"Now this," and she handed me a mask while she affixed one about her own face.

I demurred to the mask.

"I will not take my lady upon an errand where we can not show our faces."

She laughed merrily, and replied: "It is the way of Paris, my lord, and naught is thought of it. Many lords and ladies wish to keep their faces from the *canaille*."

I drew a breath of resignation and put it on.

"Am I not a comely man?" the lady asked, one touch of woman's vanity showing through it all.

"Yes, by my faith, madame;" but such sayings were foreign to my awkward tongue.

She led me out of the palace by a private way, and when the street was reached we walked along as two men would. She directed our course, and as she gave no hint of her destination I did not inquire. It was but a brief walk before we came to an arched door on a side street, and there she paused and looked carefully about to see that no one watched us and then—in we went.

The lady seemed in highest spirits over her unaccountable prank, and laughed girlishly. "Now I will gratify my curiosity. You know I admit my curiosity, sometimes. These men are not alone in their thirst for excitement. It is so tiresome at court, ever the same thing day after day.''

We had now come into a fairly wide, well-lighted hall, and an obsequious attendant showed us up a stair, and opening a door, pointed out the place she asked for. Imagine my utter astonishment when we stood together within the gaming room at Bertrand's. What an infernal fool I had been to be tempted back into this very place of all others. I thought at once it was some cowardly trick of Yvard's. I seized the woman by the arm, for I supposed her then but another decoy; there was no telling how far this Spanish intrigue had gone or what high personages Madame du Maine might be able to enlist in furtherance of her schemes. I seized her firmly, and had taken one step back towards the door again, when her cold ringing voice undeceived me.

''What means my lord; I thought him a gentleman. Shall I appeal for protection to these low men here?''

There was such a truth in her low tones that I cast her free, and in some measure explained my thought.

''Well, well, we'll not quarrel here,'' and looking about her with eager curiosity, she chose a table where fewest players sat, and thitherwards we went. This table was placed rather apart from the others, against a pillar, and no gamesters sat on the side next the wall. It left but scant space to sit between. There we took our places, and the lady tumbled out a purse well filled with gold pieces, handed some to me and bade me play.

She laid her wagers, and won with the glee of a child, her face alternate flushed and pale. I could see I wronged her by supposing her in league with the place. She played in too feverish earnest.

During this while I had observed the same two men who had met me on the stair the previous night. They were walking about and carelessly looking on at the different games. Yet for all their nonchalance there was a well-defined method in their procedure, that attracted my attention. The taller man scanned every person in the hall, and when the lady and I came in he watched us intently.

His companion—the same as on the previous night—withdrew to talk. After some consultation they reached a decision. Together they came our way, and the tall man clapped his hand twice.

At the signal, for such it was, from every table rose a man or two, and ranged themselves about him who called. I could also see a guard suddenly stationed, as if by magic, at each point of exit. Where, here and there, a cloak was thrown back, the gleam of a uniform showed beneath.

"There, my lads, is our quarry; take them," commanded the tall man, pointing to us.

I cursed myself for a silly fool to run again into such danger.

The dispatches in my bosom would hang me, and I dared not explain my possession of them. It was plain, too, that the King's officers, as well as Serigny, had

7—BLACK WOLF

their suspicions of the place. It was too late now for penitence, it was time to act.

The lady arose so trembling and frightened that my courage all came back to me. She forgot her gold pieces lying on the table in front of her.

"My lord," she whispered, "you must protect me; it would be the scandal of all France were I to be discovered in such a place."

Her appeal made me forget my own imminent danger, and I bethought myself what best to do. They could approach me by but one side, and while I considered a parley with the officers, heard a glad little cry from the lady. She calmly gathered up her gold and restored it to her purse, as if the matter were already settled, though I could see no change in the front of those around us. As the soldiers would have pulled the table away, she bade them wait, and said: "I would speak to your leader."

The tall man asked: "And what would you say? We have no time to talk."

"It is not to you, I know you both; I would speak to my lord by your side."

With that, the other, who had remained rather in the background, came forward, and she took him aside where none could hear, save myself a word or two. The lady spoke to him in a low, quiet tone, and raised her mask a little. The man started back, then removed his cap deferentially. I was close enough to hear his exclamation:

"Mademoiselle la Princesse."

"Hush," she placed her finger on her lips, "he does not know," indicating me by a gesture.

I was as astonished as he, but had no further anxiety. No officer would dare arrest a Princess of the Blood in such a place.

"What does Mademoiselle do in Bertrand's gaming house?"

"It is not for you to question, my lord," she drew herself up coldly, "I chose it. Now I would go. Provide an escort for me and the gentleman who has the honor to accompany me."

She came back to me smiling. "We will go in peace; It is Vauban. It must be no trifling matter to fetch him out to-night. I wonder who it is he seeks?"

I thought I could enlighten her, perhaps, but kept a still tongue.

Vauban gave a quiet order to the tall man, who, it appears, was in command of the squad, which order he in turn communicated to them.

"We have made a mistake. Permit these gentlemen to pass out, and none else."

Vauban then interrupted:

"De Verrue, do you take ten men and escort these, these—gentlemen where they will."

A young officer stepped forward at the word, but seemed not pleased to leave in face of more exciting events.

"Nay, nay, boy do not look so glum; take my word, it is an honor a marshal of France would assume did not sterner duties bid him stay."

My lady tossed her purse to the sergeant as she passed:

"Divide this with your men, and drink a health to—well—the Princess Unknown."

CHAPTER X

IN THE HOUSE OF BERTRAND

IT would now have been a most simple matter for me to go out unmolested beside the princess. And this is what I should have done had it not been for an accident. While Vauban was talking to the princess, I glanced round the room to see if Yvard was there, or any other person likely to know of this business. There was one figure strolling about in the rear which wore a familiar look, yet I could not say I had seen the man before.

When Vauban gave the order to allow us to pass "and none else," this man very visibly took on an air of apprehension. He looked from one door to the other and, finding all guarded, was quite alarmed, then, without perceiving himself observed, he manned himself with his former unconcerned manner. There was something in the poise of his head, his walk, which came as a well remembered thing from some secret niche of memory.

Now as the princess and I walked out in front of our guard, this man fell, as if naturally, into the rear of our company, and attempted nonchalantly to saunter out behind us. The guard at the door locked their bayonets across, barring his exit.

"By whose orders," he demanded with some show of haughty indignation, "do you hold me a prisoner with this disorderly rabble?"

"Marshal Vauban's," the sentry replied, unmoved.

The man shrank back perceptibly; as I took a longer sight of him the familiarity of voice and figure recurred more strongly. I stood still to look. He turned his face. Broussard! I almost spoke the name. Yes, beyond all peradventure it was Broussard, disguised, but still Broussard.

What a world of vain speculation this opened on the instant, speculation to which no answer came. How much and what had I told him during our voyage? How had he treasured it and where repeated it? For I had now no other thought than he was the spy who brought Yvard the packet designed for Spain.

"Come my lord, are you dreaming?" the princess broke in impatiently. I had quite forgotten her.

·"No madame, I crave your patience, and beg attention a moment."

I then asked hurriedly whether she knew the young officer in charge of our escort, and whether she would trust him to see her to a place of safety. She knew the lad as a gentleman of birth and reputed honor, so with the guard and the marshal's orders felt herself safe. Despite the effort to speak coolly my whole frame and voice quivered with excitement at prospect of winding up the entire affair by one more stroke of luck. Seeing which my lady icily inquired:

"But why? Why do you fear? Surely these soldiers are sufficient to afford protection."

The half veiled scorn of her manner cut me to the quick, but I determined not to be drawn aside from my purpose. My face still a-flush at her suggestion of cowardice, I replied earnestly:

"Mademoiselle la Princesse —"

"Ah, you know me?"

I nodded.

"And yet are willing to relinquish the honor of my escort?"

"It is duty, Mademoiselle la Princesse; stern and imperative duty."

"Sh!" Placing her finger to her lips, "address me simply as Madame."

"Madame, you wrong me; I would not desert you while in danger; now I may give you into safer hands with honor. A most urgent matter demands my presence there," pointing inside, "it may cost my life. Had I better not acquaint M. de Verrue with your character? He will then be more circumspect?" She thought a space.

"No, you may tell him I am a woman—tell him of the stupid folly which led me here to-night and brought a brave gentleman into danger—but not my name."

She would have thanked me further, but I was all impatience to be inside, seeing which she graciously bade me go. I bethought me then of the packet yet in my bosom, and knowing all those within were to be searched I took a hasty resolution, born of my confidence in the

Princess. It may be said here that the lady whom I escorted on that memorable night was known throughout the kingdom for her eccentric tastes, and noted for never meddling with intrigues of either state or love. Her passion lay with her dogs and horses, the hunt, and not in the trifles of a court.

"Madame, will you not render me a service in return?" I felt my whole attitude to be imploring, so warmly did I bespeak her grace.

"I have here some papers of the utmost value to myself, to no one else. My honor requires that they be delivered to M. Jerome de Greville before to-morrow's sun arises. He keeps his lodging in Rue St. Denis, at the sign of the Austrian Arms. Can Madame not dispatch a trusted messenger and secure their delivery?"

The fervor of the appeal touched her, for she listened with interest.

"Oh, Madame, I beseech you, as I have obeyed you without question this night, do not fail me as you love the glory of France. You may have M. de Greville informed how and where you came by them, in case aught of ill should happen to me this night."

She took the packet.

"Upon my royal word," she whispered, in such a tone of sincerity I felt relieved of any uneasiness concerning the papers.

I had a real regret at seeing her leave the hall. Walking so regally in front of the guard I wondered at my thick-headedness which had not before perceived in her every movement the princely pride of Bourbon. I threw my cloak, which fettered me, to one of the men, and wearing still my mask, re-entered the hall. They were already engaged in the search, questioning closely each man in rotation. None was allowed to depart without being questioned and examined. I immediately sought for Broussard. He had gone over towards another small door, the same through which I had escaped the night before. There were two guards posted here.

Broussard dawdled about with the air of a man very much bored, who only waited his turn to go through a disagreeable ordeal that he might leave. I fancied his wits were actively at work beneath so impassive an exterior. He had spoken privately to several men, one at a time, in careless fashion, and then tapping the legs of the tables, and kicking the chairs as he passed, he again came near the door. I managed to keep close to him. As he stood talking to the sentries the four men came up two by two from opposite directions, and at a sign from him, grappled with the guard. While they were thus engaged Broussard bolted through the door. I drew my sword and plunged after him.

From inside, the sentries cried out: "The two spies have gone this way," and the whole mob surged out and divided in chase. Some perhaps were in league with Broussard, others were in the service of Vauban, I could not tell.

The hall was densely dark; I knew not the way, but I had Broussard but a few feet in front to guide me; behind, some twenty or thirty stout varlets strung out in pursuit, not a dozen paces to the rear.

It so happened that there was a door which stood half open, and Broussard being hard pressed doubled by this and darted in. He was but a couple of yards ahead and I alone observed this stratagem. When he vanished to the right, I slipped in behind, just as our foremost pursuers swept by. The great noises they made and the resounding echoes effectually prevented their notice of a cessation of sounds from us. Nor did they pause to listen. Crushing through the narrow passage their pressure slammed the door behind us. I heard the clank of a heavy bolt as it dropped into place. Thinking Broussard had sought some secret means of escape known to himself, and fearing he would get away, I dashed madly on, only to fetch up with a terrific thump against a stone wall.

The shock dazed me and I fell in a heap to the floor. Perhaps it was as well, for I made no further noise. But I listened.

The place was intensely dark, and not a sound save the heightened beating of my own heart disturbed it. I was afraid to move, lest I bring upon me the crowd outside. Had not one of the men cried "*two* spies." It did look as if I too was a confederate of Broussard, and I could not have explained. The echoes of the chase died away, and all was still. My mind and ears were very busy then trying to make out what sort of a hole this was I had so unceremoniously fallen into. And Broussard? Where had he disappeared? I knew he could not be far, for there had been no footsteps since the door shut. I took it that he must be in the room, and that the reasons which enforced quiet upon me were also powerful to him.

He was worse off though than I, for he had doubtless heard me blunder into the wall, and thought one of the marshal's men had followed him. This idea suggested he would probably then lay perfectly still and wait for the man to recover and go out. Or, the thought made me shiver—he might steal up and finish me with the dagger. As quietly as I could I loosened my own knife in its sheath and got it well in hand. In spite of all the caution I used, the sheath rattled against a buckle. I knew my position was betrayed. I thought then to reach a corner where I could the better protect myself against a stealthy attack.

Immediately overhead an almost indistinguishable blur marked a high, square window, some seven feet from the floor. There was but one. In all probability the door lay directly opposite. That being true, the natural inclination of a man flying down the hall in the direction we came would be to go further to the right. Reasoning in this wise, hoping to avoid a struggle with Broussard in the dark, I edged my way along the wall toward the left. Inch by inch I went, holding my sword extended at arm's length in front of me, and lifting each foot carefully to avoid the scraping. Every few feet I made a complete sweep in all directions with my blade, to guard against approach. Proceeding in this way, I felt my sword's point at length touch something—something soft. Before I had time to wonder what it was, the sharp hiss of a blade cut close to my cheek, and struck clanging against the wall. I sprang back beyond reach.

"Broussard," and in the extreme excitement I spoke his name unwittingly, "Broussard, stand still; I had no thought to attack you. Stay where you are, and I will seek another place."

There came a voice, "Who are you to call me Broussard?" but I answered not.

In the absence of any preparation for assault, I took it that he would remain where he was. Thereupon I backed into the diagonal corner, and stood stock still.

After some period—hours or minutes, I knew not what, they were interminable—Broussard spoke again. His voice sounded sharp, and unnaturally loud.

"Who are you, and what do you want? I know you; is it Nortier, Lireux?"

"Hush, fool; dost not hear the tread of Vauban's men outside? You will call them down upon us with your babble." They were stamping through the passage as I spoke.

"Ah!" and there was a world of relief and incredulity in his lowered tone. "Then you are not with Vauban? Who are you?" I made no reply.

During the long period of absolute and profound silence which succeeded I had much time to reflect. I judged myself to be in an unused chamber, which, if square, would be about thirty feet across—calculating by the distance from the diagonal corner—if in fact Broussard lay in the corner. There was but one opening, for I could hear the wind stirring outside, and no draught came in. Did the window open on the street, or on an inner court? There was no way of telling.

If it be true that men live in thoughts rather than in deeds, if the changing phantoms of our brain carve deeper impressions than the petty part we play with our hands, then, indeed, that frightful night would form by far the longest chapter in the history of my soul.

Darkness, darkness, darkness; quivering, soundless, hopeless night.

I feared to move, and no sense save that of hearing bound me to the world of living men. Living men? What place had I among them?

A party of drunken roisterers staggered beneath the window, singing coarse songs and bandying their brutal jests. But it no longer interested me to know the window opened on a street.

Hour after hour plodded in slow procession through the night.

Outside, a clattering vehicle whipped past over the rough stones, the driver swearing at his team. The day was coming at last. Did I wish it? Perhaps the night were kinder, for it at least obscured my misery. I almost prayed the darkness might last.

CHAPTER XI

THE DAWN AND THE DUSK

GRADUALLY, so gradually the change could hardly be observed, the inner grating of the window became visible; the chinks between the edges of the stones assumed distinctness. A ghostly blotch grew into a fact upon the floor. · A leaden hue, less black than the pulsing sea of ink about it, spread and spread, lighter and lighter, until it invaded the dim recesses where I stood. My hand became once more a tangible possession, unreal and grim, yet all my own. The opposite wall loomed up, my utmost frontier of the domain of certainty. Dimmer, darker, more obscure, the door, a vast unexplored cavern gathered to itself the hobgoblins of evil and gave them shelter. As still as the creeping on of day we two men stood, glaring at each other and watched it come.

Exactly when I began to see him I could not say. Every impulse and vital force of nature centered in my eyes, and they fastened themselves upon that one irregular shadow in the opposing corner which slowly—oh! with such agonizing slowness—assumed the outlines of a man. My fascinated gaze wandered not nor wearied. When in the moist light of the morning I clearly saw

Broussard, haggard, pale and sunken-eyed, watching me thirty feet away, it seemed that I had seen him all the night.

No detail of his dress or manner but I observed. There was a scar across his forehead, fresh and bleeding a bit. A contusion rather. He had probably struck the door-facing as he rushed in. Yes, it bled. A few drops had trickled down his nose; there hung one, quite dry, from his brow. Precisely beneath this there were some dozen or so upon the floor. All could have been covered by my hand. Like myself Broussard had not moved throughout that awful night. God, how I pitied him. With such a weight of treason on his soul. And yet, looking back, the night was less awful than the coming day, far more merciful than the hideous night which followed it. With the sun Broussard heartened up, and first broke the silence.

"Who are you comrade, and what do you here?"

I was at a loss for reply. I had no faith in him, yet even a rotten stick might serve to get me out.

"I am trapped like yourself, and feared you all the night. God in Heaven what a long night it was."

Broussard had no words, his convulsive shudder expressed more than mine.

"Do you know how to get out of here?" I asked.

"Not I, except by the door, or the window," looking at that.

"I'll try the door," he continued, smiling the treacherous smile of the tiger. I remembered so well the first day he showed his teeth aboard ship. The man well knew I recognized him, he had heard me speak his name, and I feared if he found the door open he would shut me up again, and escape.

"I'll test the door softly and see what is outside," and he moved as if to put his thought in action.

"Hold on, not yet; methinks I'll try that door myself." I could see he had the same idea which had occurred to me, for he demurred.

"No, my fine sir; why you and not I?"

"Because I know you, sir, and fear to trust you."

"Verily, you have honorable intentions yourself to suspect me so readily." He was bent on engaging me in conversation, so he might perhaps recognize me from my voice. The mask still hid my features, and the entire difference in my mode of dress made recognition almost impossible. The puzzled expression of a half recollection still rested on his face as I continued:

"I do not merely suspect you, I know you for a traitor—nay do not clap your hand upon your sword until I have finished. You have now in your possession certain traitorous dispatches which were given you by one Carne Yvard in exchange for others which you brought over with you in a vessel called le Dauphin. Ah, you begin to pale and shrink, and well you may—"

"You lie!" he shrieked, convincing me I had made a home thrust.

"Softly, softly, have a care, lest you call the Marshal's bloodhounds down upon us. The dispatches with the purple seals, which you brought with such care from Biloxi, have been taken from Yvard, and are now in safe keeping for the King. The lie, ah, well, I'll pardon that for the while. You can not leave here, and I have ample time for avenging my honor after I have had the pleasure of your delightful conversation."

He leaned morosely against the wall, staring at me, as I went on.

"Now listen to me quietly. You have those dispatches upon your person. I want them, and by all the gods I will have them. If I have to kill you for them, then so much the worse for you. Now listen. Give me those dispatches. We will then get out of here together, and once outside, I will give you full four and twenty hours. That time elapsed, I will turn the dispatches over to the authorities. If you can escape with your miserable life so be it. Do you agree?"

"I have no dispatches," he sullenly replied, "and who are you to dare charge me with treason?"

There was no ring of real resentment in his tones, though he strove manfully to simulate offended and indignant innocence. It was necessary to keep him in ignorance for a while, because I feared he might set upon me, and being really an excellent swordsman, the issue of conflict would be doubtful. But the weightier reason lay in the fact that the clash of steel might draw down upon us the occupants of the house. Here I was in a much worse plight than he, though he knew it not. For whether those occupants were the friends of Broussard or the Marshal's men, the result would be equally fatal to me. A man must think quickly under such straits,

8—BLACK WOLF

and I was sorely put to it for some device. No stratagem would be too base to use against such a villain, for he would not hesitate to knife me in the back.

"Broussard, let us understand each other here and now. You know me. I am Placide de Mouret," removing my mask and looking him sternly in the eye.

"Great God, de Mouret!"

"The same. I am your master at the swords, and you know it. Now turn out those papers." I had been quietly drawing my blade during this speech, as the dazed man tried to collect his senses, so I was ready while he still stood unprepared.

"Throw up your hands."

He mechanically obeyed; the discovery of his villainy had completely unmanned him.

"Now unbuckle your belt, and drop it to the ground." He did as he was bid.

"Kick it across the floor." The weapon was tossed out of his reach.

I walked up closer to him, and forced him to loose his coat that I might find the papers, and was rewarded by the discovery of a packet, much similar to that dropped by Yvard. It was sealed in such a manner it could not be opened, and bore no address. I removed the dagger from his hip, and having, as I thought, completely disarmed him, felt no further uneasiness. The man was thoroughly cowed, and never once raised his eyes to mine. Verily treason doth rob the stoutest heart of half its courage.

"Now do as I bid you, and I will keep my promise to

let you go.   And mind that you make not the slightest
sound which may attract the soldiers.''

"Ah, you fear the soldiers too? '' he asked, vaguely
trying to puzzle out why I should be afraid of those in
whose service I was.

"It is not to our purpose to talk.   I simply want the
credit myself, and do not want to share it with those
fellows out there.   We must work to leave this place at
once.   Do you stand where you are.''

I gathered up the scattered weapons and piled them
all in one corner, farthest from the door, where I now
proposed to set about getting free.   With the fearful
blight of uncovered treason in his soul, Broussard obeyed
me cringingly as a servant, and worked as hard, for his
safety lay in mine.   We went first to the door by which
we entered, and after a tedious examination failed to
find any means by which it could be opened or broken
down.   A stout latch, of some pattern we could not tell,
held it fast from the outside.   There was no catch or
fastening of any sort within.   The age-hardened oak,
studded as it was with heavily wrought nails, forbade
the plan of cutting through.   This would require days
and days of patient labor, and I was already faint from
lack of food and the exhaustion of the night.   Plainly
the room was intended for a prison, and as such it served
well its purpose.   Baffled and disheartened I turned my
thought to the window.   It looked out upon the street;
this was so much in my favor.   The irons that guarded
it were close set, bending out toward the street in the
shape of a bow.   I judged this was in order that archers

stationed there might shoot the more easily into the
street in times of siege.

I could have reached this without trouble, but I desired to employ Broussard, that I might know where he
was and prevent treachery. For that double purpose I
reached up and grasped the sill, commanding him to
catch me about the knees and lift so I might see out.
This he did. While in that position he made a pretense
of shifting his hold, and something impelled me to
glance downward at him. He was stealthily drawing a
concealed knife from his bosom. I threw all my weight
back upon him, casting the twain of us together to the
floor. Meantime he had the knife full drawn, in his left
hand held at my breast.

I grappled with him, holding his left hand in my right,
and with the free hand clutched him by the throat, burying
my thumb deep in his wind-pipe. Instinctively he
raised both hands to protect his throat, and then we
struggled to our feet. He made futile efforts to strike
me with the knife, but his strength deserted him with
his wind. The blade dropped clattering on the floor.
My other hand closed about his neck, circling it with an
unyielding collar of steel. Desperately as a caged rat
might fight he squirmed and twisted in my grasp. To
no avail.

Tigerish now, as though I held a rabid dog, I thrust
him back against the wall, and there rigidly held him
fast. In merciless silence I listened to the precious
breath gurgling from his body; a reddish froth gathered
at the lips. I could feel his hot blood surge and beat

against my thumb under that deadly pressure. The cold sweat stood in clammy clusters upon his forehead; his head thrown back, the eyes turned toward the ceiling no longer pleaded into mine. I sickened almost at sight of the tongue swelling black, which seemed to consume all the fleeing color from lips and face. Oh God, how he struggled! His hands closed over mine as bars of steel to tear them from his throat.

Even in our mortal strife I marked the eternal harmony of the scene. Truly death had never stage more fitting whereon to play its last stern drama of dissolution. Hemmed in by four massive walls of granite, ghastly grim and desolately gray, we wrestled in a stifling stillness, while hell stood umpire at the game. No sound of trumpet, no warlike cry, no strains of martial music were there to thrill the nerves and taunt men on to glory. We fought to the scrape and scratch of shuffling feet, the labored gasp, the rattle in the throat, while echo hushed in silence and in fright.

He grew more quiet, his muscles stiffened and relaxed—he was no longer conscious. A few more convulsive quivers, as a serpent might writhe and jerk, then he hung, a limp dead thing, in my hands. My outstretched arms seemed made as a gibbet, feeling no fatigue, so lightly did they sustain him. Cords of brass could be no more tense than mine; his weight was as nothing. Softly I eased him down, and composed his limbs in decent order upon the stones.

Then I rose, and gazed complacently. at my work.

Yes, it *was* well done, excellently done, in fact. The most expert strangler of the Choctows could have done no better. Those purpling lines about the throat, those darker clots where my thumbs had left their signs, could not have been more intelligently placed. I smiled my satisfaction at the job, then—then—my own overstrung nerves gave way, and I fell unconscious across the corpse of my hands' creation.

When I came to myself I was weeping, weeping as a child might weep, over the dead, distorted face of him I had loved. How long this lasted I had no means of knowing. Uncompromising necessity forced me to action; forbade me time to dream.

The body being in my way where it lay—for I proposed now to work in earnest at the window—I moved it tenderly as possible across the floor and stretched him out near the door sill. Springing up then I attacked the bars at the window. Hours and hours I labored, impelled to greater effort by the dread of spending another night in that room of murder. I was patient, too, patient with the cunning of a maniac.

The dagger made my chisel; my sword, wrapped in a cloth to muffle the strokes, furnished me a maul. Full half the day was before me. The rough paving stones below held out the hope of escape or death. How to reach the street after the bars were removed, I did not suffer myself to consider. I should go mad if I lay idle. I leaned as far out the window as the grating would allow, and observed a guard standing in plain view at the

" Then I rose, and gazed at my work."   p. 117.

corner. It was very evident the Provost of Paris had taken possession of the house, and there was little use in my trying to make a way out the door.

I bitterly resented the intrusion of every passenger along the street, and scanned with hatred the few who came. For while they remained in hearing I was obliged to cease my chipping at the masonry and leaden cement which held my freedom. I bided my time, and, long before the shadow of the house across the way had climbed to the window where I worked, had the gratification of finding a bar give way in my hands, and found I could take it out. Removing this bar, it gave me a powerful leverage on the others, and by exerting all my strength, succeeded in bending the two on either side to such a degree I could force my body between.

While thus engaged, my eyes were ever fixed anxiously upon the street, in the hope that Jerome might pursue his plan of watching the house, and I would catch sight of him. The passers-by were few indeed, but somehow it struck me that the same persons passed several times, and in something like regular order. A patrol of Jerome's? My heart bounded at the thought. I watched more carefully; yes, it was true. I counted five different persons; some walked fast, some walked slow, but all looked about them and inspected the house with more than an ordinary glance. And, no, I was not mistaken, that simple-looking countryman yonder was Jerome.

I was quite at a loss how to attract his attention; I feared to yell, lest that give notice to the sentry. I took a spur from my heel and dropped it directly in front of him; I knew he would recognize it, for it was his own, loaned to me for my more fashionable appearance. He heard the jingle and glanced around. His hat blew off as if by accident and fell near the spur. In stooping to pick it up, the spur also found its way into his hand beneath the hat. He was truly a quick-witted gentleman, and I forgave him from my heart all his chaff in the matter of teaching me manners. It took him not a great while to comprehend, and taking note of the situation of my window, he sauntered off. Thence forward only three men passed by the house, at much longer intervals. He had taken one with him, and I was left to surmise in what method they purposed to effect my deliverance. I made myself almost merry. The long labor at the window had cramped my limbs to such a degree it pained me to move. I clambered down and took a few turns about the room as if I had naught to do but exercise. But at every turn the hideous face and whitened eyes of Broussard dogged my footsteps as a spectre. Look where I would, it was only that I saw. Hour after hour crawled by. Jerome would wait for night. Night!

Did he but know what lurking horrors filled the dismal hours for me, he would come soon. By some fatality I had drawn the body directly to the spot where the last fading shafts of light would hover about its face. Not for a paradise of peace would I touch the loathsome thing again to hide it in the shadows. I could neither take my eyes from it nor put my hands upon it. Like the basilisk of fable it held my gaze charmed, fixed it, bound it fast. Crouch as I might in the remotest corner, cover my face in my mantle, still that searching, penetrating thing pierced all obstacles, glared grisly and distinct before me.

I tried to throw off the thought which now constantly recurred. What if Jerome did not come? Would I starve here in company with this corrupting flesh? No, there was the window; a headlong dash from that would bring death and release. So I determined. Then came on the night. To me it brought no rest, no sweet surcease of the labors through the day.

Somewhere, afar off in the city, there rang a tremulous bell, launching its vibrations upon the infinite silence as a sinner's guilty soul might trembling stand in the presence of Almighty condemnation. The melancholy howl of a dog at first cleft through every nerve and fibre of my being, thrilling with a creeping chill of horror. So regular did it come, so unvaried, I grew to count the seconds under my breath, and to note its monotonous precision. Somehow this occupation in a measure relieved me, and when the howls came more infrequently and at less well defined intervals, I mentally resented the change. Time had ceased to be. I cowered in the corner with naught but death and fear and darkness to keep me company.

CHAPTER XII

FLORINE TO THE RESCUE

A SHROUD of consuming terror now possessed me. I crouched in the dank corner clutching my sword, listening, vainly listening, for some sound out of which to conjure up an assassin. A rat ran across my foot. Screaming out I bounded erect and beat about me with blind desperation. One hand touched the other and shrank from its mate. They were as ice.

Oh, God, the horrid silence! How weightily it bore upon me, stripping me of voice, of courage and of hope. How many, many times I braced myself against the wall, cold with fear at the apprehension of an attack by some demon of the night. How many, many times I sank again into the same dumb misery when no enemy appeared to do me hurt.

So long it had been since the tones of human speech blessed my ears, I almost hoped the marshal's men might come, that I might hear his stern command, "Hang him to yonder window ledge." A rasping thirst roasted my throat until my tongue gritted and ground as a rusted clapper in a bell. I touched it with my hand. It was as dry as Broussard's.

Broussard! A quiver in the musty air set me all a shudder; in every rustle I felt again the last convulsions of the dead. Dull lights gathered when I closed my eyes, and rested upon his swollen features, their white eyes following me in hate.

Coolly and logically as if it concerned someone else, the reason of it all crept into my morbid brain. I was mad; mad from hunger, thirst and terror. Yes, mad, and felt not one whit sorry of it; nay, rejoiced rather, for it meant a freedom of the spirit. So insidiously this knowledge forced itself upon me, it brought no shock, I even dimly wondered that any other condition ever existed. Verily, men are happier for a gentle frenzy. Then, indeed, are all things leveled, all barriers removed. Gone were all my pigmy troubles, vanished into nothingness. Engulfed in a common ruin lay all fragments of desire; the search for reward, the dread of punishment—all petty figments of the imagination were powerful now no more. The fall of reason crushed every human hope and dulled the edge of every human fear. What cared I now for food, for water; for honor or for shame? My mind, imperial and free from artificial restraints, plunged riotously into forbidden realms. I reveled in the exaltation of chainless thought, and drank from the deepest wells of rebellion delicious draughts of secret sin, thanking, yea thanking, this sweet madness which gave a glorious independence.

What repugnance had I now for yon piece of foul and rotting carrion! What mattered if but lately a breathing man it had strangled in my grip. By the

gods, a knightly feat and most bravely done! And I
laughed at my former fear, not loud, but such as laughed
the fiends of hell when Lucifer rose against his Prince.
Low I chuckled, then shivered at my own unnatural
voice.

Dead now to every sense of physical loathing I advanced steadfastly towards where he lay. Shorn of
human companions my wretchedness sought a lonely
comradeship with the piece of mortal clay. Turning
now and again to beat back some skinny hand which
snatched my garments, to slap in the face some evil
sprite which thrust its sneer upon me, I walked in resolution across the floor. I fancied again I heard the
tread of men in the passage. Pleased at the babble of
the children of my own imagination, I stood to listen.
Yes, by the wit of a fool, I'll indulge the jest, a joyous
jibe and a merry.

The low shuffle of cautious feet came again. The
latch clanked ever so softly as if some hand without
lifted it gently, oh so gently raised it. "Ha! there you are,
seeking to frighten me again, but I know you well. No,
no, you'll scare me no more; I'll play a merry game
with you." So I hid myself in the dark, and thought to
play a prank upon the evil Thing. Held my breath.

Elated to find I owned so wondrously fertile a brain I
saw the door open little by little without a creak. A
current of liberated air brushed by my cheek. So real
it was, I smiled. The door swung wider and wider yet,
in the dark I saw it. Verily the sight of a madman is
sharp. The wind blew more chill and strong. I saw a

gleam peeping beneath a cloak as from a hidden lanthorn; I bethought me I would catch the tiny wanderer
from the floor and hold it in my hand.   It came crawling and crawling, on and on, wavering to my feet.   So
many times that night had I manned myself valiantly to
fight a shadow, I only laughed in silence and contempt
at this.

Behold the folly of a madman's thought.   Yet the
creation of it all gave me exquisite pleasure, as a child
might find delight in some strange toy from which it
could call weird shapes at will.   On it moved with a
noiseless, gliding motion; now inside the door, now
coming, coming, coming—nearly to me.   Now it let
fall a timorous blade of light along the floor.   It reached
Broussard's body.   Its foot struck him.   It stooped,
threw the light full upon him.   Open fell the concealing
mantle, showing the barren stones, the corpse, the
ghastly upturned face of the strangled man.

The woman—for it was a woman—dropped to her
knees beside him, called him, felt of his clammy head,
and suffered but a single scream of swift affright to
leave her lips.   From the unhooded lanthorn burst out
a spreading yellow glow.   Her scream awoke me to a
consciousness of reality.   From my own unlocked tongue
of terror came its answer.   I joined my voice to hers,
defied the hush of slumbering centuries and filled that
quaking room with a perfect deluge of reverberating
shrieks.   Many others, men, with cloaks, some having
lights, some none, rushed in behind the woman.   From
that time I knew nothing.

*　　*　　*　　*　　*　　*

I awakened from a dreamy languor; a subtle essence of perfume floated through my senses. A gentle touch of some kindly hand was bathing my temples. Fearful lest this sweet illusion vanish with the others, I kept my eyes firmly closed, and soon abandoned myself wholly to the subduing influences of natural slumber.

"Has he stirred, Florine?"

"No, Monsieur, but his head is cooler now—he sleeps, hush! Perhaps another day he will be better. How he raved through the night. Poor, young gentleman, he quite exhausted himself."

"Ah, well, Florine, he is young, and with such nurses as thou and Nannette he will of a surety recover."

I turned my head and smiled a feeble recognition of Jerome and Florine. The other woman I had never seen; she was much older than Florine and had a kind, motherly face.

"What day is it?"

"The morning of Sunday."

It was Wednesday night when Jerome and I went to the ball.

I looked about me. The lodgings were those I had taken at the Austrian Arms, yet much changed in little things. The vase of flowers there in the window, the neat-swept hearth, the cheerful fire, and that indefinable something which gives a touch of womanliness to a room. Florine, perhaps.

"Ugh! I'm so glad to be here," and I shuddered at the remembrance of my prison and suffering.

"Poor dear," said the older woman in a voice full of sympathy, "don't worry; you are in comfort now, and will soon be strong again."

"Am I wounded in any wise?" I inquired, for I knew not the manner of my coming there.

"No, no, my lad," broke in Jerome's hearty reassurance, "not a bit, just worn and starved out. Truly, boy, you had a rough adventure. By 'Od's blood, I'd hate to have the like! Has he taken any food Florine?"

"Nothing but the wine, and a sup or two of broth. Here is something for him now," and she brought me a most tempting array of soup, hot viands and victuals of which I feared to eat as I desired.

Though Florine and Jerome would not permit me to disturb myself with vain conversation, yet by dint of questions and listening when they talked apart, thinking I slept, I found how it all came about. It seems Florine saw and recognized me when I returned to the gaming room, having left Madame la Princesse. She knew too, in some way which I did not learn, that neither Broussard nor I had left Bertrand's that night. This, though the Provost's men had been searching the city for us both. She kept her knowledge to herself. When the turbulence calmed down somewhat and sentries were placed to guard the house, she occupied herself in slipping about looking for my hiding place. It took but a little while for her, familiar as she was with the house, to find the room where Broussard and I had taken refuge. Listening at the door she heard our angry voices and the scuffle within. This may have been when I was choking him. Horrible! horrible!

At any rate she feared to intrude, and at once set out to seek help. The girl throughout acted with astonishing promptness and judgment. Florine had recognized Madame la Princesse—all Paris knew the eccentric lady—so went straight to her. At first denied admission she sent up a note couched in such terms as gained for her an immediate private interview—indeed the Princess herself was careful it should be strictly private.

Madame knew nothing of me except the request I made concerning Jerome, and sending the papers to the Austrian Arms. Florine went without delay to that place. This was about midday. Meanwhile Jerome, much troubled that I did not appear during the night, pursued our original plan of watching the house, and arranged his men at windows, and in the street, in such a way as not to attract attention. One of them had seen me working at the window but never dreamed it was I. Jerome found the house already doubly guarded by the Provost's men, to his infinite disgust. He was a handy chap though, and not to be outdone. Dressing himself as a clumsy lout, he found little difficulty in worming the transactions of the night before out of one of the guard off duty. A drink or two together at the sign of the "Yellow Flagon" fetched this information.

Jerome was much wearied through his long watching and anxiety when he returned to the Austrian Arms.

The hostler at the inn turned him aside from the front door by a gesture, so that he entered by another way. Claude acquainted him that a lady in the public room desired to speak with M. Jerome de Greville, and would not be denied. Jerome's custom with visitors was to see them first himself, before Claude told them whether he was in or no.

Peeping through an aperture he saw the lady walking impatiently up and down the room, tapping at the window, mending the fire, and expressing her haste in many other pettish manners so truly feminine. It was Florine. He knew the girl well from his frequenting Bertrand's during this piece of business. Jerome sent her word he would be in, and changing his costume to one he usually wore, presented himself before her in the public room.

"Is it I you seek, M. de Greville, Mademoiselle?" he inquired, politely.

"Oh! Monsieur de Greville, it is you; I'm so glad." she came forward with a pretty air of perplexity and surprise, for Florine had a dainty woman's way about her, showing even through her present trouble. She bore herself more steadily that she had not to deal with some severe-faced stranger, but a gallant gentleman, whose mien was not that from which timid maidens were prone to fly.

"Oh, Monsieur de Greville, I know not what to say, now that I am well met with you."

"And by my faith, Mademoiselle, I am sure no word

9—BLACK WOLF

of mine would grace those pretty lips as well as thine own sweet syllables. So *I* can not tell you what to say.''

Florine pouted her dissent, yet was not in earnest angered—she was a woman. Jerome saw her business lay deeper than mere jest and badinage, so he spoke her more seriously.

''I pray you Mademoiselle—Florine?—am I right? Be seated.''

Florine had no thought for gallantries; she declined the proffered seat, and, standing, proceeded at once to the point of her mission,

''There is a young gentleman in our house,'' and she blushed a little, Jerome declared to me afterwards, ''in Bertrand's wine room—you know the place? locked up, and I am not certain whether he lives or is dead. I can not tell Monsieur his name, but you know him. Oh, he was kind to me, and I would willingly do something to save him. It is so hard to be only a woman. The Provost has the house guarded.''

''I know it,'' Jerome put in drily.

''This gentleman gave your name and lodgings to the lady who was with him there last night, and she it was who sent you the packet.'' Florine had run on hurriedly, unheeding Jerome's blank look of astonishment. This was probably a shrewd guess on her part, yet it squarely struck the mark.

''Lady? Sent the papers? Who? What lady?'' Jerome asked before she could answer anything.

''That I must not tell, Monsieur. Oh, come, quick; get him away from there; if our people find him they may do him harm. Monsieur is a brave gentleman, a friend of his, is it not true? Come.''

Jerome drew the facts pretty well out of the excited girl, knowing somewhat of the circumstances and guessing the rest—all in an exceeding short space of time. Florine told him as accurately as she could in what room I lay, leaving him to locate the window from the street. From this point the plan was simple enough. Jerome and Florine arrived at Bertrand's by different routes, Florine passing in unconcernedly, and Jerome, clad again as a stupid country knave, walked by the house to discover my outer window.

It was at this time that the falling of the spur conveyed to him the intelligence of my life and place of confinement. After this Jerome had to depend greatly upon the quick-witted woman.

It would be a long story, and a bootless, were I to tell how it fell out that Florine had a friend, the same kind-faced woman who helped her watch beside my bed; the window of this friend's garret room opened almost directly opposite Florine's own poor apartment. Only a narrow, dingy alley lay between; so scant was the space the upper stories came near to touching across it. Florine's friend, after some tearful persuasion, consented to aid the rescue of such a gallant gentleman as I was described to be. The girl could come and go at will. The friend permitted Jerome and three of his men to hide in her room. From her window Jerome cast a light cord into Florine's window, she drawing a stouter rope across with it, and made fast. It now became a trifling feat for these nimble adventurers to swing themselves across to Florine's room, but twelve feet or so away. Once inside Bertrand's they proceeded with abundant caution, all of which near came to naught through Florine's sudden shriek and my own nervous clamor. It shamed me heartily.

"Truly, comrade, thou hast good lungs," Jerome told me days afterward. "It took all our strength to shut thee of thy wind."

When the four men found me a helpless body in their hands, they were greatly troubled. However, Florine insisted that I be carried to her room where she could conceal me.

Once there they found means to truss me up like a bale of merchandise and sling me across the alley again, whence I was conveyed, still unconscious, through out-of-the-way streets to the Austrian Arms.

And so it was I came to my strength, safe in my own lodgings in Rue St. Denis, with Florine and her kind-hearted friend to nurse me.

CHAPTER XIII

THE GIRL OF THE WINE SHOP

YOUTH and health do not long lie idle. Even while I lay recovering my health, Jerome and I were busy with our plans. Not the least unforeseen item in what had befallen, was the chance that carried me into a house where I saw again the "black wolf's head," which brought once more to mind the history of the d'Artins. But there was still to come that other happening, the one which bound my whole life, heart and soul, my love and happiness forever, in with the fortunes of that black wolf's breed.

As I grew stronger Jerome and I had a long talk. He told me the morning after I left him, which was Thursday, a veiled woman had brought him a pair of gauntlets, with the request that he preserve them carefully. Jerome naturally wanted to know who had sent such a present. The woman answered no questions, only impressed upon him the importance of keeping them himself and letting no one have them. She would not tell whence she came, and when she departed Jerome made a sign to Claude, who followed. He returned and reported she had entered the apartments of Mademoiselle de Chartres by a private way.

Verily this was coming close to the King, and to Orleans; these gauntlets coming from the house of this
haughty Bourbon Princess. One of the gauntlets, of
course, contained the papers taken from Yvard, the same
I had confided to Mademoiselle la Princesse. I smiled
my satisfaction that she had been so discreet.

The other packet Jerome found upon me when I was
disrobed for bed.

It was many days before Jerome asked me for any
details of my imprisonment, or how it came about there
was a dead man in the room with me. I related the
whole circumstance briefly as possible, who Broussard
was, and all, to avoid further questioning. For I hated
to dwell upon the occurrences of that night, yet ever returned to them with a sort of secret fascination.

"You choked him well, comrade," was Jerome's only
comment, regarding the affair, yet I fancied I saw him
shiver somewhat at the ghastly recollection of Broussard. The matter being thus dismissed, we never spoke
of it again.

Our fire burned warm, filling the room with a homelike glow, so with good wine and clear consciences
Jerome and I drank and talked and stretched the lazy
evening through.

"There is just one other thing we can do, Placide, to
put the finishing touch upon our success."

I turned an interrogative glance toward the speaker.

"That is to find out, if possible, who is back of this
scheming. That fellow Yvard, dare-devil though he is,
has not brain enough to concoct such a plan, even if he

had courage and energy to fight it through. Depend
upon it, some powerful person is behind Yvard. Most
likely Madame du Maine. What say you to an adventure?''

My blood was in the humor for sport, the wine heated
me somewhat, and recking not of consequences I caught
at his idea.

''Willingly, comrade, but what?''

''Let us to Sceaux, to Madame's court, and see what
we may discover, for two fools like ourselves might perchance stumble blindly upon what a wise man would
overlook,'' he continued with mock humility.

''Yes, and two fools like ourselves might perchance
get themselves hanged for what a wise man would keep
his skirts clear of. There's a peril in meddling with
the affairs of the great.''

''Seriously, now. I have means and ways of learning
things in Madame's family. My head has been fast set
on this matter for some time. If you agree to take the
risk with me, you should know how we are to act. Now
mind you,'' he pursued, rising and stretching his back
to the fire, facing me, ''mind you, I tell you all I want
you to know, and you must promise me to make no inquiries on your own account.''

By this time I had grown accustomed to trust de
Greville, so I simply assented.

''A lady you know—it might get me into trouble,''
he further explained; with that I made myself content.

Jerome averted his face as if he would first frame
his speech carefully before he gave it me. Here Se-

rigny's final remark about making friends of the
ladies recurred to me, and I wondered what this fair
unknown had to do with such a rough game as we
played. Before the hand was out, though, I understood
how truly it had been said that women's wits now
swayed the destinies of France. Since this day, too,
our country has suffered much through women, when
under the next, and more pliant Louis, they ruled with
even a scantier pretense at concealment or of decency.
Jerome spoke slow and guardedly, when he turned to
me again. He began in a tone subdued by the intensity of his feelings—which, as I soon learned, were quite
natural.

"I was a mere lad; I had a sweetheart whose family
lived near our own in the vicinity of a certain small
provincial town, it matters not where. She, much·
younger than I, shared all my childish games. It was
the will of God that we should love. My family was
rich, is rich; both were noble. I had two older brothers
who stood between me and a title or wealth. Her
parents were ambitious for her future; I was put aside.
They sent her away, away from me, and married her
here in Paris to a man she had never seen. A simple
marriage of convenience, as we say here. Her heart was
numb and dead; it made no rebellion. I went to the
army; gained nothing but my rank. My brothers died,
and I being the next heir can live as it pleases me.
Here I am in Paris; she is at Sceaux, two leagues
away. I love her yet, and, God forgive her, she loves
me. Her old husband who is attached to the Duc

du Maine cares nothing for her. She amuses herself half in idleness with the intrigues of the court.
Nay do not look so black, Placide, for even this can be
innocent enough. There is much excuse for her, too,
my friend. A woman must needs have love to feed
upon. They can never, like ourselves, fill their hearts
entirely with ambition, with glory or with adventure.
Men may make of their lives a cloister or a camp and
be content; but women, whatever else of gaud and
glitter they may have, yet require love and tender-
ness and gentle sympathy beside. Happy is she who
receives all these from her husband; and that husband
treads dangerous ground who denies it to her. I see
your wonder at hearing this from me; but I have
thought constantly upon such things. Peste! this
touches not our business; let us go on. Through this
lady's husband, and by another source of information, I
hope to find the truth concerning Yvard. Do you follow
me?''

"Yes, but how?" I put in. "When I run my neck into
a halter, I want to know whose hands are playing with
the cord.''

"Never fear for her. Madame—that is, the lady—
has a firm hold upon the Duc du Maine himself, in. fact
she is quite indispensable to him. Don't ask me for
more. Once let the Duc be made Regent, and my old-
time sweetheart of those innocent days in Anjou will be
the most powerful woman in France. But with all that,
Placide,'' and the man's quivering voice went straight
to the very tenderest core of my heart for the depths of

bitterness it contained, "in spite of it all she'd rather be
back in the country breathing the pure and peaceful air,
a guiltless and happy girl, than to live as she does, and
rule the land. God knows I wish we had never seen
Paris."

I held my tongue; there was nothing I could say. He
felt his trouble keenly enough, and I refrained from
molding my undesired sympathy into words. Directly,
Jerome took heart and spoke again:

"Those are the conditions, I merely make the best of
them. There is still another friend of mine at Sceaux,
the Chevalier Charles de la Mora, a most gallant soldier and kindly gentleman. Verily, they are scarce now
in France. He has fallen into misfortunes of late and is
about to take some command in the colonies. I love
him much, and am sorely tempted to cast my lot with
his. But, you understand why I stay," and he lifted up
his hands with a gesture of perfect helplessness.

"His wife, Madame Agnes—almost a girl—is one of
the most beautiful and clever women in France, and who,
by way of novelty, loves her own husband. Women
are queer sometimes, are they not? To-morrow we go
to Sceaux; it will at least be an experience to you, even
should nothing good come of it. Do you agree?"

My curiosity was thoroughly aroused, and scenting
sport of a rare character I agreed to join the chase. It
was judged best that we should make all things ready
for an immediate journey to Versailles upon our return
from Sceaux.

Before we slept, my few serviceables were put in position for instant departure.

*   *   *   *   *   *

When I arose in the morning Jerome had already left his bed. I supposed it was out of consideration for what he was still pleased to consider my weak condition that he refrained from waking me. Claude came tripping in later with the message that M. de Greville had gone to make some last arrangements for our journey. I slept so restfully through the night my fatigue and all unpleasant reminders of the episode at Bertrand's had quite worn away, and I felt refreshed and strong again. When Florine came to inquire for my health she found me busied about the packing. I greeted her kindly, for in truth my gratitude was deep and sincere.

"Monsieur is preparing to leave?" she asked as if more than afraid of a reply. I could see she had some purpose in the question.

"Yes, I leave Paris to-day."

"To-day?" she echoed.

Yes, but I would return and find you again; I could not depart from France without finding and thanking you for all your kindness. In truth I am glad you came, for———." I tried to say more, but the words left my lips sounding so cold and meaningless the sentence died away incomplete.

Florine stood there, vaguely watching me as though she did not understand.

"Leave France?" she repeated, her tone expressing the hope she had not heard aright.

I had already said much more than I intended, for I was not fully aware of Jerome's intentions, and desired to say nothing which would reveal them.

"Leave France?" she urged again, "Monsieur—" she halted for the word quite naturally.

"De Mouret," I supplied, and for the first time she knew my name; surely it was little enough to trust one with who had given me my life.

"Monsieur de Mouret is to leave France?"

"Yes," I answered her truly, "but not to-day, possibly not for several days. I would not go away without seeing you again."

I felt my tone become warmer as I thought of all this girl had risked for me, and so blundered on uncertainly. What was I to do? What could I offer her in repayment? Not gold; she had refused that with the air of a grande marquise the night she first helped me from Bertrand's.

Heartily wishing for some of Jerome's finesse and tact, I gazed at her, stupid and silent, watching the tears gather in her eyes. I could only guess the thought which was passing in her mind, and even there I wronged her.

"Oh, Monsieur!" she spoke as from the fullness of her heart, while her voice trembled with excess of emotion, "Monsieur is going back into the great world; Monsieur has honor and fair fame; I must return to the wine shop."

The poor girl must have been wearied out with her watchings by my bed, for she burst into such an uncon-

trollable weeping as I fain would have prevented. I
did my rough best at comfort, but had to let her sorrow run its course.

"Oh, Monsieur, think of it! I must go back to that
dreadful wine shop, to the gaming tables; must continue to draw men there to be despoiled of their money,
perhaps of their lives; must laugh and be gay, though
my heart break at its own debasement. There have
been mány, ah, so many, I have lured to that place;
and it came so near to costing you your life—you who
were so kind to Florine."

She had sunk to the floor, and catching my hand
poured out all the bitterness of her heart.

"Yet, Monsieur, what can Florine do? There is no
way for a weak woman to do anything in this wretched
Paris. If I do not bring players to the house my aunt
beats me. See," she drew up her sleeve, and exposed
the welts of cruel cuts across the bare white flesh. "She
denies me food in my garret. So I must work, be
merry and work—and weep all the day for the misery
of the nights." My heart went out to the girl with all
sympathy, but, every whit as helpless as she, I only
wondered what could be done.

"Monsieur, it was not of my choosing, believe me,
believe me, it really was not. My father thought his
sister so well off in this fine Paris, when she offered to
bring me up as her own child, and sent us presents, he
made me come with her. We were so poor, so cruelly
poor. My mother could not come for me, and now
how can I go back? I dare not let her know how I am

treated. It would break her heart, and she is so old and tottering. If I seek other employment no one will take me, no one would give me a character for service. All the world is open to you. You go where you please, do what pleases you. All the world is shut to Florine. And you, Monsieur, my only friend, I hoped when you were well again, such a rich gentleman could find me a place among his friends; find me some quiet place where I might live and be of use, not bringing evil to all I touch. What an evil life, what a wicked life I lead. Oh, Monsieur, save me from it; save me! The horrible man you defended me from that night pursues me everywhere; my aunt is jealous because of him. She hates me now and would like to drive me out upon the streets —ugh! the terror of it. But her husband won't let her; he is kinder than she. See, I am pretty, I bring custom. She can not tell her husband why she hates me. No, no. Bertrand would kill her. And I dare not tell him. They would kill me—''

Her speech rambled on now, disconnected and incoherent. Still by catching sentences here and there the whole pitiful story was clear to me. My eyes would always overflow at sight of woman's suffering, my throat choked up; I could speak no word to her. Of a truth what a horrible life it must be; what iron webs do sin and circumstance weave round their victim. The cowering girl sobbed convulsively on the floor at my feet. I laid my hand tenderly upon her head.

"Florine, I have but two friends myself in all this land of France. You have served one of these faith-

fully in helping me. I will commend you to him, and
am sure he will reward you well.''

"Monsieur, I seek no reward; I served you not for
money.''

She shamed me, though I persisted.

"Not a reward, Florine, but surely you can let him
send you back to your mother. Here is money; his
money, not mine; he is rich, I am poor. He can pay you
for valuable service, I can only give you my undying
gratitude.''

I bent down and kissed her pale forehead, whereat
she wept afresh.

"Claude's wife will keep you here safe until we come
again. Then we will find means to protect and provide
for you.''

I bade her rise now and calm herself, for a bustle in
the street announced the noisy arrival of several horsemen. A few moments, and Jerome's voice called me
from below to make all ready.

I called Claude's wife up and delivered the girl to her
keeping, then turned to look out into the street. There
were now drawn up in front of the door four sturdy
equerries, well mounted, and leading two excellent nags,
which I took to be those Jerome had provided for our
own use.

Jerome obliged me once more to dress with exceeding
care, but I fretted much for my own easy garments
which permitted a man to use his limbs with the freedom
God had given them. Verily there would be no regret
when all this frippery could be cast aside, and by my

faith, it was much simpler to lay it off than to array one's self in. I never did learn all the eccentricities of that remarkable rig my fashionable friend had adorned me with.

"Had we better not strap on our pistols?" I asked, not knowing what he purposed.

"No; gentlemen do not wear them. Beside, at Sceaux one sharpens one's wits, and lets even his good blade dull and rust."

We mustered six stout swords as we clattered away from the Austrian Arms, and I could not but note, despite what Jerome had said, he took good care to provide trusty fellows and swift horses.

"A lean hound for a long race," Jerome laughingly remarked, noticing my inspection of the not over-fed nag I bestrode.

We took that road leading past the heights of Ville-juif, which in hardly more than an hour's brisk ride brought us to the park of Sceaux, overlooking the beautiful Fontenay valley of which I was destined to learn much. During this ride I had leisure to speak with de Greville of Florine, for the girl's story had roused a real desire in my heart to see her bettered.

"There are thousands such in Paris," he replied, shrugging his shoulders unconcernedly. "The few tell you truth, the many lie to you. You know not when to believe them. If you like, though, I will see what may be done. At least she may be placed in la Salt-peterie where no present harm can reach her, to earn a living. It is not a pleasant life, and no wonder young and pretty girls prefer the gay world to the seclusion and labor of Saltpeterie. Yet we will try.''

He treated the matter lightly, as a thing of common occurrence, yet was Jerome tender-hearted. Men who live in great cities become so hardened to the vice and crime about them that they no longer feel keenly, as we provincials do, the appeal of misery.

I might say here that Florine was one of the next ship-load of girls who were sent to the colonies. There she found a very worthy young planter who took her to wife, and after the manner of the mistreated girl in the fairy tales you children used to read, ''lived happily ever afterward.'' She became, from all accounts, a good wife and devoted mother; her children yet live in Louisiana, happy and prosperous.

CHAPTER XIV

THE SECRETARY AND THE DUKE

THOSE reflections which I set down at the end of the last paragraph drifted me somewhat from the regular thread of my narrative. This, perhaps, is not the only reason why I should stumble and shy along like a balky palfrey when I approach one of the trifling accidents which transpired immediately after our arrival at Sceaux.

Thinking now this matter over, my withered cheeks lose their ashen hue, and burn again with the hot, tumultuous blood of youth and shame. But I may as well tell it with all the resolution a man summons before plunging into an icy bath at midwinter. It came, the unexpected prelude to one long, sweet song. It was in this wise:

Jerome seemed a welcome guest at Sceaux, and from the hearty greetings, yet respectful withal, which were accorded him, must have been a man of more consideration in the world than I had heretofore supposed. Before this, I received him at his own worth, and our short acquaintance had been so filled with matters of serious moment, I made no inquiries beyond the scant

stray bits of information he had himself volunteered.
However that might be, his welcome at Sceaux was sincere. Nor did I wonder at his being a favorite, from
the jovial jests and flings he cast at those who crowded
round, which set them all a-laughing. His familiarity
with the doings of the day, and the quick repartee he
used to men of different parties, astonished me greatly.

Having disposed of our horses, and given quiet orders
to the groom, Jerome made me acquainted with his
friends. Some part of their good-fellowship fell to my
lot as a friend of Jerome's, and put me upon my mettle
to return it.

As good luck would have it, Jerome's friend, the Chevalier Charles de la Mora, was then at Sceaux, and came
up early on learning of our arrival.

He was a splendid fellow of thirty-five, stalwart and
unusually graceful for a man of his inches. His frank
and cordial manner was his greatest charm to me,
though a woman would doubtless have raved more over
those dark, dreamy eyes, which while mild enough, betimes gave promise of fire and to spare.

He spoke most affectionately to Jerome, and bade us
both be sure his wife would receive us with sincerest
pleasure. Several of the gentlemen had seen service,
and with them I was immediately on easy terms.

Before entering the Villa I paused in a doorway at the
head of a short flight of steps, bowing and posturing
through my new catalogue of behavior, anxiously
watching for Jerome's approval, or a cue. The rascal,
I could not for the life of me tell from his expression

whether he applauded my fine manners or laughed secretly at the folly of it all.   But I went on as I was
taught, bending myself pretty well double, half backing
into the door which led to an inner hall.   Holding this
position, which however elegant it might have appeared
to those in front, was certainly neither graceful or attractive viewed from within, I felt a sudden jar from the
rear, and being thus struck at a point of vantage, came
near to plunging forward upon my face.   Before I could
recover my equilibrium and turn about, I heard the
jingle of a tray of glasses and a cool shower of spray
flew about my ears.   Then the dazed and bewildered
eyes of a timid girl looked full into mine; she courage-
ously paused and essayed to stammer out an apology.
Her gaze, though, wandered past me, and one sight of
the drawn features of those who had seen it all and now
sought in vain to restrain their laughter, was too much
for this startled fawn.   She turned and fled as the wind,
just when their merry peal burst out.

"Well, my little lady had best look where she goes,
and not run through a door with her eyes behind her,"
roared de Virelle, when the girl had well escaped.

"His clothes are ruined, and so fine, ah, so fine,"
drawled Miron.

"By my soul, Captain, you have flowers to spare,"
chimed in Le Rue.   "That's right, gather them up, for
Mademoiselle is not usually so generous with her guer-
dons that any should be lost.   The little icicle."

His speech was suited to my actions, for, like a fool,
I had already dropped upon my knees, busied about

picking up the scattered roses and replacing them in the vases from which they had fallen. The tray was still rolling and rattling around on the floor. Verily, I felt my shame must consume me, and took refuge in this humble occupation to hide my face. There is some sort of a confused recollection now abiding with me, that a man-servant at length came to sweep up the fragments, while I watched him vacantly, a tangled bunch of roses in my hand.

In all their laughs and jests and jibes hurled at my embarrassment, Jerome never for a moment lost sight of the main purpose of our visit. As all roads led to Rome, so did he adroitly turn all topics of conversation into those channels where might be supposed to run the information we wanted.

I felt myself, especially in my present frame of mind, ill-fitted for such a play. The blunt and awkward directness of the camp suited better my ways and speech. Though I might discreetly hold my tongue, I could never use it with the credit I could my sword. Nor could I rid my mind of the childish vision which for one short instant confronted me at the door. Even then I pondered more on her amazed expression and youthful innocence than upon our own chances for success or failure.

From the comments of those about me, I gathered she was a protege of Madame's, whose reserved manners made her no great favorite with the dissolute throng which collected at the gay Villa of Sceaux. I took little part in their conversation, and was glad when Jerome by a gesture called me to follow him away.

"Let us go to see Madame," he said simply, when we were entirely out of hearing.

"Du Maine?" I inquired, vaguely wondering why we should venture into the lion's den.

"No — Madame — the other," he replied with some degree of hesitation.

I followed him without further questioning. He led the way, which was doubtless a familiar one, and the maid at the door, knowing him, admitted us at once to Madame's apartment. The woman, who sat alone in the dainty silk-hung boudoir, rose and came swiftly forward to greet Jerome, the radiant girlish smile changing quickly when she perceived me enter behind him. It was more the grande dame, and less the delighted woman, who acknowledged my presentation with courtly grace. Intuitively I felt her unvoiced inquiry of Jerome why he had not come alone. Yet was she thoroughly polite, and chatted pleasantly with us concerning the news of the day.

"We are to have a fete this afternoon; you must both come. Each guest is expected to contribute in some way to the entertainment of the company. You Jerome — M. de Greville," she begged pardon with a sudden glance at me, "You, M. de Greville, will doubtless favor us with a well-turned madrigal. And you, my dear Captain de Mouret, in which direction do your talents lie?"

"I have no talents, Madame; a plain blunt man of the camp."

"Ah! a soldier; so interesting in these stupid times, when men are little but women differently dressed. Ah, it has been too truly said that 'when men were created, some of the mud which remained served to fashion the souls of princes and lackeys.' But surely you could give us a story?" and so she talked on, not discourteous, but heedless of my protests. I was really alarmed, lest she seriously call upon me before that stately company.

The tiny clock upon her table chimed the third quarter, and she volunteered that at eleven she expected other callers. Acting upon this hint Jerome proceeded at once to tell her why we came, yet I noted in all his confidences he ever kept something to himself for safety's sake. The maid's reappearance interrupted us. She announced, "M. de Valence."

A gleam of anger swept across Madame's face.

"Bid him wait my pleasure in the ante-room. He is ten minutes early. No, the sooner he comes the sooner it is over; wait; bid him come in. M. le Captain, de Greville, will you gentlemen please to retire in that small room for a short space? I will speedily be free again."

And so it came about we overheard matters which opened my mind to the way affairs of state are managed, and I grew to learn upon what slender threads of love, of malice, of jealousy and of hate the destinies of nations must often hang. From our situation we could not help but hear all that passed between Madame and her caller. The maid withdrew, in the slow hurry of a truant on his way to school, but hastened at a sign of annoyance from Madame.

"Monsieur de Valence, you are full ten minutes early. You know I bade you be always exactly punctual," was Madame's petulant greeting of the handsome man who bore himself so meekly in her presence.

No tone was ever colder, no demeanor more haughty than hers, and this proud man who bent before no storm, who held the fortunes of many within his grasp, bowed like an obedient child to her whim.

"Yes, Celeste, I know, but—"

"Madame de Chartrain," she corrected. (I use the name de Chartrain, though it was not her own.)

"Yes—Madame, I know, but, it is so hard to wait; do you not understand how I count the minutes every day until—"

"Yes, yes, I've heard all those fine excuses before. To your business. The other can wait, business first, then—"

"Pleasure?" he supplemented with an eagerness strangely at variance with the rigid self-control he had hitherto shown.

"I did not say pleasure," she gravely broke in, "your business."

The man submitted with the patience of one quite accustomed, yet not wholly resigned to such a reception, and spread numerous papers upon the table before her. Selecting one he began to explain:

"Your wishes in regard to this matter have been carried out; I had the man detained in the city where he is at your command. He suspects nothing, though fretful at the restraint."

"Very good. And the other?"

"Yes, here it is. You see this has been so arranged that the Duke quite naturally selected Menezes to bear these dispatches. You may remind him that Menezes is a brother of the man Perrault, whom he had hanged some years ago. Here is the man's history, which you can look over at leisure. The Duke has forgotten all this in his impatience to remedy the Yvard fiasco. It will serve, however, to make him think you even more clever and devoted to him."

I listened closely at the name "Yvard."

"Well, now so far so good. And the question of finance? That is of more importance."

"And of more difficulty. The Madame often dabbles herself in these dealings involving money, and she is harder to deceive. However she is not accurate at figures, clever though she be otherwise. Look over this; this calculation. See, there is a simple transposition of an item, which results in a difference of near ten thousand livres. It appears there to have been made by the money lender for his greater gain. You can study this copy before the Duke comes. Then you will be quite prepared to point out this error and make the correction. Here is his copy which he will sign."

"Ah, good," she said looking over the memorandum he had given her of the amounts, with the correct calculations all neatly carried out.

"Well, that is enough for this morning; you may go; these things weary me."

"Celeste, Celeste, how long is this to continue? will you never— "

"*Madame*," she corrected positively, rumpling and smoothing out again the paper in her lap.

"As you will," with an air of hopeless protest. "Do you mean always to send me away when our business is completed—?"

"Was it not our agreement?"

"Yes, but I thought—"

"You had no right to think."

"A man must needs think whether he will or no, what is of life itself. Are you a woman of ice? Do you not realize I sell all I hold most dear, the confidence born of a life-time's honest service to my King, my own honor, only to serve you, to be with you?"

"I am weary. It is time for you to go."

"Yes, but is there nothing else? You agreed—"

"Oh, I know, why remind me?" She turned upon him fiercely. "Do you wish to make me hate you? Now you are only an object of indifference, objectionable to me as are all men who make love, and sigh, and worry me. Do you wish me to hate and despise you more than the rest?"

"God forbid! But—"

"You still insist?"

"Yes, I must have my thirty pieces of silver, the price of my treachery," de Valence returned bitterly; "men die in the Bastille for lesser offenses than mine."

"That is your affair," the woman replied, without a shade of concern.

I thought I could perceive a growing embarrassment in her manner as de Valence came closer to her, remembering, for so she must, that we could hear every word through the portiere. She collected herself bravely; de Valence must not suspect.

"Come, I'll pay you," and she put her lips upward so coolly I wondered he should care to touch them. Jerome raged silently, for I confess we were both guilty of looking as well as listening. De Valence leaned over her, but lifted his head again.

"Celeste—Madame, so cold. I'd as lief kiss the marble lips of Diana in the park."

"Oh, as you please; you may kiss them, too, if you like," she shrugged her shoulders, and was not pretty for the instant. "I pay as I promise; it is a mere barter of commodities You may take or leave it as you choose."

The man's attitude of dejection touched even me, but the woman gave no sign of feeling or compassion, only intense impatience

"Well, Monsieur, am I to sit waiting an hour? Are you come to be a sordid huckster to wrangle over your price?"

De Valence bent over her again, touched the lips lightly, and strode away, gathering up his papers from the table as he went. Two only were left, and those Madame held listlessly in her hand.

We felt thoroughly conscious of our guilt, Jerome and I, when we put aside the screen and re-entered the room. There was a certain air of resentment in his manner, as if he would call her to account, and I heartily wished myself otherwise. Perhaps it was all for the best; my presence prevented, for the time, explanations, and I fancied the woman was grateful for the respite. Her lassitude, and effort to overcome it, smote me to the quick, and right willingly I would have aided her had I but the power. To Jerome she spoke:

"You heard—all?"

He nodded.

"And saw?" Less resolutely this question came. The words conveyed the wish, unexpressed, that he had not heard. To me she gave no thought. Again Jerome nodded, and looked away.

"It is the penalty and the price of power. Oh, Jerome, how fervently I have prayed that this all had not been," she went on oblivious of my presence.

Jerome's resentment faded away at her mute appeal for sympathy, and I am very sure he would not have me chronicle all that then occurred. Suffice it, that I employed myself by the window, some minutes perhaps, until a hasty rap on the door, and the maid bore a message which she delivered to her mistress in secret.

"Bid him come in at once if it please him."

"He is already here, madame," the girl replied.

We had barely time to gain our former hiding place before a man richly dressed, and limping, entered; the same I had seen in the gardens of Versailles. I was now intensely interested in this little drama, which, as it were, was being played for my own benefit, and gave closer study to the Duke of Maine who hurried in.

The weak, irresolute face bore no trace of the dignity and power which made his royal father at times truly great; it showed, too, but little inheritance from the proud beauty of de Montespan. Vastly inferior to both, and to his ambitious wife whose schemes he adopted when they succeeded and disowned when they failed, the Duke trembled now upon the verge of a mighty intrigue which perchance would make him master of an empire, perchance consign him to the Bastille or to the block. Well he knew that the abandoned Philip of Orleans, though he sometimes forgot his friends, never spared an enemy. With these thoughts haunting him, his timid mind shrank from putting his fortunes to a decisive test, and he looked forward, dreading to see the increasing feebleness of the King hasten that day when a quick stroke must win or lose.

He approached Madame at the table with a semblance of that swagger affected by the weakling in presence of women, yet permitting the wandering eye and uncertain gestures to betray his uneasiness. Something had evidently gone wrong with my lord.

"Have you heard, Celeste, of Yvard?" he inquired, dropping into a seat.

My ears quickened at the familiar name.

"Well, what of him?"

"He has lost the Louisiana dispatches, and I know not what they contained."

"What!" exclaimed the woman, as if genuinely alarmed, and learning the bad news at first hand.

"Yes, the cursed fool lost them in some drunken brawl in the city. We have had the place thoroughly searched, but—"he finished the sentence with a shrug to express his failure.

"What if they should reach Orleans?" he continued evenly. "My men fear he has gone to him anyway, hoping to play in with both for pardon. I'd feel much safer could we only lay our hands upon him. He is the one man beside ourselves here who knows—who knows, anything," the Duke went on with growing trepidation.

"Well, make yourself comfort, my lord, I took the responsibility to detain Yvard in Paris."

"You?" he sprang from his chair in astonishment. "You? Why? How?"

"I thought your safety demanded it. My lord is too generous, too confiding," she threw toward him a glance of concern poor de Valance would have periled his soul to win. You see, when we entrusted him with this business, it was so delicate a mission, I set a watch upon him—some of my own people of Anjou—and when he acted negligently they reported to me. He began drinking, too, and freely, so I feared his discretion. I now have the man safe in Paris. What would my lord with him?"

Du Maine fixed his cold eyes upon her, for a short space, then,

"It would be prudent to put him quietly out of the

way," he suggested, the thin lips closing cruelly. "No, hold him, we may have further need for his sword. But have a care that he talks to no one."

Madame had raised no objection to the Duke's cool command that an end be made of Yvard, yet I did her the credit to suppose it was because she well knew she might do as she liked, and he be none the wiser.

He now settled himself upon a divan near Madame, with all the complacency of a man whose own foresight has saved him a serious trouble, and said after mature deliberation, gazing thoughtfully at the sportive cherubs on the ceiling:

"Well, it could not have been so bad after all, for I observed the caution to prepare a warning for our friends across the frontier, and had arranged for a friend of ours to be entrapped by Orleans, betraying misleading dispatches to him. A fine plan, think you? Menezes you know is devoted to me, and I have promised him a patent."

"Who did your grace say was to be this friend?"

"Menezes."

"Why Menezes?"

"I have done much for the fellow, and he is not over clever; clever enough for the purpose, you know, but —"

"Does my lord not remember Menezes is a brother of the Perrault whom you had hanged some years ago? I fear you have been badly advised."

"No! I do not recall him."

"The rogue who cast a stone at your horse?"

"Ah, I bring him to mind. Short, thick-set fellow, who whined something about hunger, children, and the cold. Ugh! What concern have I with the rabble? But how do you know this, Celeste?"

"I have long misdoubted him, and had the rascal overlooked. He is of Picardy, and his father was attached to St. Andre, who likes not His Grace, the Duke of Maine."

"No, by my faith, he hates me. Ah, I see it all. Celeste, you should have been a man, a man's wit almost you have. Really, so much brain is wasted in that pretty head of yours. Madame will come to comprehend she does not know it all—yet she torments me till I give in. I think I shall take firmer hold, and manage my own affairs to better advantage than she. Ugh! What a scrape she was like to get me in."

He gradually regained the expression of complete satisfaction with himself, and prepared now to show the masterpiece of his work, the contract with Antonio of Modena, the money-lender.

"Here are our financial plans; the usury is high, but there is great risk, so thinks Antonio; egad! perhaps he is right, though it is possible we may pay him. Altogether a most excellent plan, my own work——."

Madame interrupted him, thinking perhaps it was wise that he should not be committed too far that he could not throw the blame on other shoulders. She took advantage of a pause to examine the document with apparent care.

"Yes, excellent, but let us see. Three, seven, twelve,

fourteen, twenty-three—here is some mistake. Let us
go over it again. Yes, here it is. This is not your accounting. The miserly Lombard would cozen you of
your honor if he could but sell it again. Here is an
error of near ten thousand livres; let me correct it for
you.''

And while he stared at her she deftly copied the correct amounts from the slip she held concealed in her
hand. She knew the figures were his own, but gave no
token.

''I doubt not you would have looked over it more
carefully before you signed it, and these matters would
have been detected by your own eyes.''

''Yes, yes,'' he replied nervously, reaching out his
hand for the paper lest she observe—what her quick
eyes had at first seen—that the contract already bore
his signature and seal. She gave it him and he replaced it carefully in his breast.

''I will give those careless secretaries a lesson they
sorely need,'' and in this disturbed condition of mind
he blustered out of the apartment, forgetting his usual
gallantries, which Madame so diplomatically put aside
without giving too serious offense.

Jerome leaned against the window-facing, his unseeing eyes resting on the park beyond the little garden at
our feet. His brow lowered, not as of a storm, but
with the murkiness of a settled and dismal day. Perchance his thoughts wandered with his childhood's
sweetheart amid the fertile vales of far away Anjou.

11—BLACK WOLF

Nothing was more distant from him than the gilded furnishings, the frescoes, the marble Venus at his elbow. Beside her table, alone, and abstracted as Jerome, the woman toyed with a dainty fan; her impassive beauty, born of rigid training, betrayed not the inner desolation. Her face was calm and serious enough, the skin lay smooth and glowed with all those delicate tints that women love.

Her quietude reminded me of the slumbering ocean, glassy and tranquil, whose unmarred surface conveyed no hint of sunken ships beneath, of cold dumb faces tossing in the brine, of death-abysses where wrecks abandoned lie.

I slipped away without rousing a protest from Jerome, and closing the door softly left them to their meditations and to each other.

CHAPTER XV

NEW HOPES

NOW, that I was well out of their way, it came to me to wonder what I should do with myself until Jerome might please to seek me again, but accident favored me with occupation. Passing through the hall I heard a woman's shrill voice, lifted in anger, berating some unfortunate attendant.

"You wretched hussy, to speak rudely to a guest of mine, who did but make to you a pretty speech. I'd have you be most charming to Monsieur Viard. Remember, you are only a hireling, and need give yourself no such fine and unseemly airs."

The door just ahead of me was thrown violently open, and out strutted a tiny lady in a most disproportionate rage. She was beautiful neither in face nor figure; she was diminutive, and petulant of manner, but bore herself with an air of almost regal pride. It was she whom I came to know as Madame du Maine, a daughter of the proud and princely Condes. Following her, weeping bitterly, came the sweet maid who had spilled the tray of flowers on me at the door. I stepped back into an alcove, lest, perchance, she look behind, and aimlessly I straggled out into the gardens as best I might.

(163)

The Villa being a strange ground, it fretted me to be alone therein, with nothing to think of but this trouble of my friends. And Madame de Chartrain, did I blame her? Blame Jerome? Yes—no. I hardly knew. Viewed at a distance and impartially, such things strike us with aversion, and we are quick to condemn. But the more I thought the nearer I came to concluding it took something more than a mere mummery to make a wife. All the ceremonials and benedictions and lighted candles and high-sounding phrases could not bind a woman's heart, where that heart was free, or called some other man its lord. Yet the bare fact remained, this woman was a wife, and to me, at least, that name had always been a sacred and holy one.

To what vain or wise conclusions my cogitations may have led me, I conceive not, for another small matter now quite absorbed my whole attention. It was the beginning of that one dear hope which speedily banished all others. It is said the trippant tread of Fate doth leave no print upon the sand to mark its passage, nor doth she sound a note of warning that the waiting hand may grasp her garments as she flies.

A gleam of white in one of the summer houses caught my roving eye, and quite aimlessly I passed the door. A chit of a child crouched upon the floor, and leaned forward on the benches, weeping as though each ' sob were like to burst her little heart. I grant it was no affair of mine, yet my tears were ever wont to start, and eyes play traitor to mine arm at sight of woman's trouble. Without thinking one whit, I stepped in be-

side her, and laying my hand gently upon the lassie's
shoulder, implored that she weep no more.

Up she sprang to face me, flushed and indignant.
Verily was I abashed. Yet there was that of sympathy
and sincerity in my voice and mien—or so she told me
after—which turned her wrath aside.

"You, Monsieur; I thought it was old Monsieur Viard,
he pursues me so."

It was the same little maid I had seen in the hall, and
that was why I trembled. She wept now for the scold-
ing she had got. I caught my breath to inquire why
she wept.

"Oh, Madame, Madame—it is the humor of Madame
to humiliate me of late; she reminds me ever of my de-
pendent position. And Monsieur," the child straightened up proudly till she was quite a woman. "Monsieur, I come of a race as old as her own—and as honored." "Charles is poor—the Chevalier de la Mora,
you know. But now he goes to the colonies, and will
take me with him."

It was a silly enough thing to do, but about here I
stalked most unceremoniously off, leaving her to her
sorrow and her tears. Since that day I have often smiled
to think how foolishly do the wisest men deport themselves when they first begin to love. Their little starts
of passion, their petty angers and their sweet repent-
ances—all were unexplored by me, for Love to me was
yet an unread book.

At the door of the house M. Leroux hailed me graciously:

"Well met, my dear Captain; we go to the park, and would have you bear us company. Where is M. de Greville?"

I explained as best I might his absence, and followed them in lieu of better employment, forgetting for the time the threatened fete. Before I could extricate myself, these new friends had led me into a brilliant circle, and duly presented me to Madame, who sat on a sort of raised platform in the center.

She showed no traces of her recent anger and spite, vented upon that patient girl who now claimed all my thought. Her ladies, some languishing literary notables of the day, and officers, stood about discussing the news, and talked of naught but some fetching style or popular play, through all of which I struggled as bravely as my dazed condition would permit. It seemed I would never grow accustomed to the like, though it is said many men find great delight in such gatherings. But one thing I searched for most eagerly.

Behind Madame's chair, after a little, appeared the sweet shy face of my weeping Niobe of the park. I felt she saw and recognized me, and my face grew warmer at the thought. I made bold to ask one of the gentlemen standing near me who the lady might be, and not desiring to point at her, simply described her as well as possible, and as being in attendance upon Madame.

"That, Monsieur, is Madame Agnes, wife of the Chevalier de la Mora; the wittiest and most beautiful woman at Sceaux, and the chilliest."

Noting the change of countenance which I sought in vain to control, he went on banteringly.

"Beware M. le Capitaine, half the men at Sceaux are in love with her, but she has the execrable taste to prefer her own husband. Such women destroy half the zest of living. Beside, the Chevalier has a marvelous sword and a most unpleasant temper. Bah! how ludicrous it is for men to anger at trifles.

"But," I faltered, "she seems a mere child."

"Yes, but none the less charming," and he turned away to continue his interrupted conversation with the daring young Arouet, the same who was to acquire universal fame under the name Voltaire.

Thus rudely were my new-awakened hopes of love cast down. A wife, and the wife of a friend! She had spoken to me of "Charles," and of going with him to the colonies. A wife, yet for all that, I knew I loved her.

They say the road to hell is paved with good intentions. My intentions were the best that ever made excellent cobblestones toward the infernal gate. Only a few days and I would be gone; surely those could be passed through in peace. She was a wife—I would never let her know that all my heart was hers. This I determined. But man is weak, and the very atmosphere of France dried up the springs of every honest impulse. Everywhere was scoffing, raillery and disbelief. Honor, friendship and virtue were regarded as the vain chimeras of a fool. Why should not I enjoy life while I might?

Directly Madame Chartrain entered without intrud-

ing, and composedly took her place among the ladies
who made room for her near Madame. Nothing in her
manner bore evidence of her recent conflict. It was
really marvelous how the life these women led schooled
them to a stoicism any Choctaw brave daring the stake
might envy. She nodded to me gaily, and I stopped
to touch her hand .

"Where is M. de Greville? Is he not to be with us
this afternoon?"

I looked her in the face, wondering, for could she not
answer her own question far better than I? She read
my meaning, but her glance never wavered.

"Ah! There he is, among the gentlemen. I feared
he found Sceaux too dull after Paris, and he had promised us a bit of his work. You know he composes famous verses to some fair and distant inamorata."

"Indeed, Madame, I suspected not his talents," I
replied. Our conversation lagged, for the programme
had already commenced, and we gave our attention to
the reading of some curious letters, said to have been
written by two Persians of distinction then traveling in
Europe, which were being published anonymously in
Paris. At first, I could not bring myself to listen to
such twaddle, dubiously moral, which, under the guise
of light, small talk, struck at the foundations of government, religious beliefs, and all which I had before held
sacred. Listening only to contradict, I grew interested
in spite of myself, and only at some allusion more than
usually out of place, as it seemed to me, among so

many ladies, did I take my eyes from the reader's countenance, and suffer them to roam about the company.

Feeling again the subtle influence of Agnes' gaze
fixed full upon me, it caused my cheeks to flush, my
knees to quake, and verily, my legs were as like to
carry me away as to sustain me where I leaned against
a tree. The girl was looking straight at me; I dared
not return her stare which had something more than
mere curiosity in it, and disturbed me greatly.

The reading was finished without my knowledge, a
piece of buffoonery, or play acting gone through with,
which I did not see, when my own name, called by
Madame, brought me to my proper good sense again.

I found myself, before I was quite aware, bending before Madame and receiving her command that I should
do something for the amusement of the company.

"M. Jerome has favored us, you know—we have no
drones here," she went on pleasantly, "and it is the
rule at Sceaux that all must join our merriment."

"Jerome?" I answered in a bewildered fashion, for I
had no recollection of seeing aught he did; then I remembered hearing him recite some languishing verses
about a white rose, a kiss, a lady's lips—some sighs,
and such other stuff that now escapes me—but I had
paid no attention to it all.

Jerome, the villain, seconded Madame's request so
vigorously I could not decline, though he well knew I
was no carpet knight capable of entertaining ladies fair
on the tourney field of wit.

"The Captain sings divinely, Madame, but is becomingly modest, as you see." The wretch laughed in his sleeve; I could have strangled him.

"Ah, so rare," she retorted, "you men are vainer than my ladies."

I knew myself the target for dozens of curious eyes, under the heat of which I near melted away.

"Sing, comrade, sing some sweet love ditty of a lonely forest maiden and her lover, robed in the innocence of Eden."

Had the fool no sense? I caught the imploring expression of interest on the girl's sweet face behind Madame, and determined at all hazards they should not have the laugh at me. I saw it all then; they were in league with Jerome to play a game of "bait the bear," with me for bear.

So I pitched in and sang, such a song I warrant as my lords and ladies had never bent their ears to hear before, a crooning death incantation of the Choctaws, which fell as naturally from my lips as my own mother tongue.

Their laughter hushed, for even in the court of France, sated as it was with novelties, laying a world under tribute for amusements, that wild, weird melody never rose before nor since. One stanza I sang translated into French that they might understand;

"Yuh! Listen. Quickly you have drawn near to hearken;
Listen! Now I have come to step over your soul;
You are of the Wolf Clan;
Your name is Ayuni;
Toward the Black Coffin of the upland, in the upland of the Darkening Land your path shall stretch out.

With the Black Coffin and the Black Slabs I have come to
cover you.
When darkness comes your spirit shall grow less and dwindle
away never to reappear. Listen."

And they did listen; yea, attentively did they
hearken, for a great pall of silence lowered upon them,
so new, so strange to them was the song.

When I had quite finished, the soft, Indian words
dropping as the splash of unknown, unseen waters,
Madame besought me with earnestness to tell her more,
and the others crowded round to hear. I do not know
what evil genius of folly prompted the childish deed,
but feeling safe in having found what we wanted, and
moved more than I would admit by the now admiring
eyes of the girl, I gathered up half a dozen daggers
from the gentlemen who stood about. Selecting those
whose weight and balance commended themselves most
to my purpose, I cleared a small space, and having sent
a serving man for a pack of cards, chose a five spot and
pinned it to a tree. Standing back some ten to fifteen
paces, I cast the four knives at the corner pips in quick
succession, piercing them truly, then paused a minute
and cast the fifth knife at the center, striking accurately
between the other four. It was an act of idle vanity,
yet I hated for Jerome to taunt me on the way home.

By these petty means I gained a cheap applause from
the belles and gallants at Sceaux, and Jerome opened
not his lips to jibe me, as I feared, but like the rest, applauded.

I had now quite regained my courage, but for the

girl. I loved to think of her as but a girl; that she was also a wife I barred out of our castle in Spain. Why should I be afraid of such a timid child? Verily, I knew not.

My folly had one result I could not then foresee; it told some of those present, whose hand it was had cast the hunting knife which struck Yvard. I did not learn this for days after.

The approving and pleased look on the little lady's face fired me with an insane desire to further win her notice, whereat I chided myself for a vain coxcomb, and drew imperceptibly away from the company, until I gained a shady and secluded walk which led to a retired nook overlooking the valley.

The quietude of the evening's close jarred on my turbulence of spirit. For the first time a woman's voice lingered in my ears after her speech was done, a woman's smile played as the fitful summer's lightning before my eyes. Oh, fool, fool! What place had women in a soldier's life. What a discordant harmony would one angel create amid the rough denizens of Biloxi. So I reasoned, forgetful that reasons never yet convinced the heart.

CHAPTER XVI

THE UNEXPECTED

AS one who pauses at the threshold of some fabled palace of the houri, so did I stop, bewildered by the beauty of this virgin field of love, by fancy decked with blossoms, now spreading all the allurements of fetterless imaginings before me. A sudden whiff brought me the perfume of her presence, and, turning, she appeared before me, whether in the spirit or the flesh, I could hardly tell, so transported was I by the swift changes of my thought, merging beauties ever new, ever sparkling, with those scarce tasted ones but just discarded. Yet there she was, a dainty thing in white. White of dress, white of face, white of spirit.

In frightened tones of far-away sweetness, her voice mingled with the air, so low, so melodious one could scarce determine when she commenced to speak.

"Monsieur, quick, listen. You are in danger. I was in Madame de Chartrain's chamber and overheard. You have letters. M. de Greville will take them from you—for her sake—they compromise her. There is other danger," she spoke breathlessly on, "other more deadly danger lurking for you here; I beseech you to

(173)

leave—at once.   M. de Greville will take those letters
from you by force or guile.   Oh, tarry not, there has
been so much of blood, and this place so seeming fair;
the assassin, the poison and prison houses.''

The eloquence of fear trembled in her words.   Half
starting forward I drank in every syllable, not for the
warning she would fain convey, but for their sweetness.
All I could realize for the moment was that she had
sought me, sought me freely.   Then she was gone.
Swiftly, noiselessly as she came, she disappeared.   The
distant flutter of her skirts among the sombre trees
marked the path she went.   Through it all I spoke no
word, returning, as one who has received an angel's
visit, to my reverie.

I was not suffered long to spend my time alone.   The
old beau, de Virelle, in his bluff and hearty way directed the attention of a party of ladies who were with
him to where I hung over a marble balustrade enrap-
tured at the broad expanse of valley, rosy tinted with
the hues of ebbing light, boundless as the dim horizon
of my own sweet dreams.

"By my faith, Captain, you should have heard the
clamor over your departure.   Already famous, and so
soon weary of your laurels.   Ah! a tryst," he exclaimed.   "Verily you do better than I thought," for
he had picked up a muslin handkerchief, edged with
lace, which sought in vain to hide itself among the
leaves.   So busied had I been it escaped my notice.
Instinctively I reclaimed the prize and with no gentle

hand I doubt, for his touch and jeering manner dese-
crated the sacred relic of my vanished saint.

De Virelle scowled somewhat at my precipitation, but,
meeting a no less determined air, passed the matter by.
His ladies affected not to see. They in their turn plied
me with inquiries about the savages in America, asked
all manner of silly questions, and completed with their
foolish simperings the disgust I already felt at such an
interruption to my thought. Yet so great is the force
of novelty to women they clung about me as if I were
some strange tame animal brought to Paris for their di-
vertisement.

"Zounds, Margot dear," de Virelle blurted out aside,
for even his dull senses saw I was not pleased, "our
good Moliere must have had this hermit captain in his
mind when he made Alceste to rail so at the hypocri-
sies of the world, and urge the telling of truth and looking of truth at all times."

"How brutally frank! What bad breeding," assented that young woman.

"This captain seems so full of weariness at our coming,
and lacks the grace to veil it decently; let us go."

Finding no hand of mine raised to hinder them, these
fair dames and demoiselles, with many pretty pouts and
flutters and flounces, betook themselves away, followed
by their faithful squire.

I began then to feel sorry at having disgraced
Jerome's gentle teachings. The light dying away
across the distant fields and streams, I resigned my solitary communion and set out slowly toward the villa.

The meaning of all the girl had said now forced itself upon my attention. If this were true, and it seemed plausible enough in view of all that had transpired here, I was indeed confronted by a new and serious danger. Happily danger was not a new fellow-traveler; I merely turned over in my mind the best means to meet it.

Going rather out of my way, I found the grooms without much difficulty, and telling them we were to leave Sceaux at once, ordered the horses saddled, and made ready at a side door where I directed them to wait. My own mind was to tell Jerome nothing of it, but simply to mount the best horse and ride away alone —if that course became necessary.

*   *   *   *   *   *

I will break in a bit just here to speak of an incident which occurred that very night in the modest boudoir of Madame de la Mora. Had I but known of it at the time, it would have saved me many weary months of suffering.

Madame Agnes de la Mora sat placidly, her work basket by her side, busied about some lace she was mending. The Chevalier studied a number of military maps of Louisiana at his table. It was a pretty picture of domestic harmony, then quite unfashionable at Sceaux. A timid rap at the door, and a voice:

"Sister, may I come in?"

"Yes, child," and her sister Charlotte slipped silently in and sat herself upon the floor at Madame's feet. There was a striking similarity between the two. Madame, for all her dignified title, being but a year the elder, and she scant of twenty. Charlotte, somewhat slighter and more delicately colored, was even of greater beauty than her sister, with much promise for the years to come. To the casual observer, though, especially when viewed apart, they seemed almost reflections one of the other. There was something of a loving guardianship in the attitude of the elder, of confiding trust in that of the younger, as she leaned her head upon her sister's knee in pensive meditation.

"Sister, I must tell you of something; I know not that I did well or ill," and she lifted her face with a surety of sympathy.

"What is it, dear, what weighty matter troubles you now?"

The Chevalier looked up long enough to say:

"Have you torn your frock, or only quarreled again with the good Abbe over your task?" The girl very evidently had nothing to fear from his harshness.

"No! No! Don't tease; it's really important. This day at noon Madame Chartrain was in her chamber—you know the young man who came with M. Jerome?" de la Mora nodded.

"The same I ran into at the door?" and she flushed again at the memory of our discomfiture.

"Well, to-day noon at Madam Chartrain's I heard that danger threatened him concerning some papers or something which he has—and Madame du Maine, too, they mean him harm; and—and—well, I told him. Did I do ill, sister?"

12—Black Wolf

"What is that, Charlotte? Come here."

She crossed the room obediently and stood before him.

The Chevalier asked: "How did it happen, child? Tell me all about it, where you saw him, who was there, and all."

So she went on to tell of her seeking me in the park, and her hurried warning.

"Well, what did he say to all that?"

"He didn't say anything; I gave him no chance; I just ran up near him and told him as quick as ever I could that he had better go off somewhere, and then—and then—well, I just ran away again. He looked so startled and surprised he could not say anything. When I turned again to peep through the hedge he was still standing there with his hands stretched out as if he would have liked to stop me, but I was already gone."

The girl laughed a short little laugh and tucked her hand closer into his.

"Did I do wrong, Charles? Tell me, was it so very, very—bold?"

The Chevalier could not quite suppress the smile already twitching at his lips, though he soon looked grave enough.

"Yes, child, it was not well; beside, the affair is not yours, and it is always dangerous to meddle. There, now, don't worry, it does not matter much after all. Soon we leave here and you will never see any of them again, I hope. This is no place for lassies fair and

young as you. I hope to take both you and Agnes to
a new and purer land.''

"Soon we leave?'' she repeated, ''oh, I forgot; but
I don't want to, I like it here.''

"Like it?   I thought you hated Sceaux?''

"Yes, I did—but—''

"But, what?''

"But, nothing, I just like it—now,'' she insisted illog-
ically.

"Who is this young man, Charles?'' asked Agnes
when her sister had gone.   And he told her.

CHAPTER XVII

THE FLIGHT FROM SCEAUX.

THE responsibility brought by the possession of such valuable state papers oppressed me greatly, to say nothing of the perils which would beset their custodian if it became Jerome's purpose to reclaim them. I thought it most prudent and proper under present conditions to see the dispatches safe in de Serigny's hands— then, at least, I would be absolved from any blame in the matter. Serigny held me responsible, and it would perhaps be the part of wisdom to act independently of Jerome, report fully to Serigny, and if it were then his wish that the investigation concerning Yvard and Madame du Maine be pressed to further discoveries, nothing would be easier than to return to Paris almost before Jerome could miss me. I need tell Serigny nothing of my suspicion of Jerome; even if true, his animosity would vanish with the cause which gave it birth.

There was much to acquaint Serigny with, much perchance he knew already. Paris swarmed with rumors. Every lip was busy with second-hand gossip coming, as each relator declared, from the most reliable sources. "My cousin, who is laundress to the Countess de Lanois, says," and upon this immaculate authority the

(180)

butcher upon his morning rounds detailed the most delightful and impossible gossip to his customers.

"Pierre, my son, the valet, who is in the confidence of the Duke of Gesvres, heard His Grace say with his own lips"—and so the wine-room stories flew, gathering strength and falsehood as they went. But the story of to-day gave the lie to that of yesterday, and no man knew the truth.

War with Spain filled every mouth, yet none had a why or a wherefore. The King said "war," and all his nation echoed. No, not all. Many there were who gave voice to the cry with hearts that rebelled, with clear brains questioning the right of one man to plunge a whole people into renewed slaughter. These held their peace for the sake of their necks. *"I am the State,"* Louis had declared, and such ideas were not for the canaille to have; they must curb their tongues to cheat the gibbet. Being a soldier and under orders, I had no right to form opinions, but, sobered in some degree by these reflections, paced about until it came time to take horse and away.

"In the name of the wandering Ulysses, Placide, where have you been these two good hours?" said Jerome, suddenly coming toward me.

"Has it been so long? I tired of the crowd and strolled alone through the gardens."

His quick eye caught sight of the handkerchief tucked snugly in my belt.

"A lady? And so soon?" he bantered me.

My tell-tale flush permitted no denial, nor did I care

to discuss it.   As we talked we drifted into a small room just off the main hall.

"By the way, Placide, had we better not place our dispatches in some safe hiding until we leave here?   It might be suspected we have them.   The devil only knows what that scheming de Valence and du Maine may not unearth.   Their spies are everywhere."

I agreed with him.   It was as well; anything to gain time and allay suspicion.   But I understood my lady's warning was true; his earnestness convinced me.

"Where do you carry them?"

"Sewn in the lining of my cloak," I replied.   A lie, but pardonable.

"Why, you careless fellow; they may be lost.   Where is your cloak?" seeing I did not have it.

"In charge of Damien; he is trusty."

"Better have it yourself; wait here, I will go and fetch it."

I congratulated myself on this diplomatic stroke, for Jerome was about to start off in all haste when Damien himself appeared, and before I could stop him, delivered the message.

"The horses are saddled and at the door."

"Go and wait with them."

Jerome had taken my cloak from the fellow's arm, for in fact he had it, and now laid it across his knee.   His blank expression showed utter astonishment at the disclosure

"What does this mean?   We are to rest here tonight?"

"No; I ride to Paris."

"Why?"

"I am afraid."

"Of what?"

"Of everything. We are in the house of our enemies, and it is the quality of courage to be discreet."

During this brief dialogue Jerome was stealthily running his hands through the lining of my cloak until he comprehended I had misled him. I could almost put his thought in words. Together we arose, laying each our hands upon the half-closed door, he to hold it, I to open it, steady-eyed, and each reluctant to cause the breach we knew must come.

"Placide, the papers are not here," he said in a quiet tone, yet full of determination.

"I know it."

"Why have you deceived me then?" for he could mask his purposes no longer, "Hand me those dispatches."

"No. My orders are to place them in the hands of Serigny."

"But I *must* have them."

"And I tell you as firmly, you can not."

"Listen, Captain," he begged in altered tones, "those dispatches may compromise Celeste. Let us take from them anything which implicates her in this miserable intrigue, and deliver the rest. That is easy. I can open and close them again so it can not be told."

"My orders are not to open them."

"By God, you will!" he burst out with volcanic fury,

"no, no; I am too hot. We can lose them; tell Serigny they were never found; tell him Yvard carried
them off; tell him he never had them. We can fix a
tale."

"It would be a long story, and a liar must needs have
a good memory."

I was playing for time, time to think, time to get
away.

"But I will go with you to Serigny," he insisted, "tell
the lie and make him to believe. 'Pshaw, man, you
know not the ways of the world, at least not at the Court
of France."

"Think, Jerome, of the war, of our people in the colonies, of our honor?"

"I care not for it all," the wild passion in his voice
made me almost fear him. "All that is as nothing to
me where Celeste is concerned. Oh, Placide, think of
it! I love her, love her, love her—do you comprehend
what that means to such a man as I? I, who have
loved her almost from her birth, have seen her taken
from me and sold—yes, sold by her money-loving father,
sold, sold! I, who have borne all her husband's leers
when, flushed with the insolence of rank and wine, this
shriveled bridegroom bore her as a piece of ornament
to his house in Paris. Can I bear to lose her now?

"But, Jerome, you would not be such a coward as to
permit our brethren in the colonies to be slaughtered,
while you tell your pitiful lie to shield a woman? It
can not be done. What a fool you are come to be. Man,
man, where is your courage?"

"I care not. Love for such a woman would make of Truth a liar, and of Jove a fool. Think, Placide, think of her, Celeste, in the Bastille, the irons cutting into her delicate hands, those hands which I have so fondly held within my own—the cold stones for her bed. Or, worse: The block, the headsman and the jeering rabble. Have you no feeling, man? Suppose there was some woman whom you loved—a guilty love, I grant—but so strong, so deep, so overpowering, you could not master it? Suppose *she* were threatened, would you not protect her even if you lost your life; yea, bartered away your honor?"

A pale little tearful face thrust itself before me as he spoke, and I knew my own weak heart. I confess his pleading staggered me, and I hesitated. He came closer; all the love and fear of a strong and desperate man wove itself into his words.

"Could you only have seen her two hours ago when you left her chamber; have heard her sobs, felt the tremble of her heart when she threw herself, just as when a child she used to do, into my arms pleading for protection! Those dispatches will ruin her. She so calm, so proud, so brave to all the world, wept like a terrified baby upon my breast. Placide, I'd die and go to hell to save her. She so cold and pure, her very name is a reproach to this flock of butterfly women. This woman loves me, loves me even though that love be what men call dishonor. Bah! I hate the word. Her father never sold her heart. No, that was mine, forever mine. Had I but foreseen this I'd have left you rotting in Bertrand's dungeon. No, no.

Placide, I meant it not; I'm not myself; forgive me, comrade; pity her and pity me.''

I vaguely wondered what there could be in the packet to cause him so sincere an apprehension. But I must think of my people and be strong. I denied him once for all He sprang at me with the fury of a demon. Being the cooler and stronger, I threw him off easily and reached the door as he came again with his sword. It was a delicate predicament. I could easily kill him. Wild with a lover's fear, he left his front open to my blade, but I'd had enough of death. He paused to shove a table from his path, which gave me time to open and slip through the door.

In a moment he rushed out behind me, pale and panting. The corridor, deserted, echoed to our flying steps. I ran on ahead making my way toward the horses. Meeting people outside, we had to slacken our gait, smile, and conceal the realities of the situation, the necessity for which he apprehended as quickly as I.

Four horses stood ready, and choosing the one I thought best fitted for a hard chase—it was evident we could not afford to fight it out at Sceaux—and to fight seemed now his purpose—I vaulted lightly into the saddle, and before Jerome could hinder, had jumped the low wall and taken the direct road to Paris.

Practiced horseman as Jerome was, it took him no time to follow, and his grooms joined in the chase.

On, on, we sped. Trees, fences, walls and people all melted into one motley and indistinguishable stream. In the open road we strung out, according to the speed of our mounts, one of the grooms dropping farther and farther in the rear. The distance between Jerome and myself, despite his frantic belaborings of his brave steed, grew steadily greater.

Just before we passed a crooked lane off to the left, leading whither I knew not, Jerome turned in his saddle and called to the two grooms now well to the rear.

"That way quick; to the Versailles road. Cut him off."

The fellows obeyed, reining their horses into a swinging lope, as, less hurried, they took the lane indicated. Jerome thence rode on after me alone. The situation was now becoming awkward. I had acted without cool consideration heretofore, taking the Paris road because it was the only one I knew, and trusting thereafter largely to fortune. Now, as I caught occasional glimpses of the city spires, the towers of Notre Dame, I must perforce remember I had no hopes from them. The crazed man behind knew the city well, while to me it was a labyrinth of difficulty. I had no friends, while he counted many. I must act, and that quickly. Had I but known enough to turn down that lane into the Versailles road I could have reached the palace without molestation, thanks to my good luck in picking the best horse of the lot. Thinking of the lane brought an idea which promised well.

Moderating my speed gradually I suffered Jerome to draw nearer. I then called over my shoulder that as we were now man to man, we might dismount and fight it out upon a piece of level sward beside the road. His horse was nearly spent, and inflamed to fury by the fear of my escape, he eagerly agreed. While we parleyed, I worked myself into a position near his horse's head, and as he prepared to alight, snatched my sword and with a quick upper cut severed one rein near the bit. The blade having cut his horse slightly under his throat, he reared and plunged, and finding himself uncontrolled started madly off down the road, Jerome cursing, screaming and clinging to his mane.

I had to laugh at the success of my stratagem, for though it was a scurvy trick to play an old friend, it was much the simplest way out of the difficulty to dispose of him in this bloodless fashion. I put my horse about now without interference. When I wheeled down the lane toward Versailles, Jerome's clatter and dust was just dying away over the crest of a distant hill, making most excellent time in the direction of Paris.

Now that this new danger was past, I rode on heavy-hearted enough, for I had grown to love Jerome, and blamed him little for his sudden touch of fury. For I was nearly in the same boat, borne on by the same strong currents as Jerome.

Verily, what will man not do for woman? Love had turned him from a courteous nobleman of France, a brave and kindly gentleman, into the frenzied coward who would lie to his master, slay his friend, and turn traitor to his countrymen. A god could not love and be wise.

I jogged along slowly, seeking to rest my horse, for I could not tell how soon I must look to his speed for safety. It was necessary also that I should see the two fellows who watched the Versailles road before they caught sight of me Possibly an artifice might avail me where force would fail.

Presently from a slight eminence the broad highway could be seen winding out of Paris, glistening in the starlight, for it was now after dusk, twisting in dusty undulations toward the distant palace of the King. I drew rein among some trees which served for shelter, and scanned the way to see if the watchers were in sight. The lane, before it entered the Versailles road, branched out into two portions, one bearing away toward Paris, while the other traversed a piece of low ground that struck the main road several hundred yards in the other direction. Within the irregular triangle thus formed the two grooms had thrown themselves upon the ground, being distinctly visible in a little clearing.

Their position commanded quite a considerable stretch of road toward the city, and as by going that way it would take a good hour and a half of hard riding to get so far, it was certain they did not expect me to pass for some time. That cut-off through the lane must have been ten miles the shorter journey.

This reflection gave me some hope that I might be able to slip by in a gallop before they could take horse. Yet I could not afford to waste much time, for Jerome might perchance find means to follow, and would not be in a pleasant humor. There could be no accounting for the lengths to which his desperation and folly might carry him. I had need for both haste and caution.

I was now at the top of a slight hillock, the grooms resting at the foot. As ill fortune would have it, my horse's hoof loosened a stone, and one of them looking up recognized my figure clear drawn against the fading colors of the sky. They both jumped up with an alertness which would have done credit to old woodsmen, and before I could dodge by, had remounted and taken possession of the road. My more elevated position and perhaps better hearing, too, enabled me to detect the coming of persons along the road from Paris. Certainly as many as three or four horsemen, perhaps a vehicle. It could hardly be possible that Jerome had made the trip so quickly, yet I did not know what other and shorter way he might find. At any rate every instant intensified the danger, for if it were Jerome, then, indeed, I could not hope to make Versailles that night.

Listening more critically I decided they were travelling too slowly to be Jerome's party.

I would then most gladly have charged the insolents in front and taken all chances, but my half hour of quiet thought had brought me the conclusion it was too much to risk my life, at least until Serigny was acquainted with the information we had gained. I, too, was the only person who knew of the traitors on board le Dauphin.

"Who are you, and what do you mean stopping a gentleman's path?" I called to the twain who had drawn a little away from the foot of the hill seeing the

disadvantage of their former position in case I charged
them, and preferring to receive me on the open ground.

"No harm, Monsieur, we only mean to detain you
until M. de Greville comes up," the slender man spoke
quite politely.

"M. de Greville will not come up this night—may
God have mercy on his soul," I added solemnly.

"Why not, fine sir?" the gruffer fellow on the big
bay questioned with some heat. I made no quibble on
his manner, but replied:

"I doubt I have slain him. He lies back yonder in
the road to Sceaux, and I know not whether he be dead
or still lives."

They hesitated and consulted together in a low tone;
I saw my opportunity to press their indecision.

"What excuse can you make and what authority have
you for halting an officer of the King with dispatches
to the King? With M. Jerome de Greville to stand between you and harm it was dangerous enough; now it
is a matter of hanging."

"But M. de Greville is not dead," they protested
together, "we left him a few minutes since alive and
well." I seized upon the vacillation manifest in their
voices and proceeded with confidence.

"Then how think you I came along this road? Think
you M. Jerome would let me go so easily? You know
his temper too well. Does he change his mind like a
woman? I turned about to take the nearer path, and
see, his blood is not yet dry upon my sword."

"We do not believe you. It is some trick."

"If you will but move this way and give me clear passage to Versailles, I will go and say nothing. You can then return and minister to your master."

"Nay, we'll hold the road an hour, which gives him time to come up. An hour gone and you may pursue your journey."

"Then, forsooth, one of you can make his peace with God. I'll shoot your stoutest bully and try blades with the other."

I raised the pistol which had been concealed unknown to Jerome, and to say the truth, it looked formidable enough all a-glitter beneath the rising moon, though I doubted much if I could strike my mark.

As I started resolutely onward I warned them: "Pull your nags off in yonder level space, leave the left fork free, or by the gods, you burly black-haired rascal, I'll take the first shot at you, you make the fairest target. Way there, in the King's name!"

As is ever so with low-born churls, and no gentleman to command, each looked to the other for some act of heroism, and each sought his own safety.

They stood their ground only an instant, then pulled aside as I had bidden them. As soon as I passed them a decent distance as if I had no fear, I put spurs to my good steed, and, breathing more freely than I had done for many days, heard the merry pounding of his hoofs upon the open way to my mission's end.

CHAPTER XVIII

SERIGNY'S DEPARTURE

THE clocks were striking, one after the other in monotonous imitative fashion, the hour of nine when I delivered my horse to a sleepy groom at the little tavern just outside the Versailles gate.

Serigny was already in his rooms, intent on some business, and opened his door himself. There was no need for concealing his gratification and the intense impatience he felt to know results, nor did he make any attempt at concealment. On the contrary, he was as urgent as a school child. Everything about him, packed in boxes and traveling bags, seemed prepared for instant journey. Upon his table a few disarranged papers were scattered beside a leathern portfolio, through which he had evidently been looking when I arrived. Without stopping to replace any of the documents he hastened me to a seat, and drawing his chair close, commanded me to begin. My coming had been so sudden I had given no consideration to the nature of my report to Serigny, and found some difficulty in gathering ideas together in such shape they would be understood. I had hardly begun my statement when quick steps sounded along the outer passage followed by an almost imperative knock on the door. Jerome, I thought. So it was. Jerome, bespattered and soiled from his hard ride, a raw bruise across his cheek, his clothing awry. He was pale and determined, yet quiet withal.

I instinctively rose and laid my hand to my hilt. A glance reassured me. His purpose, lying deeper, I could not divine; it was plain though he brooded not that kind of quarrel. Nor do I to this day know what he intended when he first entered Serigny's room that night.

"I rode after you in all haste, Captain."

"Indeed you did," I mentally agreed.

"And met a fall, which, as you see, has somewhat disfigured me," and he laughed, while I agreed with him again.

Serigny, being so intent on the important transactions of the hour, accepted his explanation without question. The welcome, though cordial, was brief, Serigny being a man of no unnecessary words.

"Go on, Captain," and I picked up the broken thread of my narrative where Jerome had interrupted.

As I went on obediently, Jerome would now and again supply some link wherein my memory failed, or suggest something I had left unsaid, until having so much the nimbler tongue he took the telling out of my mouth entirely. I could not complain, for he detailed the various adventures far better than I, and gave me more of the credit than I would have claimed for myself. We had, by common consent, forgotten our late strife, and becoming much interested I broke in upon a glowing account of my heroism:

"Hold, Jerome, by my faith, you grow more garrulous than a fish-wife of the barriers; tell but a plain, straight tale, and leave off all that romantic garniture of thine," and thence I reclaimed my straggling story and brought it to a conclusion. All this while the dispatches for which we had risked so much lay safe in my breast. I rather hesitated to produce them, dreading what the hot-headed fellow might do to get a hold upon that which peradventure would cause trouble to his lady love. I could not decline when Serigny asked for them, but hauled out both packets, one taken from Yvard, the other from Broussard, casting them upon the table. Jerome eyed them so I that knew from the look his late fury was not yet dead, and I watched him in readiness for any move he might make to repossess them.

He sat as unconcerned as if the whole affair interested him no further, now that the main object of his solicitude was safe in the keeping of his superior. I misdoubted whether this was not all a sham, and could hardly believe him the same frenzied Jerome who had pleaded so hard, and fought so desperately for this selfsame packet of Yvard's, which at this time reposed within easy reach of his hand. Once he reached out and took it up negligently, inspected the seals and marks, then replaced it. His examination seemed one of mere idle curiosity, or would have so appeared had I not known that he was already perfectly acquainted with every mark borne by our charge. The eyes, half closed in dreamy contemplation, spoke apparently of a man who has been relieved of some grave responsibility and enjoys the relaxation, yet, for all of that, he was listening most intently to what Serigny and I were talking of. Serigny was now fondling the instruments which were to be the restoration of his own and his brother's influence. His words were addressed to neither of us in particular.

"Here is the seal of Spain. Cellemare again, Egad! They are bold, or must have great confidence in their emissaries. Here, too, is Madame. Ah, my clever little lady, you have outdone your own cleverness at last. I fancy even the King's old love for his son's mother will not save you now. I would I knew what was in them."

"We can easily see, and close them snug again," ventured Jerome, but noting Serigny's frown, he turned it off with a laugh, "or so our friend Madame would advise."

"It thus became manifest he had not abandoned his idea of intercepting whatever might compromise Madame de Chartrain.

Serigny continued: "These must be placed before the King unopened by any of us. Yes, it's a risk," he caught Jerome's knotted brow of indecision, "I grant you it is a risk, for I know not what complications are here contained. I will myself seek the King, and with these am sure to gain his own ear."

Jerome all this while uttered no other word, nervously

flicking the mud splotches off his boots, and lifting an earnest look now and anon to Serigny.

My own mind was busy devising means to foil any contemplated treachery upon his part, and wondering whether it was not my duty to acquaint Serigny with the whole truth of the matter. The test came when I least expected it. When all our adventures had been detailed again and again, his dozens of incisive questions answered, our conversation naturally drifted toward the future. My mission in France completed, there was nothing now but a return to the colonies, and the uncertainties of a campaign which I no longer doubted was imminent. Somehow the thought of a great and glorious war did not appeal to me so forcibly as such a prospect would have done some few weeks agone.

There was ever a shy little face, a brave girlish figure which stood resolute and trembling before me in the park, that intruded between me and the barbaric splendor of our western wars. Nor did I raise a hand to brush the vision aside. It toned down the innate savagery of man, softened the stern, callous impulses of the soldier, and all the currents of my being trickled through quieter, sweeter channels of life and love. Even the shame of it made not the thought less sweet.

There was but trifling period to spare for such gentler musings, for Serigny, by a gesture, called attention to his well packed luggage.

"See, I am ready. I only waited your coming and report to put out at once for le Dauphin. My people have already gone forward to arm and provision her for the struggle. We must be prompt. There is much to lose in a day. I myself will go on to-morrow and have all in complete readiness for the voyage, and, who knows, for the fighting on the other side. Now give heed Placide—Captain de Mouret,'' for he was always particular to distinguish the man from the soldier, and in giving orders to address me by my proper title. ''The war has been decided upon; you will remain here and watch developments''—he was proceeding to acquaint me with what was expected of me. I knew not what he might say, but felt impelled to throw out a silent warning, which even though he understood it not, he was quick enough to take. He paused and looked me inquisitively in the face. I glanced awkwardly from him to Jerome and back again.

The thought then dominant was a growing distrust of Jerome, and the desire to have our movements secret. I remembered Bienville's words ''We know not who to trust,'' and being ignorant of what orders Serigny meant to give, or how much information they would convey to Jerome, deemed it best to let all the occurrences of the day come out. I could not forget the lad's gallantry, nor must I lose sight of the fact that as affairs now were, he might very well have gone over to the other side for the sake of Madame; things stranger than that took place every day, and I had learned to be discreet. He might thus come into valuable hints and afterward cast them into the scale against Bienville, for every means good or bad would be used by them to save their own influence, to uplift the Duke of Maine.

If Bienville were involved in the general ruin, why, what mattered it to them?

While I remained hesitating for a word, Jerome's ready wit had already comprehended my purpose. He took the words from my lips. His countenance first flushed, then became hard and fixed, compelling me for the time into silence.

"Monsieur de Serigny, I perhaps can speak you better our good Captain's mind. He mistrusts me—."

"You?" burst out Serigny greatly surprised. "Why you have ever been our staunch and loyal friend. What is this, Captain de Mouret, surely you are above a young man's jealousy?"

Jerome gave me no time to explain.

"Softly, softly, sir. The Captain has good cause. Give me heed, my friends. To you, M. de Serigny, I will say upon my honor, which until this day was never stained by thought or deed, I will say,—this day I would have betrayed you. Nay, do not look so pained and unbelieving; all men are mortal, and passions stronger even than duty, stronger than loyalty, yea, stronger than honor itself, may tyrannize over the best of us. I repeat, this day would I gladly have betrayed you, betrayed my friends to save—well it boots not whom, but a woman. For the woman I love may lose her liberty if not her life when those accursed papers reach the hands of the King. I was mad, and at this moment doubt and fear myself. It is better not to trust me with your plans; the Captain is right. Jerome de Greville never yet deceived a friend, but for the love of God, Messires, do

not tempt him now," and he faced about with unsteady
step and started toward the door. Before we could detain him he was gone, leaving Serigny staring in the
most unbelieving and bewildered fashion at me."

"In God's name, Captain, what piece of folly is this?
Tell me all, for ofttimes the success of the most careful
plans is governed by just such undercurrents as this, of
man's love or woman's spite. Go on, I listen."

I explained briefly Madame's position, Serigny nod-
ding his acquiescence; it was an old tale to him, except
he did not know Jerome's relations with Madame. Of
her domination over the Duke of Maine he was well
aware. When my story was fully done he pondered
for a long while in silence. His sorrow was deep and
sincere.

"Poor fellow; poor fellow; as noble a lad as ever
drew a sword, but in his present frame of mind it is
safer not to trust him; he is capable of any act of
desperation. We will do our best to protect his lady,
though. Where was I? This matter has disturbed me—
Oh, yes, about to give your orders. You see I am all
ready to leave. I have but waited your return. The war
has been decided on and the news needs only to be given
out. The King hesitates and wavers; Chamillard is a
mere reflection of the royal whim. If we do not attack the
Spaniard he will attack us; it is simply a question of
whether we want the war at Biloxi or Havana. For my
part I would rather see Havana in siege than Biloxi.
This matter can not be long delayed, a few days more
at most. These dispatches may decide. With these

before the King he will no longer doubt my brother, but will place the blame where it most properly belongs— for in the main, Louis is just. I would not desire any greater pleasure than to see the gibbet whereon these traitors of the itching palms, these thieves who sell their King for Spanish gold, will take their last dance. Do you remain here for as many as six days, this room is at your disposal. Be quiet and discreet; learn all and tell nothing. A still tongue is the safest in these times. The moment war is declared make all speed for Dieppe and we will up anchor and away."

`Serigny was as happy as a boy at the prospect of action; the atmosphere of court ill agreed with his fiery temper. This was the gist of our plan of operations, and it was so arranged in detail.

In a few moments Serigny left me, taking the packet with him, and I in excess of caution followed him at a little distance, locking the door behind me and keeping the key in my pocket. I bore his tall figure well in sight until he passed out of the unfrequented halls into that portion of the palace where the many shuttlecocks of fortune congregated to laugh and talk and plot and lie. Not long after he came back, sorely nettled and disappointed.

"It is done; the King has them in his own hands; yet he does not talk; promises nothing; is closeted with his ministers; they must be of considerable importance. It is all secure for us, for I told him of my departure in the morning to the colonies, and he assented. I judge, then, it is something of a very delicate nature, touching

the royal honor of the King's own blood. Besides much
is in cipher which it will take time to read. Louis,
you know, would not admit, save to those nearest his
throne, the possession of the secret Spanish cipher.''

The night passed by dismal and uncertain enough.
I must confess to a great sinking of the heart when I
saw Serigny's carriage roll away in the gray of the early
morning, leaving me absolutely alone in my father's
land of France, where in the short space of two weeks so
much had transpired; much to be ever remembered,
much I would have given worlds to forget.

It must have been a most forlorn and dejected looking creature that stood in the great square that sunless
morning, peering into the mists which had absorbed the
carriage.   The solitude of vast untrodden forests breeds
not that vacant sense of desolation which we children of
nature feel in the crowded haunts of men.   Face after
face, form after form, voice after voice, yet not one
familiar countenance, not one remembered tone, not the
glance of a kindly eye; all is new, all is strange, all
at seeming enmity.   The defection of Jerome, my only
comrade, was indeed a cup of bitterness.   I dreaded to
meet him, not knowing what tack he might cut away on.
Yet I could not blame him; it was more of pity I felt.

I recall with great delight some of the minor occurrences of the next three or four days.   After Serigny's
departure, every afternoon at imminent risk I would
take horse to Sceaux, and pursuing a by-way through
the forests and fields, through which a wood-cutter first
led me, ride hard to catch a glimpse of her who now

occupied all my thoughts. I wonder at this time how
I then held so firm by the duty of returning to the colonies, when the very thought of war and turmoil was
so distasteful to me. When I rode to Paris and
clothed myself once more in my own proper garments,
their friendly folds gave me a new courage to meet
whatever Fate might send.

It may be pertinent to chronicle here, what history
has already recorded, the result of placing those dispatches in the King's hands.

The Duke of Maine, as all the world knows, dis-
avowed his wife's act in treating with Spain, and thus
saved his own dainty carcass from sharing her captivity
in the Bastille. But both he and Madame were im-
prisoned until he made most abject submission and apology to Orleans.

Madame de Chartrain was sent to a provincial fortress,
and bore her incarceration with great fortitude, winning
even from her enemies the admiration always accorded
to firmness and virtue.

Philip of Orleans being once firmly established in the
Regency, changed his usual course, and pardoned many
of those who had conspired against him. Their prison
doors were opened, and the Duke of Maine, becoming
reconciled to his haughty lady, forgave her and gained
great credit thereby in the vulgar mind. They spent
their lives quietly at Sceaux during the Regency, and
naught else of them concerns this history.

Philip of Orleans possessed some of the virtues of a
great man, and many of a good man but these he kept

ever locked within his own bosom. His mother, the rigid and austere Madame, said once of him:

"Though good fairies have gifted my son at his birth with numerous noble qualities, one envious member of the sisterhood spitefully decreed that he should never know how to use any of these gifts." Such was the character of the Regent.

Of Jerome and Madame de Chartrain I would fain tell more, but during the troubled times in America I completely lost sight of them, and my inquiries developed nothing of sufficient verity to give credence to here.

All Frenchmen know of Jerome's gallant death at Malplaquet. It is a fireside legend now, and young French lads turn their moistened eyes away at the hearing. Marshal Villars being sorely hurt and in peril of capture, there fought beside his litter an unknown gentleman who, without name or rank, yet bore himself so commandingly, the discouraged guard rallied again and gave him willing obedience. Arrived at a narrow bridge he urged the litter-bearers safely across, and fighting at the rear to be himself the last to reach a place of safety, he was struck and fell. Prince Eugene, the courteous enemy, who had himself witnessed the incident, sent a guard of honor to the Marshal at Valenciennes the next day with the body, deeming it that of a man of consequence. His letter congratulated the defeated Villars upon having such chivalric friends.

It was poor Jerome, and no one knew him then. He rests now with his fathers.

I loved the lad truly. As knightly a gentleman as ever died for his King, or lied for his lady.

CHAPTER XIX

THE CASTLE OF CARTILLON

TWO days, four, passed. Serigny had departed for Dieppe to arm and equip le Dauphin, yet still there was no official declaration of war. I was waiting, as he had ordered, for the formal declaration, on the publication of which I was to join him on board at once and we would set sail instantly for Biloxi.

Another anxious day, during which I vacillated between an ignoble love and a noble duty. Then, late in the evening, the whole court was fanned into a blaze destined to spread throughout Europe and America, by the announcement that the war had been formally decided upon.

Men may long look forward to a crushing calamity, and when it comes be surprised and unprepared. So, though I well knew I must leave France with all speed, and possibly never see her shores again, I put it from me as persistently as men do the certainty of death. Every day did I ride to Sceaux, by the old wall, and catch a glimpse of her I loved. When war was at last declared there was no time for parleying with duty. My path lay straight and clear before me; yet for once a soldier's duty and a soldier's adventure gave me no pleasure. All my thoughts were otherwhere.

(205)

Hot-foot to Sceaux again I rode on my way to Dieppe, and from the same embrasure at the wall where my horses had trampled down the foliage many times, I watched her coming. It was not for long. More hurriedly than was her custom she glided, a glorified young creature, in and out amongst the shrubbery, until the envious chapel door hid her from my sight. No living thing was in view. The sound of no discordant voice broke the holy peace of God. Temptation came never to our first erring mother in more insidious guise than this.

Where was the harm, I reasoned, it was but for an instant's speech with her, ere the bounding seas would roll between us. So with nervous haste I tumbled from my horse and tethered him stoutly to a tree. Over the wall and to the chapel door took another instant, and there, inside, at the rail, she knelt. I paused, as a sinner might, hesitating to mar with heart profane the devotions of a saint. My foot struck a cracking board in the entry, and drew her glance toward me. She sprang up as I entered, with a swift cry of surprise, and, as I fancied, some whit of gladness in the tone.

"You, Monsieur? You here? I thought you away from Sceaux."

"Yes, Madame, true; but I returned to speak with you before I leave France forever. I came here to—to —" I could not tell her why; my heart, so full, clogged my utterance. But women ever understand.

As I cast about me for a word, we had drawn closer, and taking the hand which half-hid in the folds of her dress, gleamed more white and pure, I would have raised it to my lips. Even at such a time I noted the device upon a ring she wore, a device grown so familiar: *A wolf's head, sable.*

"An old thing of my mother's," she explained, "Charles has one, and I."

I eagerly seized upon a subject which might so naturally prolong our interview.

"Aye, I know the device well; are you of the d'Artins?"

"Yes, my mother was; there are now none of the race. The last is a wanderer; I know not if he lives."

"I know, perchance, of such a man, Madame; would you tell me more of him, of yourself?"

"I never saw him, my mother's father. Her marriage displeased him greatly. When her first child was born, a girl, she sent it to him for his blessing. He denied it, saying he wanted no more of women. The child died in infancy. Of my sister's birth and mine he was never told. Then he went away, where, none know."

It thrilled me with a new hope. Who could guess but my relations with Colonel d'Ortez might throw me again in her way. I took her hand again, making pretence to examine the ring more curiously. She made slight demur, and I pressed my first fervent kiss upon the hand of woman. Man's fortitude could stand no more. Tossing honor, discretion, duty to the winds, I folded her close, closer yet, and kissed her brow, her hair, her eyes—her lips, she struggling like a frightened nest-ling all the while. It was done.

Ashamed but impenitent—it was too new, too sweet to wish undone—I loosed her gently, and kissed her hand but once again, then left her standing where the light from the mullioned window in halos wreathed my saint. It was thus I ever afterward remembered her.

She made no other sign; I withdrew swiftly as I came. From across the wall, unobserved, I watched her leave the place, downcast of eye and slow of step. In rebellious and uncertain mood I rode away.

Though the relish in my task was done, I made all haste toward Dieppe. Scarcely stopping for food, changing horses as often as I could, I pushed on with-out adventure until I reached the Chateau Cartillon, then a formless ruin.

Here my saddle girth broke and I was nearly thrown to the ground. I scrambled off, walked to the little inn where I inquired how far I had yet to go.

"Three leagues yet to Dieppe," the host replied, "but Monsieur can not go on to-night; he must wait the morrow; he can go with comfort in the morning."

I sent my groom for a new girth and found it would take quite an hour to procure one from the village.

"Probably Monsieur would visit the castle upon the hill there," persisted the landlord, pointing across the way, "it is worth his while. It is said to have been de-stroyed by the Great Henry in his wars with the Duke of Mayenne. True it is that sounds of battle and

screams are yet heard there on stormy nights. Probably Monsieur would rest here several days——.''

I essayed to silence the fellow, for I was in no mood
to listen to his chatter. Yet there was something in his
eulogy of the locality, which he gave as a hawker cry-
ing his wares, that fixed my unwilling attention.

"And, Monsieur, perchance you may see old mad
Michel. What! you know naught of him? Country
folk do say his grandam witnessed the murder of the
Count, and that it sent her feeble mind a-wandering.
Her child through all her life did fancy herself the
Count, and made strange speeches to the people's fear.
And now this grandson of hers has grown old in frenzy
like his mother and grandam, possessed of an evil spirit
which speaks through him betimes—it is a curse of the
blood, Monsieur, a grievous curse of the blood.''

It aroused something of a curiosity within me, yet I
was loath to pause upon my journey. Forced, though,
to wait an hour, I thought to walk over to the Chateau
a couple of hundred yards distant. Taking a lad who
lounged about the inn, to show me the way, I sauntered
up the path, pausing a while at a long-disused spring,
and idly plucked an apple from a branch which over-
hung it. A little further up, and mounting the steep
acclivity, I stood within the ancient fortress.

This castle, since rebuilded, you, my children, are of
course familiar with, for you were all born here. At
that date the great central tower alone stood erect
amid the universal destruction. A black wolf's head

reared itself high above the portcullis. The moat was filled with drift of crumbling years, and the walls, fallen in many places, ran hither and thither in aimless curves and angles, much as they do to-day.

Up to this hour my chronicle has been only of such adventures as might befall a soldier upon any enterprise, but now a strange thing happened. Until that moment I had never seen the Chateau Cartillon, still there was not a corner or a passage which did not seem well known to me. My feet fell into paths they seemed no strangers to. I seemed to know intuitively what each building was for, and even imagined most vividly scenes which had transpired there. The whole place had the most intense personal interest for me, why I knew not.

I am not superstitious, but the ruin oppressed me, made me restless and uneasy; yet I was loath to leave. The loneliness of it all filled me with vague apprehensions as I picked my way across the grass encumbered court-yard toward the road again. A thousand haunting fancies of half familiar things thronged from out each dismantled doorway. Faces I all but recognized peered at me through the broken casements; voices I almost knew called to me from many a silent corner. Yet all was still, all was solitude. Heartily shamed at my quickening step I hurried on and having consumed a quarter of my hour sat down by the spring mentioned before, just beyond the castle's utmost boundary.

The haze of late afternoon had deepened into night upon the peaceful meadows and lazy sweep of river. A distant peasant's song came faintly from the fields.

While sitting there beside the spring, gazing listlessly into its placid depths, an uncanny figure made its way through a breach in the bastion, and stood before me. At first I confess I was startled, the wild uncouth thing, bent and decrepit, with hair of long and tangled gray, fiery sunken eyes, seemed born of another world than this. He bent his gaze with searching scrutiny full upon me.

The lad whispered: "It's old mad Michel; he lives up there," pointing to a tumbled down tower, "and believes himself the Count—the Count, and him long dead lying yonder in the well."

The boy shuddered and crossed himself.

The old man gazed steadily at me for some moments then bowing low, he cried:

"Hail! Son of d'Artin! Hast come to view thine own again? Let us into the walls."

"Let us go, Monsieur, quick," urged the lad, tugging at my coat, "it is late."

The dusk in fact was coming on apace and climbing shadows crept round the grotesque masonry. Unheeding the lad's fear, I was strongly impelled to talk with the daft creature. It was an impulse born not wholly of idle curiosity. I felt strangely moved.

"What do you want of me, old man?" I asked.

"I am Henri d'Artin, by murder's hand laid low; I would tell you much."

"Let us go, Monsieur, let us go. He speaks of unholy things," the boy pleaded fearfully. Meeting no response he turned and fled down the slope, away in the twilight beneath the trees.

"Dost hear the clanking arms, the rolling drums of war? List unto the shouts, the cries within. Dost not know it is the day after the feast of the most Blessed Saint Bartholomew?"

The man's wild earnestness fixed a spell upon me, and to the end of his narrative I listened until the tale was done. I can not hope to set down here as I heard it what the madman said, nor to have my lines breathe forth the vigor of his speech. Carried beyond mortal energy by his frenzy, overmastered by some mysterious Power of which we men know naught, he threw into his strange, weird story a life and action which entered my very soul. And as he spoke he seemed to live through the scenes that he so vividly described. It was as though some grim drama were being enacted for my enlighten-ment. So well as I can tell it, the tale ran thus:

On yestermorn my wife, my daughter and little boy, committed to the charge of old Gaston, had driven into Rouen to spend the day. I rode along after them to learn the news from Paris. We of the Reformed Faith hoped for great things from the meeting of our leaders with the Duke of Guise and the Queen Mother, for King Charles seemed kindly disposed toward us. But, God of Mercy! what scenes there were in Rouen; every-where was slaughter, everywhere was murder. I found my carriage overturned in the streets, covering the dead and mutilated bodies of wif and daughter; the babe,

" The old man gazed steadily at me for some moments."   p. 211.

unhurt and unnoticed in the carriage, had escaped.
Throughout the city were prowling bands wearing the
white cross in their caps, the white sash on their arms,
which designated the followers of Guise, and with cries
of "Death to the Huguenots" and "No quarter to the
enemies of Holy Church," they slew without mercy.
I had now no idea but to put my boy in a place of
safety, and with him before me rode straight for the
nearest gate.   I passed unmolested through the streets,
and by avoiding the public places, drawing out of the
way of murdering bands, thought to evade them and
reach the river gate south of town.   My whole soul re-
volted at leaving the bodies of wife and daughter in
Rouen, but the living child must be considered before
the dead.   At the turn from out the obscure Rue St.
Croix into the open square at Vieux Marche I heard a
shout, "Here he is, this way," and saw a man at arms
stationed in the square beckoning to his comrades who
came clattering down the Rue de Crosne. This blocked
the path along which I intended to leave the town.

Riding at their head I recognized my old time enemy,
my half brother, Pedro Ortez, a man of whose prowess
and cruelty terrible stories were told.

Right willingly would I have paused to give him
fight, but for the babe.   The fellow who had raised the
cry now threw himself full in my way with the evident
purpose of engaging me until the others came up.   I
made straight at him, but he stood his ground bravely,
and encumbered as I was with the child, he succeeded
in wounding me twice before I could pierce him through

the throat and drop him from his horse. Verily, his courage was worthy a better quarrel.

This, in full sight of the oncoming band, fixed their attention, and, raising the shout of ''Death to d'Artin,'' they spurred their horses to a gallop. I had barely disappeared down the deserted Rue Corneille when they debouched into the square, spreading out and circling round as hounds hot upon a scent. Here they were at fault, not knowing whither I had turned among so many narrow and irregular streets. Before they found me again I was well upon the high road to Cartillon. The superior speed of my horse gave me easily the lead.

I soon overtook Gaston, drawn aside in the bushes, wounded and bleeding, waiting for me. At first I upbraided him fiercely, but a frightful gash across his head, dabbling his gray hairs in blood, stopped my wrath. On the ride home he told me of the day's disaster. Pedro Ortez and his cut-throats had set upon them in the name of the church. He was soon cut down and left upon the street, recovering consciousness only to find his murdered mistress lying dead beside him. He had then crawled away to warn me, for the whole object of Ortez seemed to be to take my life.

Gaston's distress was pitiful; as his mute eyes now and again sought mine, I could not find it in my heart to censure him. Having distanced my poorly mounted pursuers I stopped to water my horse at the spring before riding the few hundred yards to the gates of Cartillon. While yet waiting by the spring I was horrified to see men struggling on top of the great tower. Their fight was brief and decisive. Two of them, one being Maurice my most trusted man at arms, were thrown violently to the courtyard below. Of the others some were killed, some overpowered and carried below again.

All of this took only an instant, for it appeared but the end of a desperate encounter which had been raging elsewhere. The time, however, was long enough for me to see that those of the larger party wore the white sash and cross which distinguished my assailants in Rouen.

"God in heaven, what murder's work have we at Cartillon?" I cried aloud in my misery. Then one who could answer came running toward me from the castle, gashed, with snapped sword in hand.

"Oh, master, master, the Catholics, the Catholics," was all he could speak out before he fell a senseless mass at my horse's feet.

Cartillon was not now a refuge.

Immediately the distant sound of hoof beats came loud and louder yet, from the direction of Rouen. Ortez was coming.

"Quick, Gaston, we must fly.'

My overtaxed horse failed me now. Pulling the rein he only sank slowly to his knees, and after a few spasmodic twitches, stiffened out forever upon the rocky road. I stood erect a moment, child in arms, irresolute. There was short shrift to think. My blood rebelled at flight.

"Here, Gaston, take the boy; hide in the wood. Carry him to the Abbot of Vaux, and conjure the good priest, by our fathers' love and ours, to save my baby."

Gaston had hardly passed from sight among the trees before a dozen well-armed horsemen, bearing the same white cross in their caps, spurred round a curve in the forest road, coming suddenly upon me beside my fallen steed. Sword in hand, I fronted them, determined, come what would, to fly no further. The evil face of Ortez shone with gratification at so unexpectedly finding me alone.

"Now, yield thee, sirrah," he cried, as his men surrounded me. A quick sword thrust through the body of his horse, brought him to the ground.

"Not yet, thou slayer of women; here, upon equal footing, thy life shall pay for those of wife and child."

I verily believed the Almighty vengeance was in my blade, and doubt not I should have slain him despite his troopers but for a crushing pike blow over the head, so swiftly did it all come about.

My brain reeled; the sword dropped clanging from my nerveless hand. When I recovered, I found myself bound upon a horse behind one of the men.

"On with him, men, to Cartillon; there we rest this night in the King's name."

In this wise we rode along; Ortez openly exultant, I silent and scornful.

"Aha, my fine brother," he spoke low at my saddle, "thy father's son has thee in his power now. And shall I not revenge upon thee the wrong our father did my mother for thine? Didst know the story?"

I made no reply, but he went on unmindful.

"To *my* mother he gave his love but dared not give

his name; to *thy* mother he gave his name but could
never give his love. So thou art the proud Lord of
Cartillon, and I the outcast soldier of fortune, the
nameless adventurer, slayer of women—what thou wilt.
But things are changed now. Before many hours I
will be the Count d'Artin, and thou a dishonored
corpse, sweet brother."

"Thou! *Thou* my brother?"

I turned upon him a look of incredulous contempt,
yet, for I had heard some such tale of my father's
youth, I asked:

"Thy mother was—?"

"Nanon Esculas, whom thy father abducted in Spain
to desert in France."

"My heart sank; I had seen the woman, and knew
her son for one of the most courageous and unprincipled
adventurers who hung about the Court and held their
swords for hire. When the noisy troop rode up to the
gates of Cartillon their leader paused, a head appeared
upon the battlements.

"Guise," cried Ortez, giving the watchword of that
day of slaughter. The drawbridge lowered, and open
swung the gates.

"Welcome to Cartillon, d'Artin," Ortez bowed.
"Here at last we find rest and refreshment. Let a feast
be spread in the great hall, ransack the place for good
cheer. We've done brave work this glorious day, my
lads, and a merry ending we'll have before the night is
gone."

Everywhere in the courtyard were evidences of bloody

conflict. Singly, in groups and in hideous crimson-splashed piles lay Catholics and Huguenots together, peaceful enough in death.

"By my faith, and a gallant set of gentlemen we have here," laughed Ortez. "What think you, brother mine?"

And even as he spoke he leaned from his saddle to strike down a half dying wretch who lifted his head from among the slain.

"Perez," he called to his sergeant riding behind him, "dispose of these bodies. Throw the heretic dogs into the old well yonder. Give our martyred friends Christian burial."

He sat his horse idly toying with his dagger, and forced me to watch my servants, the wounded and the dead, being cast into the yawning darkness of the well.

"God's blood! here is our sweet young Philip. What, not yet dead! Why, it matters not, cast him in." This in answer to a questioning look from the more merciful Perez.

The men at arms had extricated from a heap of slain the limp body of my youngest brother, a boy of twenty, his pallid face gaping open from a cut across the cheek. He lifted his eyes languidly to mine.

"Oh brother, you are come. Some water, water," he murmured.

"Throw him in, men," Ortez interrupted.

Perez yet hesitated.

"Shall we not first dispatch him, sire?"

"No, I would not harm my gentle brother; throw

him in. Be not slow about it either, thou chicken-hearted bullies; pitch him in.''

The men started to obey this savage order.

"Hound of hell!'' I screamed, tortured beyond endurance, and struggling at my bonds.

Ortez slapped me in the face with his gauntlet, then laying his hand upon my shoulder said with assumed gentleness:

"Calm yourself, my dear brother; think of your unbandaged wounds; they may bleed afresh.''

Philip was conscious as the men bore him to the edge of the well, but powerless to resist four stout fellows who cast him headlong amongst the dead and dying to mingle his groans and blood with theirs. Oh, that God should permit to men such deeds, and grant that men should witness them! When the last body had been disposed of, Ortez led the way to the banquet hall, inviting all his rabble to join the feast. The banquet hall, used as it was to scenes of turbulence, never perhaps had looked upon such a throng as that. I occupied the head of my own table, strapped helpless in my seat. On either side were vacant chairs. Ortez sat at the foot. Between, the soldiery ranged themselves as they pleased. One of the troopers coming in late would have taken his place beside me, but his Captain stopped him:

"Not there, Gardier; we have other and fairer guests for whom those seats are kept.''

Almost as he spoke the chairs on either side of me

were slipped away, and after awhile as silently returned to their places.

Sacrament of passion! In one of them was bound the mutilated corpse of my queenly wife, her fingers hacked off and her ears torn out for the gems which had decked them. Upon my left sat little Celia. But for one lurid stripe of crimson across her girlish breast she might well have been asleep, so lightly death had touched her. Behind them I saw a tall, gaunt woman, wearing a man's helm and carrying a pike. She directed the men. This was a woman's hellish work.

Ortez rose with studied politeness:

"Your wife and child, d'Artin; our charming family reunion would be incomplete without them." And the woman laughed aloud.

My brain burned; something seemed to strain and give way. I lost all sense of pain, all capacity to suffer. How long this lasted I know not. When the revelry was at its height, when the wine had dulled every human instinct of these rough "Soldiers of the Church," Ortez raised his voice above the tumult; he knew his men were in the humor for a diversion he was about to propose.

"Now comrades," he said, "for the crowning joy of this most blessed day, now for our last sacred duty to Mother Church."

He came round the table and taking a cord from the hands of one of his men he threw the noose over my head. With feet bound together, hands free, I stood amongst them, this throng of butchers, each with the white Cross of Christ in his cap, the white scarf of Guise upon his arm, drunk and eager for blood.

"Henri Francois Placide d'Artin, what hast thou to say why we shall not declare thy blood attainted, thy name dishonored, thy estate forfeited, why we shall not hang thee for a Huguenot dog, traitor to King and church? Speak."

All the defiance of my race burned fearless in my eyes; I felt my face flush an instant at the shame of such a death, but replied as steadily as might be:

"Not a word to you, thou infamous one, thou base-born coward, murderer of the helpless; not to you!"

The cool, polite manner of Ortez fell from him like a mask. He seized the cord with his own hand, jerking me prone upon the floor and commenced to drag me from the hall. A dozen willing hands lent aid. I clutched instinctively at everything which came in my way, being torn from each hold by the ruthless villains at the rope.

Desperate, I grasped the leg of a trooper, but a savage kick in the face wrenched him free, and down the stair they started for the open court. At the end of the cord came tumbling, rolling, bumping down the stone steps this almost senseless heap which was yet a man.

Arrived beside the well, whose great overhanging sweep offered a convenient scaffold, Ortez paused to look at his victim. My breath came slow, I could hardly hear their words.

"Think you his senses will return?"

"Possibly, sire," replied the man to whom this was addressed.

"Then we will wait; my sweet brother would weep to miss so brave a spectacle as his own hanging."

He sat there upon the edge of the well, whence came the groans of the dying, the hot, fresh odors of the dead, and waited, fiendish in the patient ferocity of his more than mortal hate.

After a little I opened my eyes and stared about me, scarcely comprehending where I was or what had happened. Ortez called upon his men to raise me. Being placed erect the cord was drawn just taut enough to sustain me standing. Now the ghastly woman I had seen in the hall pushed her way through the crowd.

"Her son," she hissed, and savagely struck me in the mouth until blood followed the blow. The cord instantly tightened and I felt myself swing across the well. First only a dizziness and a parched mouth. Then the tumultuous blood surged to my throat, beating, struggling, gurgling like some pent-up mountain stream against the rocks. I threw both hands up to grasp the rope—heard a laugh, not a human laugh, yet it sounded so far, so very far away, away back upon the earth.

A gigantic merciful hand seemed to take my head within its gripe and press out all the pain.

Fiery circles swam before my eyes; great crimson blotches floated about in restless clouds of flame; then dreams, dreams, long delicious dreams. And out of endless years of rhythmic music, the laughter of low-voiced women, and many colored lights, came at length oblivion.

Thus the tale ended. It was the same I had heard in far away Louisiana, told again with all the grim earnestness of desperate truth.

I stood now in the great courtyard again, beside the ancient well, drinking eagerly every inspired syllable. When the speaker had done, he shrank back into the darkness, and was gone.

It was as though I witnessed in my own person the wretched death of Henri d'Artin, and stood within his castle's court when the ruthless deed was done. Verily man knoweth not the rebellious vagaries of an unhinged brain; knoweth not what be but unmeaning phantasies, or what be solemn revelations from the very lips of God.

In the deep gloom the ruined castle loomed darkly, a ghastly monument of evil deeds. I looked about for the madman but saw him not. The weirdness of the place, the horror of its secret, crept into my blood. I became afraid. Down the bleak road I picked my way, glancing fearsomely over my shoulder. I fain would have fled as had the lad.

I found my horse re-equipped. Still shuddering I mounted, scarce daring to look backwards at the cursed pile. Then, with the madman's story surging in my brain, I dug savage spurs into my steed and galloped desperately onward through the night.

CHAPTER XX

IT was about ten of the clock when I reached Dieppe. Soon thereafter I was well aboard le Dauphin, Serigny himself meeting me at the vessel's side.

"Hullo, Placide," he cried. "All goeth well, and the passing night gives promise to us of a brighter day."

Later, in his own cabin, he told me of a brief meeting he had with Louis.

"For the time we are safe. The King is restless about the safety of the province, and he trusts Bienville as a soldier. The Spanish intrigue keeps our enemies so busy they have not time to disturb us. The King has no man who can take Bienville's place. Well, it's all happily over, and I am as delighted as a child to be at sea again. We would sail at once, now that you are come, were it not for de la Mora; he, with his wife and another lady, are to bear us company. The Chevalier is a thorough soldier, and I welcome him, but like not the presence of the ladies We may have rough work betimes."

I knew my face grew pale, and thanked the half-light

(224)

for concealment, or he must have noted. Who that "other lady" was, possessed for me no interest, and I never asked.

De la Mora. This was terrible, and so unforeseen. Full well I knew I could not spend five long weeks in daily contact with Agnes and give no betraying sign. I must needs have time to think, and that right speedily.

"When do they come, sire?"

"Any moment; they left—or should have done so— the same time as yourself. His orders were the same."

Rapidly as a man could think, so thought I.

"How long will you wait for them?"

"Until dawn, no longer. Then we sail."

A glimmer of hope—de la Mora might be delayed. Without any clearly defined purpose I went on and carefully gave Serigny every detail of information which could be valuable touching the expected trouble in the colonies. Of this my hands should, in any event, be clean. I even handed him the King's new commission directed to Bienville, whereof I was so proud to be the bearer. Whilst ridding my mind of these matters, I could not have said what course I meditated. A boat grating against the vessel's side set me all a tremble, but it was only a letter of instructions. Making some poor excuse to Serigny for the moment, I entered the yawl as it left the ship to go ashore. A well-known voice hailed us ere we made the land.

"Ahoy there, the boat," and through the shadows I made out the form of him I dreaded most to see.

15—BLACK WOLF

"Boatman, can you put three of us aboard yonder vessel?"

"Aye, sir, it is from her I have just come."

"Is thy craft a fit one to carry ladies?"

This dashed down the hope he had left his wife behind.

"Aye, sir, it is a safe craft, but not a fine ladies' barge. We can go with care and run into no danger. The wind is low."

" 'Twill serve."

I jumped ashore and would have slipped by without speaking had he not recognized me.

"By my soul, de Mouret, it is you; and we are to be companions on the voyage. Bravo."

He approached me frankly, with outstretched hand and hearty greeting. I would fain have avoided touching his honest palm, but there was no way for it.

"I see you are surprised. Yes? I was suddenly ordered to sail in le Dauphin, and report to your good Governor, Bienville. A most sturdy soldier from all report. Heaven send us a sharp campaign, I am weary of these puny quarrels. We will have brave days in the colonies."

This open-hearted way about him struck a new terror to my heart; I could face his sword but not his confidence. His cheeks glowed with martial enthusiasm and I almost caught again the hot lust of battle.

"And Agnes, with her little sister, is at the inn. Yes," he continued, noting me step back a pace in protest, "it is a rude life enough for tender women, but they come of stock that fears no danger, and it's better there than at the Court of Louis.''

I hardly heard the man. To meet his wife day after day, to associate on terms of cordial intimacy with this honorable gentleman, to enjoy his confidence, my heart filled the while with guilt too strong to conquer—the thing was torture not to be endured.

''Come with me to the inn; let us get the ladies and their luggage aboard. Agnes will be glad to meet you; she says she has great curiosity to see what you are like.''

I excused myself most lamely upon the plea of some duty to be performed.

''Ah well, on board then; she will have abundant time, aye, abundant time.''

From a dark place near the inn door, I watched their departure. Poor weakling that I was, I could not deny myself. The Chevalier, with Agnes and another lady, took their way toward the waiting boat, a flickering lanthorn being borne in their front. His words, ''Agnes will be glad to meet with you; she has great curiosity to see what you are like,'' recurred again and again.

So she had deceived him, and he knew nothing of our meetings? Ah, well do these women manage, and we are ever dupes. And I, who all my life had detested small deceptions, found myself heartily applauding this—was it not for *my* sake. This secret was *ours* —*mine* and *hers;* the bond which we two held in common apart from all the world. A sweet reflection.

The little weaknesses of women are very precious to their object, and if the deluded one knows it not, why where's the harm? Small comfort came to me, however, for all the while conscience, like a burning nettle in the side, gave the lie to each excuse.

All that night I paced about, and up and down. At length came gray dawn, but not decision. An early fisherman disposed his net upon the beach. I watched him long in silence, then abruptly asked, so fiercely that he dropped his work:

"Old man, do you know of any other vessel sailing soon for the American Colonies in the South?"

"Aye, sir, there's a brig fitting out at Boulogne-sur-Mer for the Spanish seas, to sail in a week or thereabout. But, sir," the old fellow looked cautiously about to assure himself that no one else could hear, "they say un-Christian things of that brig and crew. She bodes no good."

"A freebooter?"

"Aye, sir, or a privateer, which, they say, is the milder term."

My resolution was formed.

"Await me here; I will pay your gains for the day if you will but do me a slight service." ·

"Aye, aye, sir," he responded, touching his surf-stained cap.

I returned briefly from the inn bearing a note for M. de Serigny. Therein I explained that a most important matter had transpired to detain me until another vessel sailed, some few days at most. I would tell him of it more at length when I joined him at Biloxi.

I gave it, with a broad gold piece, to the old fellow, and directed that he give it to Serigny. There I remained until I saw the man clamber up le Dauphin's side, when I left at once, fearing further communication from Serigny.

Entering Boulogne at daybreak, the undulating valley of the Liane claimed not one appreciative glance. The ancient city trembled in its slumber at my feet. Already it became restless with the promise of another day which clad its gables in flame and burned the rough old towers with the shining gold of God. A little beyond, the waters glimmered in the sun's first rays, and writhing seaward tossed themselves in anger against the dim white cliffs of our hereditary foes.

As a picture laid away in memory this all comes back to me pure and fresh, but on that morning I gave it no heed. From the heights I passed along through quiet streets into the lower town, thence to the beach, where I was soon inquiring among the sailors for the privateer. These women looked askance at me, and regarded my unfamiliar uniform with suspicion, but after great difficulty one of their number was induced to carry me alongside an ominous looking craft lying in the harbor—a black-hulled brig of probably six hundred and fifty tons burden. Of the sentinel on deck I asked:

"Your captain—"

"Is here," and at the word a dark, wiry man, who

had evidently been watching my approach, appeared at the companion way.

"A word with you, sir, if you are the captain of this craft. I am told you are refitting for a trip to west Florida. What your errand is I care not; I want to go with you."

"We do not take passengers," he answered positively.

"Then take me as a marine, a seaman, what you will. I am a soldier, familiar with the handspike as with the sword, though knowing little of winds or currents."

Captain Levasseur eyed me closely, asked many questions concerning my life and service, to which I replied, truthfully in part. He seemed satisfied.

"Well, we do need a few more stout fellows who can handle a cutlass; when could you come aboard?"

"At once; I have no baggage but the weapons at my side."

"Good. Your name?"

"Gaspard Cambronne," I answered at random.

The freebooter laughed.

"We care nothing for your name so you will fight. We sail the day after to-morrow one week." And surveying my well knit frame, for I was a sturdy youth, "If you know any more stout young fellows like yourself we can give them a berth apiece."

So I scrambled aboard without more ado, and became at once a member of the "Seamew's" crew. I hardly knew at first why I gave a false name. But the character of the vessel was doubtful, its destination uncertain, and knowing not what mission she was on I shirked to give my real name and station. The chance was desperate, yet not one whit more desperate than I.

The Seamew sailed more than three weeks behind le Dauphin, armed with letters of marque from the King commissioning her to prey upon Spanish commerce in southern seas, and especially to take part in any expedition against Havana or Pensacola.

Our voyage wore on drearily enough to me, almost without incident. After four weeks of sky and sea we rounded the southernmost cape of Florida and turned into the Mexican Gulf. I grew more and more impatient and full of dread. Le Dauphin had twenty-three days the start of our faster vessel, and Biloxi was probably at that moment in a fever of warlike preparation. It was just possible, too, that the Spaniards had not yet been informed of the war, and nothing had been so far done by them.

Cruising by Pensacola harbor, just outside the Isle de Santa Rosa, a pine-grown stretch of narrow sand which for twenty-five leagues protects that coast, Levasseur called me to him.

"Do you know, my lad, what vessels those are at anchor in the harbor?"

Two of them I recognized as I would my own tent, two French men-of-war which Bienville had long been expecting from France. The rest were Spaniards, full-rigged, four ships, and six gunboats. Levasseur put the Seamew boldly about and entered the harbor. He signaled the Frenchmen, lowered a boat, and sent his lieutenant aboard the flagship with credentials and a letter signifying his readiness to engage in any enterprise.

From Admiral Champmeslin, in command of the squadron, he learned that Bienville and Serigny, combined with the Choctaws, had invested Pensacola by land, and on the morrow a simultaneous attack by land and sea would be made. The Spanish forces consisted of four ships, six gunboats, a strong fort on Santa Rosa Island, and the works at Pensacola, the strength of whose garrison was unknown.

That night on board the Seamew was spent in busy preparation and in rest. I alone was unemployed, my awkwardness with ropes and spars forbade it. I sat moodily upon a gun at the port, and fixing my eyes on shore vainly endeavored to make out what the French and Choctaws were doing there. To the left were the meager camp fires of the Indians; further up the hills a more generous blazing line marked the French position.

Gradually a low wavering sound separated itself from the other noises of the night, coming faint but clear upon the light land breeze, the first quivering notes of a Choctaw war chant. How familiar it was. Was I mistaken? I listened more intently. No. It was in very truth the voice of Tuskahoma, my old friend on many marches.

I cared nothing for the Seamew or her crew, and determined to seek my old friends to fight out the day with them.

What little thought I gave it justified the deed. My position as an officer of the King would palliate deserting the ship which had brought me over.

CHAPTER XXI

THE FALL OF PENSACOLA

I SLIPPED down the anchor chain without noise into the throbbing sea, and swam ashore to a point some three or four cable lengths away. Guided by the single voice which still sang of war, of glory and of death, I pushed easily into the ring of hideously painted savages who surrounded the singer. To unaccustomed eyes this would have been a fearful sight.

Two hundred warriors sat motionless as bronze idols about their chief; two hundred naked bodies glinted back the pine knot's fitful glow. In the center of this threatening circle moved Tuskahoma, two great crimson blotches upon his cheeks, treading that weird suggestive measure the Indians knew so well. Round and round a little pine-tree, shorn of its branches and striped with red, he crept, danced and sang. His words came wild and irregular, a sort of rhythmic medley, now soft and low as the murmur of the summer ocean, now thrilling every ear by their sudden ferocity and fearful energy. Now it was the gentle lullaby, the mother's crooning, the laughter of a child; again, the bursting

(233)

of the tempest, the lightning's flash, the thunder's rumbling roar.

His arms raised to heaven like some gaunt priest of butchery, he invoked the mighty Manitou of his tribe, then dropping prone upon the ground he crawled, a sinuous serpent, among the trees.

For awhile his listeners wandered away upon their chieftain's words to the waiting ones at home, to hunting grounds of peace and plenty; melodious as a maiden's sigh that song breathed of love and lover's hopes, it wailed for departed friends, extolled their virtues, and called down heaven's curses upon the coward of tomorrow's fight. Then the fierce gleam of shining steel, one wild war-whoop and all again was still. His words faded away in the echoless night till a holy hush brooded o'er beach and forest.

Then the solitary dancer wound about the ring as the crouching panther steals upon her prey, while peal after peal came the frightful cries of barbaric conflict, the shrieks of the wounded—a wild, victorious shout blended with a hopeless dying scream.

With a master's touch he played upon their vibrant feelings; not a key of human emotion he left unsounded —fame, pride, hate, love and death—his song expressed them all.

Thoroughly frenzied, warrior after warrior now began to join him in the ring; voice after voice caught up the dread refrain which terrorized the trained soldiery of Europe and filled their imaginations with the nameless horrors of unrelenting war.

High above the din Tuskahoma lifted now his fero-
cious battle cry; advancing upon the blazed sapling he
sank his tomahawk deep into the soft white wood, then
moved swiftly out of the circle to his own fire.   This
was the act by which he announced his assumption of
supreme authority.

Frantic with excitement the unleashed throng rushed
upon this fancied enemy, and soon but the mangled
fragments and the roots marked where it had stood.

And the forest slumbered and the sentry paced his
lonely path.

It is not my purpose to speak in detail of those matters of history which have been so much better described
by men of learning.   I would merely mention in passing such smaller affairs as relate directly to my own narrative.

Short and sharp was the conflict which, under God,
gave our arms the victory at Pensacola.   Swarming
over the palisades or boldly tearing them down, the
Choctaws, led by Tuskahoma, swept the Spaniards from
their works.   It so happened that Tuskahoma and I
mounted the fortifications together.   As I essayed to
drop down upon the inside my sword belt caught upon
the top of a picket, leaving me dangling in mid air, an
easy prey to those below had they only noticed my
plight.   Tuskahoma paused to sever the belt with his
knife, and by this accident I was first within the Spanish works, sword and pistol in hand.   Soon a hundred
were by my side.

The Spanish troops, inured to civilized warfare, could

not stand before these yelling demons, springing here and there elusive as phantoms, wielding torch and tomahawk with deadly effect.

In the very forefront, shoulder to shoulder, with a laugh and a parry, a lunge and a jest, fought the Chevalier de la Mora. Merry as a lad at play, resolute and quick, I could but stop betimes to wonder at the fellow. Gallant, gay and debonnair, he sang a rippling little air from soft Provence, and whirled his blade with such dainty skill that even the stoical Indians gazed in awe upon the laughing cavalier. Fighting through a bye-street, he met, steel to steel, a Spanish gentleman, within the sweep of whose sword lay half a dozen of our good fellows.

De la Mora glanced at this silent tribute to the Spaniard's prowess; his face lighted up with a soldier's joy. He planted one foot staunchly across a prostrate corpse, and right jauntily rang out the hissing music of their steel. Instinctively I paused to watch, and as instinctively understood that though pressed to his best, de la Mora desired to be left alone. Verily it was a gentleman's fight, and no odds, for love and glory's sake, though the Spaniard might have had a whit the better. As I fought on, I heard the swift hurtle of a flying knife, and saw the Spaniard drop his sword. De la Mora glanced round with indignant eyes to the Choctaw who had made the cast, now looking for approval from this gentleman who sang like a woman and fought like a fiend. The Chevalier was like to have wreaked summary vengeance for striking so foul a blow. Through the press I could see him go up to his late adversary, bare-headed and courteous, to extricate him from the motley, bleeding group wherein he had fallen. Throwing his powerful shoulder against a door, he broke it down, and tenderly carried the wounded gentleman within. I could then see him quietly standing guard at the door, waiting for the turmoil to cease, for it was then quite evident that the day was ours.

Already the Choctaws were busy tearing the reeking scalps from the living and the dead. De la Mora's face grew deathly pale at the sight; his cheeks did play the woman, and one might deem him my lady's dapper page, catching his maiden whiff of blood. This generous act kept him from being in at the close of the fray, and robbed him of the greater meed of glory which he might have thereby won. Twice that day, as he struck down a pike aimed at my breast, did he make me to feel in my heart like a lying thief—I, who was weak enough to imagine his dishonor.

Just at the last there was a trifling incident occurred which my lads insisted was greatly to my credit. News of this was carried straight to the Governor, and much was made thereof.

Bienville, with his Frenchmen, battered down the gates, and before many minutes the proud Castilian pennon lowered to the milk-white flag of France. On sea and land were we alike successful.

An hour after Pensacola fell, the Spanish ships struck their colors to Champmeslin. Our greatest loss was the total destruction of the Seamew, blown up by a red-hot shot, which fell in her powder magazine.

At the surrender I caught my old commander's eye. He motioned me to draw nearer. I obeyed most reluctantly, for I expected a stern rebuke from the rugged soldier who never forgave the slightest deviation from his orders. Instead, Bienville overwhelmed me with praise. He grasped my hand, and spoke loud enough for all the troops to hear:

"Before our assembled armies I am proud to acknowledge your share in France's triumph this day; proud and grateful for your fidelity at Versailles and Paris. Your example of loyalty and courage is one worthy to be emulated by all the sons of France. The King shall have your name for further recognition."

This was a great deal for Bienville to say, especially at such a time. My own lips were dumb.

"Take your proper place, sir."

And mechanically I walked to the head of my cheering guards. I was amazed. And Serigny? Had he made up his mind to overlook my defection? Had the Governor forgiven my failure to return in le Dauphin? Surely not. The noble voice of Bienville broke into my puzzled thought:

"Captain de Mouret, you will receive the surrender of Don Alphonso, our knightly and courteous foe."

It thrilled me with pride that I should receive so famous a sword, for knightlier foeman than Alphonso never trod a deck nor tossed his gauntlet in the lists. I stepped forward to the Spanish lines where their vanquished admiral tendered me the insignia of his command, when on a sudden thought I put back the proffered sword, assuring him so noble a soldier ought never to stand disarmed, and no hand but his should touch that valiant blade. My delighted lads cheered again like mad, and Bienville himself seemed much pleased at my courtesy.

"Bravo! Placide," he exclaimed, clapping his hands, his rugged face aglow with martial joy. His countenance changed, however, when his eye fell upon the cringing figure of Matamora, the commandant of perfidious memory.

"You, too, Matamora? What, not yet killed! Hast saved thy precious skin again? More's the pity. And do you think to merit the respect accorded manhood and good faith? By the name of honor, no. Here boy," and he beckoned to the negro slave who stood at his elbow, "do you take yon dishonored weapon and break it before the troops."

And Matamora, full glad to escape with life and limb, willingly yielded up his sword to the black who snapped it under his foot, obedient to Bienville's nod, then cast the tainted pieces from him.

Upon the long march to Biloxi, de la Mora was the life of the command, and drew to our camp fire every straggler who could make a fair excuse to come. He knew good songs, and he sang them well; he knew good cheer, and he kept us all in radiant spirits. All, save myself. I was bitterly dejected.

"Cheer up, lad," he'd say, "What ails you? One would think you'd met reverse, instead of winning glory and promotion. It was a brave day, and bravely you did bear yourself. Would that Jerome could see."

But the consciousness of dishonor had torn elation from my soul, though, God knows, it had before been stainless in thought or deed.

"We'll have many sweet and tranquil hours at Biloxi when days of peace are come. My cottage can be your home after the barracks no longer claim your care. Agnes is the sweetest of wives; her little sister, too, a child, but fair, and clever too, beyond her years."

Verily I cared nothing for a baby sister. But Agnes?

He repeated his invitation to their cottage many times, and mentally I prayed, "O God, lead not Thy children into temptation."

When we had settled down again at Biloxi, for days I remained to myself in the barracks, and saw no one, making pretense of being busy amongst my men.

De la Mora rallied me upon my ungallant conduct, in denying to the ladies the sight of so famous a soldier.

I had now firmly determined to make it necessary to be away from the post for a season, either in campaign with the Choctaws against the Natchez, or by taking part in the coming siege of Havana. Any pretext to get away. Anything but the truth.

CHAPTER XXII

THE CONTENTS OF THE BOX

ONE day very soon thereafter my servant presented me a box, which he said had been brought there by an Indian from Colonel d'Ortez, with the request that it be delivered into my own hand. And further, to beg I would make him a visit as soon as my duties would permit.

The evening being far advanced I could not go that night, so contented myself with the promise I would cross the bay on the morrow.

Later, my company being my own, I gave attention to the box, such a metal receptacle as was commonly used for articles of value. It responded easily to the key, and opened without difficulty.

The reasons for d'Ortez's fear and retirement lay bare before me, if I would but search them out. Within the box, bound together by deerskin thongs, were many writings, some on parchment, some paper, of different dates and degrees of preservation. Some were well worn from age and handling, others more recent, were in better condition. Some there were which appeared quite new and fresh; these must have been the latest to find a resting place in his keeping.

16—BLACK WOLF   (241)

All were arranged in due and systematic order; of whatever age, each bore a careful superscription, giving in brief the contents of the paper written by his own exact hand. Beside this, each document was numbered and placed in sequence. Verily, it was most methodically done, so any child could read and understand.

It was with much misgiving I approached the task of making myself familiar with my old friend's secret. Had he committed some youthful crime which weighed heavily upon his trembling age, and had driven him to these savage shores, where, shut out from all companionship with his kind, he did a lonely penance? If so, I preferred to remain in ignorance, for his was a friendship so dear, so pure, I desired not to taint it with the odor of guilt.

He had, however, made his request in such urgent terms, even pathetic, I could not disregard it, and putting aside the reluctance I felt, I took up the paper which lay on top, directed to myself, and began its perusal. It was as follows:

My dear Placide:

The great feebleness of my worn-out frame warns me again that time for me is almost past. It may be, when you recross the seas, I shall have gone to final judgment. * * * remember my request, and carry on to the end that work which generations of cowards have left undone. * * * All is here contained in these papers, except some recent news I have of the Pasquiers from the northern colonies.

Possibly if you went to Quebec and sought out the Cure of St. Martin's (who wrote this last letter, No. 32) you may right it all, and give to my soul its eternal peace. * * * With the strong

affection which my bodily infirmities have in no wise diminished,
I am,

> Your old friend.
> RAOUL ARMAND XAVIER D'ORTEZ.
> of Cartillon, Normandy.

Having carefully read this letter, I then proceeded to
peruse the various documents in the order he had arranged them.

The first, written by the hand of the Benedictine,
Laurent of Lorraine, Abbot of Vaux, told of the admission to the monastery of a child, son of Henri
d'Artin, to whom the good monks gave the name Bartholomew Pasquier. This child, though designed for
orders, left the monastery, cast his fortunes with the
King of Navarre, and became a great officer in the
household of King Henri the Fourth.

Other documents gave an account of the posterity
of this child down to one Francois Rene Alois de Pasquier, who fled to America in 1674 to escape the vengeance of a certain great lord whose son he slew in a
duel. This was he who was reputed to have been killed
in battle, and to have left no issue. And this was he
whom I afterward found to be my own good father.

There was also contained an account of the later life
of Pedro d'Ortez, who, profiting not by his blood-gotten
gains, threw himself, while in delirium, into the same
old well whereon he had hanged his brother, Henri
d'Artin.

Some further notes by the good abbot told of how
Raoul, the second son of Pedro, slew his own brother,

before their father's eyes, in order that he, Raoul, might be Count of Cartillon. And this same Raoul, some years later, did have the locket made and forced his own son to swear that he would restore the real sons of d'Artin, the true children of the Black Wolf's Breed, to their own again. All of these accounts are of surpassing interest, old and quaint, to a perusal of which I recommend my children.*

For the first time, in reading these manuscripts, did I begin clearly to associate the name d'Ortez with the name used by the madman in his story at the old Norman ruin. With this new light, link by link did the whole knotted chain untangle. Curiously enough, the tale I had heard at the ruined castle tallied in the main with the monkish documents here preserved. Indeed it supplied me with knowledge of much which otherwise I would not have comprehended so completely. The horrible reality of that weird recital was still fresh and distinct before me, undimmed by time and unforgotten through all my troubles.

I had sought refuge many times from brooding over my own affairs by turning to this for interest and occupation. Every further detail was supplied by a number of quaint documents, which Colonel d'Ortez had digested into this:

*These documents have been included in an appendix to this volume.

TABLE SHOWING THE MALE DESCENDANTS OF

HENRI d'ARTIN   AND OF   PEDRO ORTEZ.

Henri Francois Placide d'Artin, died Aug. 26, 1572.	Pedro d'Ortez, suicided 1604.
Bartholemew Pasquier (son of above), died 1609.	Charles Pedro, killed by Raoul 1602. Raoul, died 1618. } Sons of above.
Bartholemew Placide Pasquier killed in wars of the Fronde. Henri Louis John (brother to above), died 1654. } Sons of above.	Charles Francis Peter (son of Raoul), died without issue. Pedro d'Ortez (brother to above), died 1663.
Francois Rene Xavier de Pasquier (ennobled), killed 1650.	Henry (son of above), killed in battle. Alphonze, killed in battle.
Francois Rene Alois de Pasquier, fled to America. Supposed to have been killed about 1681. No known descendants. Well known to the Cure of St. Martin's, Quebec.	Felix, died in infancy. Raoul Armand Xavier d'Ortez, born 1641 (myself). Died } Sons of above. ——. No children. She who was born my daughter I disowned, and she died without issue.

It appeared that the only thing to be done was to visit the good Cure of St. Martin's, and, enlisting him in the search, find whatever descendants might have been left by this Francois Rene Alois de Pasquier. The task need not be a difficult one, as many old people should still be living who might have known of the man.*

I now bethought me of this enterprise as a fair excuse whereby I could leave Biloxi for a space. I would, therefore, call upon my old friend, and having obtained leave, matters now being safe with the colony, make the journey to Quebec.

But, alas for the weakness of fallen humanity; my last act before putting myself out of temptation's way was to run full tilt into it.

While this came so near to causing my dishonorable death, yet it was, under Divine Providence, the direct means of spreading before me a long life of happiness

*A very slight investigation showed that this last named Francois Rene Alois de Pasquier was none other than my own good father, who assumed the name de Mouret to avoid the consequences of a fatal duel in France. This I learned from the pious Cure of St. Martin's, who knew him well.

and honor. After a hard battle with my weaker self I lost the fight.

Just as on the day I departed from Versailles, I determined, cost what it would, to see Agnes once again. So I wrote her a note. Such a blunt and clumsy billet as only a love-sick soldier or a country clown could have written. It craved pardon for the heat and the haste displayed by me when we parted at Sceaux; it implored one last interview before I left the colonies forever. I had not the art to conceal or veil my meaning, but told it out and plainly. Such a note as an idiotic boy might pen, or a simpering school lass be set fluttering to receive.

I bade my man deliver this to Madame de la Mora on the morrow, charging him minutely and repeatedly to see it safe in her own hands. So careful was I, I did not doubt that even so stupid a lout as Jacques understood me perfectly.

His further instructions were to meet me at the Bay when I should return in the evening from my visit to Colonel d'Ortez, and there beside its rippling waters— or so I had arranged—I was to receive her answer.

It had now turned late of the night, and I sought repose. Sleep evaded my bed. What with my own restless desires, my chiding sense of ill-doing, and the d'Ortez story I had read, I tossed and tumbled through the remaining hours of darkness. Tumbled and tossed, whilst the sins and sufferings of men long dead passed and repassed with their spectral admonitions.

Early on the morrow, while the day was yet cool, I

crossed the Bay, and climbed the slope of sand before the lonely house. It looked more deserted and desolate than I had ever seen it. The stillness of solitary death clung as a pall about the place. Pachaco, the Indian servant, sat beside the gate, as motionless as the post against which he leaned.

"How is the master, Pachaco?" I inquired, passing in.

"Him die yesterday," came the stolid reply.

"What? Dead! When?"

"The shadows were at the longest," he answered, indicating by a gesture the western horizon.

I hurried into the master's room. In the same position he had occupied, when, months ago, he had beckoned me to remain, he sat there, dead in his chair. His clothing hung about him in that sharply angular fashion in which garments cling to a corpse. Long, thin locks were matted above his brow, awesomely disarranged. But the pose of his head, drooped a little forward, suggested a melancholy reverie, nothing more.

The golden locket, which he had shown me that well-remembered night, rested within his shrunken palm. I noted that the side was open which revealed the blazing bar of red. As if absorbed in that same unpleasant thought, there sat the master, dead; dead, and I alone knew his story. How vividly the old man's sorrow came back; how it oppressed me.

I bent down in tender sympathy to look again upon his wasted features, and kneeling, gazed into his wide-

open eyes.   The calm of promised peace upon his
brow was distorted by the unsatisfied expression of one
who has left his work undone.

So are the sins of the fathers visited upon their children, for I was no longer in doubt but that the murderer, Pedro Ortez, was the sinning ancestor of my old-
time friend.   Even in his presence my thoughts flew to
Agnes; had she not spoken of her grandsire as being
such a man? The stiffening body at my side was speedily forgotten in the music of this meditation.

I gained my feet again and looked down upon him,
fascinated by the changeless features of the dead.   It
was probably natural that standing there I should re-
volve the whole matter over and over again, from the
first I knew of it until the last.   A young man's plans,
though, work ever with the living; the dead he places
in their tomb, covers them with earth, bids them "God-
speed," and banishes the recollection.   I was already
busy with my contemplated search for the last d'Artin,
and stood there leaning against the oaken table pondering over the question, "Where is the last d'Artin?"

My mind wandered, returning with a dogged persistence to that one thought, "Where is the last d'Artin?"
"Where could I find him?"   My restless eyes roamed
round the cheerless room, coming always back to rest
upon a long dust-covered mirror set in the wall across
the way.

As wind-driven clouds gather and group themselves
in fantastic shapes, so, deep in that mirror's shadowy

depths, a vague figure gradually took form and character—myself.

With the vacant glance of a man whose mind is intensely preoccupied, I studied minutely the reflection, my own bearing, my dress, my weapons. I even noted a button off my coat, and tried dimly to remember where I had lost it, until—great God—this chamber of death and revelation had turned my brain.

What face was that I saw? My own, assuredly, but so like another.

Aghast, powerless to move or cry out, I stared helplessly into the glass. Every other sensation vanished now before this new-born terror which held my soul enslaved. I closed my eyes, I dared not look.

My body seemed immovable with horror, but a trembling hand arose and pointed at the mirror. Scant need there was to call attention to that dim, terrible presence; my whole soul shrank from the ghostly face reflected in the glass. For there, there was the same pallid countenance, death-distorted and drawn, which I had conjured up in many a frightened dream as that of the murdered Count—there was Henri d'Artin.

How long I stood transfixed, pointing into the mirror, I know not. As men think of trifles even in times of deadly fear, so did my lips frame over and over again the last question I had in mind before all sense forsook me, "Where is the last d'Artin? Where is the last d'Artin? Where—?"

And in answer to my question, that long, rigid finger

pointed *directly at me* from out the dusty glass. It was as if the hand of the dead had told me who I was.

It had been no blind chance, then, which led me to the Paris house of the "Black Wolf's Head;" the girl's ring with the same device, and the grewsome narrative beneath the shadow of the Wolf at the Norman ruin— nothing less than fate had brought these lights to me.

Verily some more logical power than unreasoning accident must direct the steps of men. A God of justice perhaps had placed these tokens in my path. And soldiers call this "Fortune."

*   *   *   *   *   *

I dispatched Pachaco to Biloxi with the news of death, and long before the afternoon our few simple arrangements for his funeral had been made.

"Bury me here, Placide, beneath this great oak," he had said to me one day. "The Infinite Mercy will consecrate the grave of penitence, wherever it may be."

He had his wish,

CHAPTER XXIII.

A NOTE WHICH WENT ASTRAY.

MEANWHILE Jacques had undertaken to manage my little affair at Biloxi with tact and discretion. And this is how the fellow did it:

It seems that Jacques thought no harm of the note, and when he took it first to the house my lady was out. The honest fellow, doing his best to carry out my instructions, refused to leave it. When he returned, my lady worked, bent down amongst her flowers, in the little garden beside their cottage. The Chevalier stood some distance off, busied someway, Jacques knew not how, but with his face turned away from my messenger as he came up. Jacques handed the note to my lady through the fence, and she took it gently by the corner, fearing to soil it. She held it up to look at the name written upon it, and seeing it was her own, looked again more curiously at the writing. She did not know the hand. Then she gaily called to the Chevalier:

"Oh, Charles, come here; see what I have; it is a missive to your wife, and from some gay gallant, too. I do not know the writing. Do you come here and read it to me. My hands are so—'' She held up two small white hands dabbled in the dirt.

(251)

"Perhaps some invitation to a court ball. We'll go, eh, Agnes?"

He came like the fine, strong gentleman he was, across the garden, taking the note from her and tearing it open. He began straightway to read, my lady on tip-toe behind him reading over his shoulder, and holding her contaminated hands away from his coat. His face grew puzzled at the first, then as he seemed to finish, he stood a pace apart from my lady and read again. There was murder in his face—yet so white and quiet.

He threw down the note and ground it into the soft earth beneath his heel. Then he caught my lady firmly by both her shoulders and held her fast, at full arm's length, gazing steadily into her face.

"God in heaven," as Jacques said to me; "Master, what eyes has that Chevalier de la Mora! No man could lie to him with those eyes reading what a fellow thought." Jacques could not make himself to leave; he stood rigid and watched.

"Well, Madame?"

"She tried to laugh, but her husband's face forbade that this could be a spark of lover's play.

"Well, Madame?"

"Why, Charles, what is the matter with you, you behave so strangely?"

The Chevalier had grown an older man, his face stern and resolute, eyes a-glitter, and mouth drawn in tense, determined lines. A most dangerous man.

"Why, Charles, what is the matter?"

"When did you meet him at Sceaux? What did you do?"

"Meet who?"

"Don't lie to me, woman, I am in no mood for subterfuge."

She besought him with one frightened look, one step forward to him as if for protection, which he repelled; then she looked as though she might weep.

"Neither do you weep. Tell me how many notes like this have you received?"

"Like what? I could not read it, you held it so high," she sobbed.

The Chevalier stooped down, picked up the crumpled paper from the earth, and smoothed it out   He then handed it to her, and regarded her face intently as she read it.

"Read this, Madame, and see how careless you have been."

And my lady read the note; she, too, read it again, the first reading not sufficing her to understand. Then she looked at her husband with great wide-open eyes; she was now calm, and as quiet as he.

"Truly, Charles, I know nothing of this."

" It was always said, Madame, at Sceaux, you could take the stage and play the parts of distressed and virtuous damosels," he answered her, coldly curling his lip.

"Tell me, Madame, as you value your soul, what is this Captain de Mouret to you?"

"As I value my soul," my lady answered him direct and steadily, looking straight into his eye, her own hands folded across her heaving breast. "As I value my soul, Charles, I know nothing of him."

"What does he mean when he says here 'I was hasty and too impulsive when we parted in the chapel at Sceaux' ? "

"Upon my honor, Charles, I do not know. I never saw the man in all my life—to know him."

"Upon your *honor*," the Chevalier repeated.

And my lady's cheek flushed fire. But her form. straightened up, and her eyes met his unflinching, without guilt or fear. The Chevalier turned and caught sight of Jacques, for the lout, according to his story, had grown to the spot as firm as one of the oaks.

"Here, you fellow, come here, *come here!*"

And Jacques dared not disobey him.

"Here, fellow, how many notes like this have you brought to my wife?"

"Only that one, my lord." Jacques started in by telling the truth, and he followed it up religiously. According to his account of it, the Chevalier looked him straight through and through until he dared not tell a lie.

"Mind that you tell me the truth. Who gave you this note?"

"Captain de Mouret."

"When?"

"Last night."

"Where?"

"At his quarters."

"To whom did he say you should deliver it?"

"To Madame Agnes de la Mora."

The Chevalier stooped, picked up the envelope, and re-read the superscription, handing it over to my lady, who took it unseeing.

"Did he expect a reply?"

"Yes, my lord."

"And where did he say to bring it?"

"Bring it to him when he returned from across the Bay this afternoon. I was to await him upon the shore.'

"At what hour?"

"None was named, my Lord; he said it would be late, perchance "

Verily, as Jacques told it me, he must have drained the stupid fellow dry.

Then the Chevalier turned to my lady with the utmost courtesy:

"What say you, Madame, shall I bear your reply to this gentle captain? For by my faith, Madame, you require a more careful go-between than this, one more discreet and less glib of tongue."

"Charles, upon my honor, I know nothing of all this; I have never seen this Captain de Mouret."

He looked as if he did not hear her. He glanced at the sun, full two hours high, drew his sword and started to leave the garden.

He paused to doff his cap, and say, "I bear your message for you, Madame; verily, I am honored."

My lady neither screamed nor fainted during his questioning of Jacques; she stood and listened as one dazed, or who but dimly understood. The Chevalier strode out sword in hand.

"For shame, Charles," she called to him calmly enough, though she was deadly pale, "here is some wretched mistake—"

"Yes, there does appear to have been a mistake—in the delivery of this precious billet. I will speedily make that right."

"Charles, Charles!"

He turned. Her bearing was full as proud as his. He looked from the woman to the paper in his hand.

"Well, if you know not this man, then he has wantonly insulted you. I shall await this Captain de Mouret by the water, and there I shall know the truth. He shall explain what means this pretty letter to my wife."

Jacques watched her proudly erect figure enter the door. He saw her sway a moment in indecision, then sink beside the bed to pray. She came shortly to the door again and called him. The fellow's brain worked slowly, and he had not yet comprehended the extent of mischief he had done. That he had done something amiss, though, he began to understand.

"You had that note from Monsieur le Capitaine de Mouret?"

"Yes, Madame."

"And he said deliver it to me?"

"To Madame Agnes de la Mora. Am I not right?"

"Yes, I am Madame Agnes de la Mora, but that note was not intended for me."

She came closer to Jacques, so close indeed she laid her trembling hand upon his sleeve.

"Tell me—you know this Captain de Mouret well—tell me if you would save an innocent woman, has this Captain de Mouret a love affair here?   Answer me, answer me truly, has he a love affair, or—or a mistress?"

Her innocence and direct question abashed Jacques sorely and set him a wondering what manner of escapade was this his master had got into.

"I will go to her, be she what she may, go to anybody; my husband must not kill this innocent man. No; and here I disturb myself about my own reputation, while two lives are in jeopardy.   I must think, I must act—but how?"

And she broke down to weep again, showing the woman in her that was behind so brave a front. Her tears were not for long.   Jacques felt it was his turn now to say something, so he blundered out, "See the Governor;" then one whit better he went, "*I* will see the Governor for you."

The good fellow had in that moment for the first time realized that he could stop the affair, and do it he would if he had to quit the colony.   And she such a lovely lady, so gentle with the poor.

"Do you not fear to speak with him of such as this?"

"No, Madame, Bienville's soldiers do not fear him; they leave that for his enemies."

And so it fell out that Jacques told the Governor. And he told him all.

17—BLACK WOLF

It was ever Bienville's wont to act with quick decision.

"Order Major Boisbriant to report to me at once."
And off posted Jacques upon his errand.

That officer attended with military promptitude.

"Major Boisbriant, do you seek on the instant the
Chevalier de la Mora, and bear him company wherever
he may go until you are relieved. Put upon him no restraint, and say nothing of your having such orders
from me if you can avoid it. There is trouble brewing
here, which I want to prevent; an affair of honor, you
understand. He has gone toward the landing on the
Bay. Be discreet and delicate."

Boisbriant nodded his comprehension, saluted, and
was gone. Bienville turned to Jacques.

"Saddle my horse at once and bring him here."

It was much later than I had hoped before I could
with decency return to Biloxi. Impatient, childish and
excited I recrossed the bay, leaving a little detail of
soldiers to watch beside the body of my friend. As soon
as I saw Jacques on the other shore I knew something
had gone wrong. That senseless knave was pacing uncertainly about the beach, stopping here and there to
dig great holes in the sand with his toe, and carefully
filling them up again. The fellow, ever on the watch
for me, was at the same time watching the path from
Biloxi, and seemed to dread my coming. Instead of
meeting me at the water, he waited for me to approach
him, thus leaving the two boatmen out of hearing.

"Well, give me the note; why stand there like a driveling fool,'' for the fellow's hesitant manner angered and frightened me.

"There is no note, sir.''

"No reply?''

"The lady sent none."

"Why?''

Under my questions Jacques turned red and pale, then he blundered out:

"The Chevalier de la Mora said he would bring the answer to you himself—at the shore.''

He kept his eyes fast riveted upon another hole he was digging in the sand.

"The—Chevalier?'' I knew what that meant. Great God! and this was the end of it all.

"Tell me, you bungling fool, what knows he of this?''

"Pardon, Master; I thought no harm of it; you had never before employed me on such an errand.''

It was now my own turn to seek the ground with my eyes, so just, so humble was the rebuke.

"I thought no harm of it, sir, and gave it to Madame in the garden; she called upon the Chevalier to read it for her.''

"What said he? To her? Was he violent?''

"No sir, most polite; terribly polite, and cool; but, master, you must not meet him; he will kill you.''

Of this I had scant doubt.

"Did he make no sign as if he would do her harm?''

"No, sir, not then, but he looked so queer one could hardly say what he meditated. I would not care to have him look at me like that.''

I was paralyzed by the suddenness of the ill-fortune which had befallen, but I was to be allowed no day of grace in which to plan a line of conduct. My face had been turned all this while toward the sea, there being something soothing to me about the long, even sweep of those bright, blue waters in the south.

Jacques faced the town. I noted a deprecatory gesture, and following his gaze saw the Chevalier himself coming our way at a good round pace. My knees did quake, and the veriest poltroon might have well been ashamed of the overweening fear which possessed me. In defense of which I may say, I believe it was due in large part to my great respect and fondness for de la Mora, as well as a deep consciousness of the justice of his cause. From long habit I looked first to my weapons, but for once felt no joy in them.

"Captain de Mouret," he greeted me with a soldier's formal courtesy.

"Chevalier de la Mora."

"Captain, I have the honor to return to you a note which I believe bears your name," and he handed me the unfortunate billet.

"Am I right? Is that your hand?"

I scorned to lie, and answered him evenly:

"It is."

"Is that note properly directed? To Madame de la Mora?"

"It is, but—"

"Have you any explanation, sir, to offer?"

For the life of me I could think of nothing to say; I

could not tell him the truth, neither could I lie to him with grace. So I simply said:

"It was not her fault," probably the worst remark I could have made.

"Then, this note is true? You did meet my wife by appointment in the ruined chapel at Sceaux?"

"No, by my honor, there was no appointment; I came upon her by chance, and through no consent of hers."

"And so you presumed to meet my wife in a lonely place—which she denies to me upon her honor, as you now swear; you were there 'hot, impulsive and hasty' which this *honorable* missive of yours craves pardon for. Now you seek another private interview which you say you can not live without?"

I nodded moodily, wishing only to have the matter over, and avoid his further questioning.

"By my soul, Captain, I am rejoiced to find you so frank—rejoiced that you do not lie. The other, God knows, is bad enough."

I winced, but held my tongue.

"Our business, then, is plain enough; and there is no time like the present."

So saying he cast off his coat and began to roll his sleeves back, leaving bare that magnificent forearm of his, supple and dexterous. Imitating him we were both soon stripped for action.

I had only my light rapier, worn about the garrison, while he was armed with his heavy campaign blade. I was already a dead man, or so I felt, for there was no spirit in me for the fight. Our blades crossed, and immediately he noted the disparity of arms.

"Captain," he remarked, composedly, drawing back a pace. "This is a bad business; I shall surely kill you, but wish to do so as a gentleman. Permit me to exchange our weapons, so you fence not at such great disadvantage."

And he offered me the hilt of his own reversed sword.

"Chevalier de la Mora, you are a gallant gentleman, will you believe a man who has not yet lied to you, and who feels a word is your due?"

"Be quick," he replied, "we may be interrupted."

"I have wronged you and will render full atonement. But it has only been a wrong of the heart; one of which I had no control, no choice. Your sweet wife has never, by word or deed, dishonored the noble name she bears."

"Of course, Captain, it is a gentleman's part to make such protestations. It is fruitless for us to discuss this matter further, except as we had so well begun."

So intent were we both that neither had seen Jacques leave us, nor had either heard the swift hoof beats of a horse upon the deadening sand, until the rider was full upon us."

Bienville. Behind him, on foot, just emerging from the brush some distance away, Boisbriant and Jacques.

"Gentlemen, gentlemen, put by your weapons. What does this mean?" He had flung himself from his horse and stood between.

De la Mora sullenly dropped his point.

"A mere private matter of honor, sire."

"Are there so few enemies of France with whom to fight that you must needs turn your swords at each other to rob me of a good soldier when I need every one?"

By this time Boisbriant and Jacques had come up, and Bienville commanded:

"Major, do you accompany the Chevalier de la Mora to his quarters. You will take his parole to remain there during the night, and he will report to me at ten to-morrow. Placide, do you come with me."

He gave up his horse to Jacques, and taking me by the arm led me in the direction of the garrison. Truly, I was in no better plight, for I feared reproof from the Governor more than the steel of de la Mora. During all this time I said no word. We returned to Biloxi in absolute silence. Bienville, with all a gentleman's instinct, recognized the delicacy of my position.

The Governor took me at once to his own room, and sat me down at the table.

"Now, Placide, tell me all about this miserable affair."

"I can not, sire; believe me, I can not. I beg of you not to put upon me a command I must disobey. This wretched matter is not for me to tell, even to you."

"A woman?"

I held my peace.

"Yes, I thought as much. Is it your fault or his, Placide?"

"Mine.'

He drummed on the table with his fingers a while before he spoke again.

"Then, my lad, there is but one thing I can do, that
is to send you away from here at once. You can leave
this place to-night, seek out Tuskahoma, make your
way to Pensacola, thence to Havana, where I warrant
you will find other occupation. Or, if you so desire, I
will accredit you to Governor Frontenac in the north."

I chose Havana, there being the greater prospect of
active service there. It took the methodical Governor
but brief space to give me such letters as would insure
me fitting reception from our brave fellows at Pensacola. He placed them in my hand, and I quietly rose
to bid him good-night, and good-bye. I would not
have ventured upon anything more than a formal word
of parting, for I had the consciousness of having done
much to forfeit his regard. But the old man came over
and put his arms about me as he might a beloved son.

"Placide," he said, "it grieves me to the soul for you
to leave me. I love you, boy, as I do my own flesh.
You have served me truly, always with affection and
honor. I respect your silence now, and ask you for no
confidences not your own. Serigny has told me how
faithful you were in Paris, and what he heard from others of your interview with the King. Placide, my lad,
even now it fires my blood to think of a boy of mine
standing before the mighty Louis, surrounded by our
enemies, and daring to tell the truth. It was glorious,
glorious, and it saved your Governor. I had minded
me in an idle day to hear it all from your own lips.

Perhaps, some day, who knows, it may yet come. You will lose not an hour in leaving Biloxi, and I have your word to engage in no encounter?"

"Aye, sire, you have my word."

"Good-by, Placide."

I had dropped upon my knee, and, taking his hand, kissed it gently. He turned back into his room, shut the door, and left me alone in the hall. I walked thence straightway to my own quarters, put on hastily the garb of the forest and made all readiness. My toilet was not elaborate, and a short half hour found me completely equipped for the journey.

Leaving Biloxi, unaccompanied, like a thief in the night, I set out, and having reached the Bay winded a horn until Pachaco heard, then sat me down to wait for his boat.

CHAPTER XXIV

THE CHILDREN OF THE BLACK WOLF'S BREED

ACCORDING to the Governor's recollection, I had been gone only a short space when a peremptory knock came upon his door. He opened it, and there stood the Chevalier de la Mora, dishevelled and with evidences of haste, but courteous as was his wont.

"I desire to speak with Captain de Mouret, at once, at once."

"That you can not do; he has gone. Chevalier, I am astonished. Had I not a gentleman's parole that you should remain in your house this night?"

"You had, sire, but the conditions were urgent, and see, I have sought Captain de Mouret without arms, so no breach could occur between us."

"Fortunately, M. le Chevalier, Captain de Mouret has consented to leave this colony to-night, and before the day dawns he will doubtless be many miles away.

The Chevalier heard like one dumb and undecided, a great doubt tugging at his heart. He departed unsteadily in the direction of the barracks.

"Here, my good fellow, hast seen Captain de Mouret?" he inquired of a straggler.

The man saluted.

(266)

"Yes, sire, he but lately went the path towards the Bay."

"How long since?"

"A bare quarter of an hour. He was dressed for the forest and went alone."

During this while I, Placide de Mouret, stranger and outcast, sat upon a grassy hillock awaiting Pachaco with his boat. The echoes of my horn had died away in the night, and soon after I caught the sound of running feet, and heard a man's voice calling my name as he ran. To my utter astonishment it was the Chevalier, breathless from his speed.

"Is it you—Captain de Mouret?"

"It is—Chevalier," I replied, uncertain at the first who the man could be.

Seeing him in such a state of mind I knew the struggle had come. There be times in every man's life when he recks lightly of consequences, and this was not my night for caring. I had, in a measure, run away thus far from him, and he, not content with this, had pursued me past the limit of forbearance. So anticipating his own action, I began carefully to take off my own coat, and remembered with pleasure that it was not a slight rapier which now hung confidently by my side.

"No, Captain, not that. I have sought you this time in peace. See, I have no weapons."

Suiting the gesture to the speech, he flung wide his arms, and showed himself unprepared for battle.

"Captain, you and I have fought side by side. You are a man of courage, and if you have injured me you will render me due account upon my demand. I do demand this of you now, that you return with me to Biloxi at once, upon my assurance as a soldier that no harm will there befall you. This, sir, upon a soldier's honor.''

It was a most unexpected outcome to such an interview. I hesitated warily at his request, and then thinking it could make matters no worse, inquired:

''How long will you require me, and for what purpose?''

''The time will be most brief, a moment should suffice. The purpose I can not give, but it will bring you into no danger. I repeat, upon the word of a man of honor, that you will be permitted to return safely as you came, and no one will follow.''

I must say, in spite of these protests, I did not want to go. But he pressed his wish so earnestly that I followed the Chevalier down the winding path back to Biloxi, not without great trepidation, however. He walked rapidly in front, and not a word was exchanged between us. We passed the barracks and the Governor's house, where I thought to stop, but he led me on. Leaving the thicker portions of the little town, he soon paused before his own gate and swung it open. The wild thought now entered my brain that perhaps he had planned some terrible revenge upon his wife, and desired to torture me by forcing me to witness it. I hung back at the gate. My own good sword re-assured me, and he mounted the step to throw open the door.

"Come in, Captain. I regret that I can not give you a more sincere welcome."

Truly, there was nothing in the aspect of the room to cause alarm. Two ladies were inside, one at either end of a simple working table—Agnes and another lady, about her own figure, whom I did not know. The elder woman looked straight in my face with an anxious air.

The Chevalier did not formally present me. Agnes drooped her head somewhat, and never raised her eyes at my entrance. It was a most awkward situation. As to what de la Mora contemplated I could not venture the wildest guess; certainly no violence in the presence of this other lady who looked so cool while yet so pale.

"Captain de Mouret, as you hope for your soul's salvation, I conjure you to tell me the whole truth. I do solemnly promise you, upon a soldier's honor, at the very worst which may come, I will only leave this colony, and will not injure any one."

I had seen de la Mora on many a field, but never did he look stronger or nobler than on that night. His voice sounded full and clear despite the intensity of his suffering.

"Captain de Mouret, you are a soldier, a brave one, as my own eyes have witnessed, reputed a man of untarnished honor. Will you truly answer me one question upon the sacred Blood of Christ?"

His earnestness appealed to every better instinct of my nature, so I replied to him:

"I will."

"Have I your oath?"

"You have."

"Then, sir, to which of these ladies, if either, did you intend this note should be delivered; and which, if either, did you meet at the ruined chapel at Sceaux? Speak, in God's name, and do not spare me! Suspicion is more terrible than truth."

The very worst had come, and I felt my resolution waver. I knew not what story Agnes had told her husband, nor did I know who that other lady was. She looked enough like Agnes to have afforded shallow pretext for an evasion. Verily here was a strong temptation for a lie, and I was almost minded to tell it and relieve Agnes. Agnes, though, would give me no cue; never once did she lift her eyes to mine. I might even then have told the lie, but for the reflection it would compromise an innocent woman.

"Captain, in God's name, speak! do you not see that I am quiet and self-controlled?"

" Chevalier de la Mora, I shall tell you the exact truth, and hold you to your promise that there shall be no violence—now. What I did was through my fault alone, nor did your lady give me the slightest encouragement—she is blameless. It is a sore strait you have placed me in, but *this* is the lady who has all a soldier's love, and a soldier's respect, which she has done nothing to forfeit."

As I spoke, I indicated the shrinking figure of Agnes, and turned to meet the storm. Verily the storm did come, but from a different source.

The elder lady rose with a fervent "Thank God!"

which I could find no reason for her saying. Agnes nervously twisted at the table cover, her cheeks crimson with the shame. I could not resist a long look down upon her, and do what I might, my love showed full and strong in my face and mien.

De la Mora keenly watched us all. That other lady, for whom I had no thought, to my utter surprise, moved toward him with hands outstretched, and cried: "Charles."

For a moment he hesitated, then:

"Oh, Agnes, Agnes, a lifetime's love and service can not compensate you for what I've made you suffer —the doubt I bore my loyal wife."

He fell upon his knee before her and carried her hand to his lips as though she were a goddess, and then sprang toward me with the gladdest of glad smiles, thrust his hand at me, and came near to cracking mine by the vigor of his grasp. His throat choked up, and he said nothing.

And all this while I looked from one to the other with a most dull and stupid stare.

Agnes looked up at me once, radiant and confused, then lowered her eyes again.

The Chevalier broke a silence which was becoming intolerable, to me at least, who did not understand it all.

"Captain de Mouret, you have been in error, and have done me no wrong. This lady here is my worshiped wife, Madame Agnes de la Mora." I looked upon her incredulously, while that gracious woman took one hand from her husband long enough to extend to me her greeting.

Thoroughly perplexed by this most unlooked for denouement, I asked:

"Who, then, is *this?*"

"This chit," he replied, walking round the table, happy as a boy, and almost lifting her bodily, "this is Madame's little sister, Charlotte. She confessed this evening to having spoken with you once in the Chapel at Sceaux—and I, may God forgive me, doubted but she had done it to shield her sister   I knew the little minx had warned you in the Park, but thought nothing of it. Charlotte, come here!"

·And Charlotte de Verges laid her warm little hand in mine.   For thirty years it has rested there in peace.

*   *   *   *   *   *   *   *

Thus, through many strange perils and purifying sorrows came the abiding happiness which blessed these last two children of the "Black Wolf's Breed."

FINIS

APPENDIX

NOTE BY THE AUTHOR. I have included here the full text of the documents contained in the iron box, sent to Placide de Mouret by Colonel D'Ortez, just prior to his death. One of these papers, that showing the male descendants of Henri d'Artin and of Pedro Ortez, which proved that Francois Rene Alois de Pasquier was the father of Placide and which indicated that the wife of the Chevalier de la Mora and her sister were the grandchildren of Colonel D'Ortez, was set out in the body of the narrative and will be found in Chapter XXII. These supplementary documents (which are historically accurate) confirm, not only the story related by Colonel D'Ortez to Placide, but also the strange story told by mad Michel under the shadow of the Castle of Cartillon. While they may add little to the narrative interest of the main story, these documents serve to confirm some of the least credible incidents of the tale, and it was thought, therefore, worth while to include them here.

DOCUMENT No. 1

Document No. 1, indorsed on back, "Notes chiefly written by the Abbot of Vaux."

In Nomine Patris, et Filii, et Sanctus Spiritus. Amen.

I, Laurent of Lorraine, Benedictine, by Divine permission Abbot of Vaux, do make these writings and divers memoranda, partly from my own unworthy knowledge, and partly from facts openly notorious and resting on the testimony of witnesses as credible as there be in this world of falsehood and vanity.

All of which latter portion, concerning one Pedro d'Ortez and his descendants, is here set down at the special prayer and persuasion of said d'Ortez, a profane and sacrilegious lord, yet whose past service to the Holy Church should not be forgotten, though his late riotous and ungodly life hath much grieved the faithful brotherhood.

THEREFORE, I, Laurent, Abbot, as above stated, do make and inscribe this chronicle, beginning this, the 29th day of June, in the year of grace, one thousand five hundred and seventy-six, according to the eccleciastical computation.

And herein:

ITEM the first—(Being a copy of entries made by my own hand upon the register of the monastery, now preserved in the archives of the same.) Aug. 26, 1572. Admitted to the sanctuary and protection of the monastery this day a certain suckling babe, aged about two years.

The infirm servitor by whom said babe was tended, dying the same day, despite all efforts and prayers.

August 28th, 1572. Died August 26th, 1572, at Cartillon, Henri Francois Placide d'Artin, Count of Cartillon, Seigneur de Massignac, etc., a heretic and apostate, falling before the wrath of

(277)

God on occasion of the pious stratagem of the Feast of the Blessed Bartholomew, arranged by Her Most Gentle Majesty, and the dutiful son of Church, Henri, duc de Guise.

Note. The babe aforementioned being the son and heir of above, was admitted to communion of the church and baptized Bartholomew Pasquier.

Further note. Sept. 9th, 1589. Bartholomew Pasquier being designed for orders, but unruly and rebellious in spirit, ran away upon the murder of our good King Henri, third of that name, and joined himself with the armies of the heretic Henri, Prince of Bearne, self-styled King of France and Navarre.

Afterward, when the said Henri, repenting of his errors, reunited with the true Church, said Bartholomew appears again as a major in his guards, holding a firm place, it was said, in the King's favor.

DOCUMENT No. 2

(Abbot Laurent's writing)

Statement of Brothers Anselmo and Jehan, touching the rites of exorcism by them administered, *contra dæmonios*, to the temporal and seigneural lord, Pedro d'Ortez, Count of Cartillon—fourteenth of said lordship—a man of profane blood, dying in grievous torment of soul, possessed of foul and wicked fiends—may God protect all true Christians from the same. AMEN.

ANSELMO DI NAPOLI.

JEHAN DE TOURS.

In Nomine Patris, et Filii, et Sanctus Spiritus. Amen.

It was come the early part of the night when there arose at the outer gate such an unseemly clattering of hoofs and rattle of worldly weapons as greatly terrified our humble-minded brethren, engaged at their devotions.

The holy Abbot, being retired at his prayer and pious meditations, Brother Jehan, worthy and devout, in humility of spirit inquired of their errand. Being informed in hot haste that the puissant and mighty Lord of Cartillon lay dying in sin, possessed of frenzies and fiends, and stood in need most urgent of extreme unction, we deliberated thereupon together.

"Hurry, haste, good fathers, ere it be too late; we have here two stout palfreys to bear you to his couch."

The Abbot having in due season come forth from his closet, we were commanded to go forthwith to minister to the needs of the noble Count.

Provided with holy oil, and the ritual for casting out demons, bearing a piece of the true cross, before which no evil being can prevail, we rode away at so rough a pace withal, through constant

(279)

urging and imprecations of the men at arms, as caused us to be
sorely shaken and disturbed, both in mind and body.

Arrived at Cartillon, we made great speed to repair to his bed-
side, where, of a truth, the man lay flat of his back, weak in flesh,
but stout and rebellious of soul, contrary to the doctrines of our
most blessed religion.

Before he caught sight of us, he moaned and heaved, pointing
his fingers ever out of the window, and uttering strange heathen
blasphemies—whereat we crossed ourselves piously.

Following the direction of his gaze we saw naught save the
starlit dome of heaven.

The eyes of the demon gave him power to see diabolical and
unclean forms.

Sorely distracted thereat, he cried out in direst fear:

"Hence ! Hence ! Seek my mother in Hell, for it was her doing.
I would have spared the women."

The man being clearly possessed of an evil demon, we immediately made ready the sacred offices of the church for the casting
out of such.

Believing from the demon voice issuing through the possessed
man's lips that it was the woman fiend, Lilith, who in female
guise doth walk the earth in darkness, we resorted with much
speed to the office specially prepared for that evil and depraved
being.

The holy ritual was being devoutly read by Brother Anselmo,
when the man, turning in his couch, caught sight of us at our sacred labors. He thereupon, with many profane and blasphemous
oaths, bade us cease and begone.

"Out! Out upon you, thou shaveling hypocrites! Thinkest thou
I am become a helpless woman to profit of thy mummeries? No,
by the body of Jupiter. Get out! get out!"

"Oh, weak and rebellious son of Holy Church, calm thy troubled
spirit and take unto thyself the most blessed peace of God. Re-
pent thine errors, and prepare thy mind for the Paradise of the
just."

Verily, it was an evil and malignant demon which controlled
him, for the words but struck a pagan madness to his heart, and
he sprang from his couch.

"Hush! Hush your priestly lies, which sink a new terror in

my soul. It can not, can not be, this other world where men receive the reward or punishment drawn upon themselves in this. Thou liest, thou canting monk-faced coward ; it is all a lie of priest-craft.

"There is no God, no Hell; no, I will not, will not believe it. Get thee hence before I drive thee to the gibbet and fling thy quarters to hawk and hound."

We crossed ourselves in horror, kissing the piece of the true cross, fearing his presence and terrible blasphemy would draw a bolt from Heaven. But there he stood, for some divine purpose secure in his body from the vengeance of God.

So fierce a fire consumed his strength he sank again in mortal weakness on his couch.

We watched him long. He gazed as one fixed by an evil eye, through the open window straight toward an ancient well across the court-yard.

He mumbled words whereof we could only guess the import. He raised a long, thin finger, knotted at the joints, and pointed to the well:

"Do you hear it? Oh, mother, mother, it was your doing ! Listen now. Dost hear their cries in Hell? See, see, the body turns and swings, softly, softly," and he covered his face, uttering the most plaintive cries.

He started up again and went to the window, stretching out his arm as before. We could see nothing but the court and old well, long dry of water.

"See, there she is; see, see; I come, I come."

And regarding not our sacred relics or adjurations, he passed out the door, down the stair of winding stone, through the men who, palsied by craven fears, put not forth their hands to stay; staring before him with wide-open eyes which saw not, d'Ortez strode through them all into the vacant court-yard.

No pause he made, but straightway went toward the well, whither—at some distance be it humbly confessed—we followed.

At first he but peered within and listened ; then he stood quiet for a space, as if he waited, for what we could not tell.

None of us being sufficiently near to prevent, and the power of the demon prevailing over weak and mortal flesh, he mounted the curb, and, amid the most horrid shrieks, cursings and revilings proceeding from the foul demon Lilith, he plunged himself bodily in the darkness below, wherefrom came only faint groans for a short space.

Thus died Pedro d'Ortez, Lord of Cartillon.

Leaving the task of getting out his body to those vassals who, greatly perturbed in spirit, gathered at the spot, we hastened away horrified at such abominations of Beelzebub as we had witnessed, being for our fear and little faith made culpable before God, and hoping to repurchase peace by great penitence.

Report made and rendered to the Most Reverend and Illustrious Father in God, Laurent, Abbot of the Monastery of Vaux, this the tenth day of July in the year of grace one thousand five hundred and ninety-six.

(Signed)   ANSELMO DI NAPOLI,
                                JEHAN DE TOURS.

DOCUMENT No. 3

(Concerning Raoul d'Ortez)

Indorsed on back, "Further notes by Abbot of Vaux."

In Nomine Patris, et Filii, et Sanctus Spiritus. Amen.

Further facts having come to my knowledge, in this, the year of grace one thousand five hundred and eighty nine, which do most gloriously illustrate the dispensations of a just God, and His visitation of the sins of the father upon the children of them who hate Him, it is deemed meet and proper that they be here set down and perpetuated for that future generations may know the truth; Therefore:

Be it held in everlasting memory, that Pedro d'Ortez, the same who has been by me beforementioned as of a profane, carnal and blood-guilty life, living not with the fear of God before his eyes, but filled with evil at the instigation of the devil:—The said Pedro having at this period two sons, desired that the elder should, according to secular law, inherit his title and lands. He desired also, that the younger, Raoul, might enter the armies of the King. But Raoul, nothing loath, in so far as the fighting there was concerned, lusted yet for the gold and acres which were his father's. Pedro, the elder brother, being of a mild and amiable temper, designed more for the cloister than the camp, Raoul jested and jibed at him alway for his gentle disposition and meekness of spirit.

All of these facts being stated and related to me by Brother Julian, who went betimes to the castle for alms and tithes—which same were frequent denied and withheld, to the great detriment of our just dues.

One day, after a more than usually violent quarrel between Pedro and Raoul, their father came suddenly upon them in a retired portion of the castle grounds. The sight was enough to

(283)

startle even a man so used to shedding human blood as had been the Lord of Cartillon.

Pedro was slowly sinking to the ground, easing himself down somewhat upon his knees and elbows. His brother stood near watching, and calmly wiping the red drippings from his sword upon the grass. Not a semblance of regret did he show for the deed of blood.

The father gazed transfixed with horror from one son to the other, until the slow comprehension came to him.

"How now, Raoul, what hast thou done?" the older man demanded of Raoul.

"Canst thou not see? He stood between me and the lordship of this fair domain," the younger replied full as sturdily, hot and scornful, with lowering brow and unrepenting glare.

"Thou foul and unnatural murderer, and thinkest thou to profit by thy brother's death? No; I swear—"

"Hold, old man; swear not and taint not thy soul with perjury. Have a care for thine own safety. It is now but the feeble barrier of thy tottering age which prevents all these acres, these fighting men, these towers from being my own. Have a care, I say, that thou dost not lie as low as he, and by my hand."

The old man fell back a pace affrighted, feeling for the first time in his life a fear, fear of his own son. Yet the scornful and defiant face before him was that of his true child. Therein he saw reflected his own turbulent and reckless youth. The wretched old man covered his face from the sight of Pedro, his first born, who had settled down upon his back in the repose of death, and moaned aloud in his agony.

"Nay, sorrow not, my father," Raoul commanded harshly, "it was but a weakling who stood next thy seat of power. Behold! I, too, am thy son; I am stronger, of a stouter heart, abler and more courageous than he, and will make thee a fitter heir. Didst thou not slay thy brother to sit in his hall? Didst not thou hang him to drink his wine, to command his servants?" Have I done aught but follow thy example?"

Heedless of his father's sobs Raoul pursued his unrelenting purpose.

"What the sword did for thee it has done for me, all glory to the sword," and he raised the reeking blade to his lips to kiss. The elder man shrank away from him as he approached.

"Nay, as I tell thee, draw not thy hand away, turn not from me, or by the blood of Christ, by thine own gray hairs, I'll lay thee beside thy woman-son, the puny changeling whose face now is scarce paler than his blood was thin. Now, by the God who made ye, swear 'twill be given out as but an accident, and no man will ever know from thee the truth."

"I swear, I swear," the old man repeated piteously after his son.

And so it came to be that Raoul, the second son, succeeded his father as Lord of Cartillon.

And thus is the promise of the Lord God made true.

DOCUMENT No. 4

(Concerning the making of the locket)

Extracts from the statement of Miguel Siliceo, goldsmith, of San Estevan de Gormaz, as given in presence of Brothers Jehan and Hubert, only such portions being here set out as have relation hereto, for the sake of greater brevity and perspicuity.

Said Miguel Siliceo, Spaniard, sojourning in the town of Rouen, having come to the Monastery of Vaux to unburthen his soul of certain diabolical knowledge and happenings which preyed thereon, to his great distress and distraction of mind, having first solemnly sworn upon the name of St. Iago of Compostella, his patron, to speak truth, did say: * * *

I came to Chateau Cartillon in the year of grace one thousand six hundred and forty-two, upon the solicitation of its lord, he having known me upon the banks of the Douro for a master workman, well skilled in rare and curious devices, both of metals and precious stones. For more than two years I rested in and about the castle, seeing much whereof my soul hath need of ease and God's forgiveness. * * *

* * * One day Count Raoul, being vexed and much disturbed, commanded my attendance upon him.

"My good Miguel," he spake in voice much softer than was his wont, "I do require of you a proof of utmost skill."

I bowed my willingness to undertake a commission.

"I require a golden locket, such as man never saw before, of rare and cunning device. Do you forthwith make it for me, showing upon the one side the black wolf's head of d'Artin, and quarterings, in fairest inlaid work. Upon the other and hidden side, let it appear the black wolf's head as before, but surcharged with the bar sinister. You know. And let it be concealed by so secretly a hidden spring, no hand but mine can touch or find," and as he spoke on, his tongue flew the faster, his eyes roved about, he

(286)

kept tight grip upon his sword as if he feared. He, Raoul of Cartillon, the man whose headlong courage was an army's byword, he
feared in his own hall.

Even so, for proceeding further, his speech grew more wild, and
I fain would have fled.

"You know my oath to my father." I of course knew naught of
the matter, nor do I know it yet, though I have diligent inquired.

"My oath to forego the hall, give up my place with my fighting
men. Yea, upon my father's sword I swore, recking light of an
oath, and the old man, dying, would have it so. That oath torments me now. The evil demons of the air haunt my bed; fiends
leer at me through the day and whisper all the night. I see my
father's soul writhing in the fires of Hell, and there he lays and
beckons me to him. But no, by the heart of Mars I'll be no
craven fool to give up my castle and my name. Perhaps my son
may, I'll make him swear to me to do so. Yet I fear; I fear; I like
not that pit of scorching flame where my father suffers because he
did lay his hand upon his brother."

I could not but look him in the face, and he thought there was
wisdom in my glance, for he clutched me at the throat.

"Ah, thou prying hound, what dost thou know? Speak! Speak!"

But speak I could not, though a soul's salvation hung on my
glib and nimble tongue.

Count Raoul soon loosed me, seeing my ignorance. Yet some
dark story had I heard and repeated not—the crimes of the great
are too dangerous morsels for a poor man to mouth.

"Go now to thy shop, and mark ye, sirrah, that no man sees thy
work."

I had hardly gotten well to my forge before three stout varlets
came in on a pretense of seeing a golden bracelet which I showed
them without suspecting aught. When, my back well turned, they
slipped gyves upon my wrists, bound me by a great band of iron
at the waist, and made all fast to the huge stone pillar.

Thenceforward, all through the days and nights which followed,
one of these men stood ever at my window to see I worked with
speed, worked on the locket and not upon my chains.

Count Raoul came many times as the work progressed, but the
guards were alway at too great a distance to tell in what quaint
form my beaten gold was fashioned.

Many, many lockets I made of cunning workmanship and design, of curious chasings and most marvelous wrought intertwinings, yet none suited my lord. One after one they returned to the melting pot and my labors re-commenced.

During the long months I was thus engaged, I saw the Count often, nay, more than daily, for his whole feverish life seemed inwoven with the yellow and white metals I was busy interlacing and rounding and polishing up.

At times an abject fear sat upon his countenance, and he mumbled of strange sights he saw, of communings with the Prince of Darkness, of specters gaunt and hideous that glided through the deserted court-yard, and stood beside his chair even in the noisy banquet chamber.

For that the Count was mad I could not doubt.

Yea, of all these things he spake as he urged me on as a lazy horse under whip and goad, to finish, finish.

I inquired of this at great risk of one of the men who stood guard; he tapped his forehead, and replied :

"He does all things so. It is so in camp, on the field, in the hall. Aye, but he's a very fiend in battle," and the fellow's eye brightened with a fierce pleasure at the thought of his lord's well-known prowess—for Count Raoul had wandered much in foreign lands, and deeds of blood followed in whispers to his door.

* * * * * * * * * * * * *

It is of these dealings with the evil lord, and close association with one possessed, I seek cleansing. * * * Too often did I pass the names of Rusbel, Ashtaroth, Beelzebub, Satan and others trippingly upon my tongue—may the Saints defend—to keep my lord's temper smooth, for I verily believe he meant to slay me when my task was done.

It was for this I made my work long and tedious, that the acid I was daily using on my chains might have due season to eat them through, and I could be free.

* * * finished at length to his satisfaction, and slipped off through the night.

* * * * * * * * * * * * *

Stated and subscribed in presence of Brothers Jehan and Hubert, on this the morrow of All Saints', in the year of grace one thousand six hundred and forty-six.

MIGUEL SILICEO.

www.ingramcontent.com/pod-product-compliance
Lightning Source LLC
Chambersburg PA
CBHW030344020726
47493CB00003B/676